THE GIANT'S HOUSE

Elizabeth McCracken was born in Boston in 1966. A graduate of the Iowa Writers' Workshop, she lives in Massachusetts, where, until recently, she was a full-time librarian. Her first book, a collection of stories, *Here's Your Hat, What's Your Hurry*, was published in 1993. She was chosen as one of *Granta*'s 'Best of Young American Novelists' in 1996.

ALSO BY ELIZABETH McCRACKEN

Here's Your Hat, What's Your Hurry

Elizabeth McCracken

THE GIANT'S HOUSE

VINTAGE

Published by Vintage 1997

8 10 9 7

First published in Great Britain by
Jonathan Cape 1996

Vintage
Random House, 20 Vauxhall Bridge Road,
London SW1V 2SA

Random House Australia (Pty) Limited
20 Alfred Street, Milsons Point, Sydney,
New South Wales 2061, Australia

Random House New Zealand Limited
18 Poland Road, Glenfield,
Auckland 10, New Zealand

Random House South Africa (Pty) Limited
Isle of Houghton, Corner of Boundary Road & Carse O'Gowrie,
Houghton 2198, South Africa

The Random House Group Limited Reg. No. 954009
www.randomhouse.co.uk

A CIP catalogue record for this book
is available from the British Library

ISBN 9780099739913

Papers used by Random House are natural, recyclable products made from wood grown in sustainable forests. The manufacturing processes conform to the environmental regulations of the country of origin

Printed and bound in Great Britain by
Antony Rowe Ltd., Chippenham, Wiltshire

for Robert Sidney Phelps
a giant of a friend

The Giant's House

Part One

See Also

I do not love mankind.

People think they're interesting. That's their first mistake. Every retiree you meet wants to supply you with his life story.

An example: thirty-five years ago a woman came into the library. She'd just heard about oral histories, and wanted to string one together herself.

"We have so many wonderful old people around," she said. "They have such wonderful stories. We could capture them on tape, then maybe transcribe them—don't you think that would make a wonderful record of the area? My father, for instance, is in a nursing home—"

Her father. Of course. She was not interested in *the* past, but *her* past.

"If I wanted to listen to old people nattering on," I told her, "I would ride a Greyhound bus across country. Such things get boring rather quickly, don't they."

The woman looked at me with the same smile she'd had on the entire conversation. She laughed experimentally.

"Oh Miss Cort," she said. "Surely you didn't mean that."

"I did and I do," I answered. My reputation even thirty-five years ago was already so spoiled there was no saving it. "I really don't see the point, do you?"

I felt that if those old people had some essential information they should write it down themselves. A life story can make adequate conversation but bad history.

Still, there you are in a nursing home, bored and lonely, and one day something different happens. Instead of a gang of school kids come to bellow Christmas carols at you, there's this earnest young person with a tape recorder, wanting to know about a flood sixty years ago, or what Main Street was like, or some such nonsense. All the other people in the home are sick to death of hearing your stories, because really let's be honest you only have a few.

Suddenly there's a microphone in your face. Wham! just like that, you're no longer a dull conversationalist, you're a natural resource.

Back then I thought, if you go around trying to rescue every fact or turn of phrase, you would never stop, you would eavesdrop until your fingers ached from playing the black keys of your tape recorder, until the batteries had gasped their last and the tape came to its end and thunked the machine off, *no more*, and still you would not have made a dent on the small talk of the world. People are always downstairs, talking without you. They gather in front of stores, run into each other at restaurants, and talk. They clump together at parties or couple up at the dinner table. They organize themselves by profession (for instance, waitresses), or by quality of looks, or by hobby, or companion (in the case of dog owners and married people), or by sexual preference or weight or social ease, and they talk.

Imagine what there is to collect: every exchange between a customer and a grocery store clerk, wrong numbers, awful baby talk to a puppy on the street, what people yell back at the radio, the sound the teenage boy outside my window makes when he catches the basketball with both his hands and his stomach, every *oh lord* said at church or in bed or standing up from a chair. *Thank you, hey watch it, gesundheit, who's a good boy, sweetness, how much? I love your dress.*

An Anthology of Common Conversation. Already I can tell you it will be incomplete. In reference works, as in sin, omission is as bad as willful misbehavior. All those words go around and end up nowhere; your fondest wishes won't save them. No need to be a packrat of palaver anyhow. Best to stick with recorded history.

Now, of course, I am as guilty as anyone, and this book is the evidence. I'm worse; I know my details by heart, no interviews necessary. No one has asked me a question yet, but I will not shut up.

Peggy Cort is crazy, anyone will tell you so. That lady who wanted to record the town's elders, the children who visited the library, my co-workers, every last soul in this town. The only person who ever thought I wasn't is dead; he is the subject of this memoir.

Let me stop. History is chronological, at least this one is. Some women become librarians because they love order; I'm one. Ordinal, cardinal, alphabetical, alphanumerical, geographical, by subject, by color, by shape, by size. Something logical that people—one hopes—cannot botch, although they will.

This isn't my story.

Let me start again.

I do not love mankind, but he was different.

He was a redhead as a child.

You won't hear that from most people. Most people won't care. But he had pretty strawberry blond hair. If he'd been out in the sun more, it would have been streaked gold.

He first came into my library in the fall of 1950, when he was eleven. Some teacher from the elementary school brought them all trooping in; I was behind the desk, putting a cart of fiction in order. I thought at first he was a second teacher, he was so much taller than the rest, tall even for a grown man. Then I noticed the chinos and white bucks and saw that this was the over-tall boy I'd heard about. Once I realized, I could see my mistake; though he would eventually develop cheekbones and whiskers, now he was pale and slightly babyfaced. He wasn't the tallest man in the world then, just a remarkably tall boy. Doctors had not yet prescribed glasses, and he squinted at faraway objects in a heroic way, as if they were new countries waiting to be discovered.

"This is Miss Cort," the teacher said, gesturing at me. "Ask her any question you want. She is here to help you. That is what librarians do."

She showed them the dusty oak card catalog, the dusty stacks, the circulation desk I spent hours keeping free of dust. In short, she terrified them.

"Fiction is on the third floor," she said. "And biography is on the second." I recognized her; she read Georgette Heyer and biographies of royalty and returned books so saturated with cigarette smoke I imagined she exhaled over each page on purpose. I wanted to stand by the exit, to whisper in every eleven-year-old ear, *Just come back. Come back by yourself and we'll forget all about this.*

At the end of the visit, the tall boy came up to talk. He seemed studious, though studious is too often the word we give to quiet odd people.

"I want a book," he said, "about being a magician."

"What sort of magician?" I said. "Like Merlin?" Recently a teacher had read aloud from *The Sword and the Stone*, and they all wanted more stories.

"No," he said. He put his hands on the circulation desk. His fingernails were cleaner than an ordinary eleven-year-old's; his mother was then still alive. "Just tricks," he said. "I want to make things look like they disappear. I looked in the card catalog under magic, but I didn't find anything."

"Try 'conjuring,' " I told him.

We found only one book, an oversized skinny volume called *Magic for Boys and Girls*. He took it to a table in the front room. He wasn't clumsy, as you might expect, but terribly delicate. His hands were large, out of proportion even with his big body, and he had to use them delicately to accomplish anything at all.

I watched his narrow back as he read the book. After an hour I walked over.

"Is that the sort of thing you wanted?" I asked.

"Yes," he said, not looking at me. The book was opened flat on the table in front of him, and he worked his hands in the air according to the instructions, without any props. His fingers kept slowly snatching at nothing, as if he had already made dozens of things disappear, rabbits and cards and rubber balls and bouquets of paper flowers, and had done this so brilliantly even he could not bring them back.

I may be adding things. It's been years now, and nearly every day I dream up my hours and meetings with James Carlson Sweatt. I am a librarian, and you cannot stop me from annotating, revising, updating. I like to think that—because I am a librarian—I offer accurate and spurious advice with no judgment, good and bad next to each other on the shelf. But my memories are not books. Blessing if they were. Then maybe someone would borrow one and keep it too long and return it, a little battered, offering money for my forgiveness, each memory new after its long absence.

My memories are not books. They are only stories that I have been over so many times in my head that I don't know from one day to the next what's remembered and what's made up. Like when you memorize a poem, and for one small unimportant part you supply your own words. The meaning's the same, the meter's identical. When you read the actual version you can never get it into your head that it's right and you're wrong.

What I give you is the day's edition. Tomorrow it may be different.

*

I lived then, as now, in Brewsterville, an unremarkable little town on Cape Cod. Brewsterville lies halfway up the spit curl of the Cape, not close enough to the rest of the world to be convenient nor far enough to be attractively remote. We get tourists who don't know exactly what they've come out to see. Now we have little to show them: a few places that sell home-made jelly, a few guest houses, a small stretch of beach on the bay side. Our zoning laws keep us quaint, but just.

Once we had more. We had James Carlson Sweatt walking the streets. Some people came out specifically to visit James; some came for the ocean and happened upon him, more impressive than the ocean because no philosopher ever wonderingly addressed him, no poet compared him to God or a lover's restless body. Moreover, the ocean does not grant autographs. James did, politely, and then asked how you were enjoying your visit.

Everyone knew him as The Giant. Well, what else could you call him? Brilliant, maybe, and handsome and talented, but doomed to be mostly enormous. A painter, an amateur magician, a compulsive letter-writer, James Carlson Sweatt spent his life sitting down, hunching over. Hunching partly because that's the way he grew, like a flower; partly to make him seem smaller to others. Five feet tall in kindergarten; six foot two at age eleven. He turned sixteen and hit seven-five the same week.

The town's talking about building a statue to honor James, but there's a lot of bickering: for instance, what size? Life-sized puts it at about the same height as the statue of the town founder, who's life-and-a-half. Some people claim it'll attract tourists, who even now take pictures in front of the founder. Others maintain that tourists will take a picture of any old thing. "Who's this behind me?" a lady tourist asks her husband, who is intent on his focusing.

"Pilgrims," he answers.

For some people, history is simply what your wife looks good standing in front of. It's what's cast in bronze, or framed in sepia tones, or acted out with wax dummies and period furniture. It takes place in glass bubbles filled with water and chunks of plastic snow; it's stamped on souvenir pencils and summarized in reprint newspapers. History nowadays is recorded in memorabilia. If you can't purchase a shopping bag that alludes to something, people won't believe it ever happened.

* * *

Librarian (like Stewardess, Certified Public Accountant, Used Car Salesman) is one of those occupations that people assume attract a certain deformed personality. Librarians are supposed to be bitter spinsters; grudging, lonely. And above all stingy: we love our fine money, our silence.

I did not love fine money: I forgave much more than I collected. I did not shush people unless they yelled. And though I was technically a spinster, I was bitter only insofar as people made me. It isn't that bitter people become librarians; it's that being a librarian may turn the most giving person bitter. We are paid all day to be generous, and no one recognizes our generosity.

As a librarian, I longed to be acknowledged, even to be taken for granted. I sat at the desk, brimming with book reviews, information, warnings, all my good schooling, advice. I wanted people to constantly callously approach. But there were days nobody talked to me at all, they just walked to the shelves and grabbed a book and checked out, said, at most, *thank you*, and sometimes only *you're welcome* when I thanked them first. I had gone to school to learn how to help them, but they believed I was simply a clerk who stamped the books.

All it takes is a patron asking. And then asking again. A piece of paper covered with notes, the pencil smudged: a left-hander (for instance, James) will smudge more. The patron you become fond of will say, *I can't believe you have this book*. Or even better (believe it or not) *you don't own this book—is there a way I can get it?*

Yes.

Even at age eleven, twelve, James asked me how to find things in the catalog. He told me of books he liked, wanting something similar. He recognized me as an expert. Despite popular theories, I believe people fall in love based not on good looks or fate but on knowledge. Either they are amazed by something a beloved knows that they themselves do not know; or they discover common rare knowledge; or they can supply knowledge to someone who's lacking. Hasn't anyone found a strange ignorance in someone beguiling? An earnest question: what day of the week does Thanksgiving fall on this year?

Nowadays, trendy librarians, wanting to be important, say, Knowledge is power. I know better. *Knowledge is love.*

People think librarians are unromantic, unimaginative. This is not true. We are people whose dreams run in particular ways. Ask a mountain climber what he feels when he sees a mountain; a lion tamer what goes through his mind when he meets a new lion; a doctor confronted with a beautiful malfunctioning body. The idea of a library full of books, the books full of knowledge, fills me with fear and love and courage and endless wonder. I knew I would be a librarian in college as a student assistant at a reference desk, watching those lovely people at work. "I don't think there's such a book—" a patron would begin, and then the librarian would hand it to them, that very book.

Unromantic? This is a reference librarian's fantasy.

A patron arrives, says, Tell me something. You reach across the desk and pull him toward you, bear hug him a second and then take him into your lap, stroke his forehead, whisper facts in his ear. *The climate of Chad is tropical in the south, desert in the north. Source: 1991 CIA World Factbook. Do you love me? Americans consumed 6.2 gallons of tea per capita in 1989. Source: Statistical Abstract of the United States. Synecdoche is a literary device meaning the part for the whole, as in, the crowned heads of Europe. I love you. I could find you British Parliamentary papers, I could track down a book you only barely remember reading. Do you love me now? We own that book, we subscribe to that journal, Elvis Presley's first movie was called* Love Me Tender.

And then you lift the patron again, take him over the desk and set him down so gently he doesn't feel it, because there's someone else arriving, and she looks, oh, she looks *uninformed.*

•

He became a regular after that first school visit, took four books out at a time, returned them, took another four. I let him renew the magic book again and again, even though the rules said one renewal only. Librarians lose reason when it comes to the regulars, the good people, the *readers*. Especially when they're like James: it wasn't that he was lonely or bored; he wasn't dragged into the library by a parent. He didn't have that strange desperate look that some librarygoers develop, even children, the one that says: *this is the only place I'm welcome anymore*. Even when he didn't want advice, he'd approach the desk with notes crumpled up, warm from his palm, his palm gray from the graphite. He'd hold it out until I grabbed the wastebasket by its rim, swung it around and offered it; his paper would go thunking in.

James was an eccentric kid, my favorite kind. I never knew how much of this eccentricity was height. He sometimes seemed peculiarly young, since he had the altitude but not the attitude of a man; and yet there was something elderly about him, too. He never returned a book without telling me that it was on time. Every now and then, when he returned one late, he was nearly frantic, almost angry; I didn't know whether it was at me for requiring books back at a certain time, or with himself for disregarding the due date.

He'd been coming in for a year when I finally met his mother. I didn't know her by sight: she was an exotic thing, with blond wavy hair down her back like a teenager, though she was thirty-five, ten years older than me. Her full cotton skirt had some sort of gold-flecked frosting swirled over the print.

"My son needs books," she said.

"Yes?" I did not like mothers who come in for their children; they are meddlesome. "Where is he?"

"In the hospital, up to Boston," she said. A doleful twang pinched her voice. "He wants books on history."

"How old is he?"

"Twelve-but-smart," she said. She wouldn't look me in the eye, and she trilled her fingertips over the edge of the counter. "Ummm . . . Robert the Bruce? Is that somebody?"

"Yes," I said. James and I had been discussing him. "Is this for James? Are you Mrs. Sweatt?"

She bit her lip. I hadn't figured James for the offspring of a lip-biter. "Do you know Jim?" she asked.

"Of course."

"Of course," she repeated, and sighed.

"He's here every week. He's in the hospital? Is there something wrong?"

"Is something wrong?" she said. "Well, nothing new. He's gone to an endocrinologist." She pronounced each syllable of this last word like a word itself. "Maybe they'll operate."

"For what?" I asked.

"For *what*?" she said. "For *him*. To slow him down." She waved her hand above her head, to indicate excessive height. "They're *alarmed*."

"Oh. I'm sorry."

"It's not good for him. I mean, it wouldn't be good for anyone to grow like that."

"No, of course not."

He must have known that he was scheduled to go to the hospital, and I was hurt he hadn't mentioned it.

"I was thinking Mark Twain too," she said. "For him to read. *Tom Sawyer* or something."

"Fiction," I said. "Third floor. Clemens."

"Clemens," she repeated. She loved the taste of other people's words in her mouth.

"*Clemens*," I said. "Mark Twain, Samuel Clemens. That's where we file him."

Before his mother had come to the library, I hadn't realized that there was anything medically wrong with James. He was tall, certainly, but in the same sweet gawky way young men are often tall. His bones had great plans, and the rest of him, voice and skin balance, strained to keep pace. He bumped into things and walked on the sides of his feet and his hair would not stay in a single configuration for more than fifteen minutes. He was not even a teenager yet; he had not outgrown childhood freckles or enthusiasms.

They didn't operate on James that hospital visit. The diagnosis: tall, very. Chronic, congenital height. He came back with more wrong than he left with: an orderly, pushing him down the hall, misguessed a corner and cracked his ankle.

He was twelve years old then, and six foot four.

• • •

A librarian is bound by many ethics no one else understands. For instance: in the patron file was James's library card application, with his address and phone number and mother's signature. But it was wrong, I felt, to look up the address of a patron for personal reasons, by which I mean my simple nosiness. Delinquent patrons, yes; a twenty-dollar bill used as a bookmark in a returned novel, certainly. But we must protect the privacy of our patrons, even from ourselves.

I'd remained pure in this respect for a while, but finally pulled the application. I noted that James had been six when he had gotten his card, five years before; I hadn't even seen Brewsterville yet. He had written his name in square crooked letters—probably he'd held the pen with both hands. But it was a document completed by a child and therefore faulty: he'd written the name of the street, but not the number. If I'd been on duty, such sloppiness would never have passed.

I decided I could telephone his mother for library purposes, as long as I was acting as librarian and not as a nosy stranger. The broken ankle promised to keep him home for a few weeks. I called up Mrs. Sweatt and offered to bring over books.

"I'll pick them up," she said.

"It's no bother, and I'd like to wish James well."

"No," she said. "Don't trouble yourself."

"I just said it's no trouble."

"Listen, Peggy," she said. That she knew my Christian name surprised me. There was a long pause while I obeyed her and listened. Finally she said, "I can't do too much for Jim. But I can pick up his books and I intend to."

So of course I resigned myself to that. I agreed with her; there was little she could do for him. Every Friday—his usual day—I wondered whether James would come in. Instead, Mrs. Sweatt arrived with her big purse, and I stamped her books with a date three weeks in the future. Mostly she insisted on titles of her own choosing—she seemed determined that James read all of Mark Twain during his convalescence—but she always asked for at least one suggestion. I imagined that it was my books he really read, my choices that came closest to what he wanted. I'd sent *Worlds in Collision* by Immanuel Velikovsky; *Mistress Masham's Repose* by T. H. White; *Hiroshima.* Mrs. Sweatt was always saying, "And something else like this," waving the book I'd personally picked out the week before.

"How's James?" I asked her.

"Fine." She examined the bindings of a row of books very closely, her head tilted to a hunched shoulder for support.

"How's the ankle?"

"Coming along."

"Not healed yet?"

She scratched her chin, then rucked up the back of her skirt like a five-year-old and scratched her leg. "He's still keeping off it," she said. "Ambrose Bierce. Do we have any Ambrose Bierce?"

I looked up the card for the magic book; James had not been in for three months. Surely an ankle would knit back together in that time. Maybe Mrs. Sweatt was keeping James from the library, had forbidden him to come. It wouldn't be the first time. A certain sort of mother is terrified by all the library's possibilities. Before he was homebound, James faithfully renewed *Magic for Boys and Girls* every three weeks. Perhaps his mother didn't like it—perhaps she thought sleight-of-hand was too close to black magic—and so he'd filed it between his mattress and box spring. But I couldn't accuse Mrs. Sweatt; though she projected fragility, I suspected she wouldn't crack under the harshest of cross-examinations.

I was meddlesome myself: I decided to cut off James's supply of interesting books. He was one of my favorite patrons—that is to say, one of my favorite people—and even this early in our friendship, the thought of never seeing him again was more than I could bear.

"This looks difficult," said Mrs. Sweatt, looking at a translation of Caesar's *Wars.*

"Oh," I said. "I thought he was bright for his age."

"Of course." She tucked the book under her arm. "Half of it's in Latin," she said under her breath.

If they ever want me to teach a course entitled *History: The Dull and the Punishing,* I have the reading list all worked out. Bulwer-Lytton, the poems of Edgar Guest, cheap novels whose morals were that war is bad but sometimes results in lifelong love between a soldier and his girl. We owned the complete works of a certain nineteenth-century lady author who drew quite a few more morals out of history than that: her books were called things like *A True Friend of Christ* and *Daisy, a Girl of the West*. I chose fiendishly well, and sent the books home with the unfortunate Mrs. Sweatt, who brought them back unread.

"This one's close," she'd say sometimes. "But not quite. How about the Civil War?"

I gave her *Gone with the Wind*, which I knew James would never be able to stomach.

Later in the week, a boy I recognized as one of James's friends came into the library. In this way we were different: James had friends, in fact plenty of them. All I ever had were patrons. Somehow his size did not make him an outcast; or, if it did, he won friends despite it. Every child in school knew him, of course. I asked the boy how James was doing, whether he'd seen James recently, and by the way, where did James live.

"Winthrop Street," the boy told me. "He and his mom live with his aunt and uncle."

"Which number?"

He shrugged with half his body. "The white house," he said. "It's got flowers painted on it."

I'd pictured a *floral* house—like a sofa, or a dress—so I almost missed the flowers that were painted on the clapboards, like handwriting practiced on ruled paper. The side of the house was punctuated with a peculiar garden of tiny blooms, each labeled, both Latin and common name, as if someone had copied them straight out of a botany textbook. They were not well painted. Even from the outside I could tell the house was too small for two people, never mind four.

The aunt met me at the door. She was as different as she could be from Mrs. Sweatt, who was her sister-in-law. The woman in front of me was dressed like a jaunty boy indulged by his mother: blue jeans held up by a western belt and a red-checked shirt. I was surprised she didn't sport toy guns in a holster.

She had a streak of dirt down one cheek; I later learned she was rarely seen without it. Only her bright red lipstick was grown-up. It matched the check of her shirt exactly. She didn't say hello, though she raised her eyebrows in a pleasant way.

"I'm the librarian," I told her. I held up the few books I had brought as evidence.

She still didn't say anything.

"Is James here?"

She opened the door, then held her hand to her lips, *sshh*. The door opened directly into the living room, no preamble or vestibule. In the dining room to my left, the late-afternoon light soaked through the colored bottles on the plate shelf and left jellied puddles on the floor. Mrs. Sweatt was asleep on the sofa, her little feet in their flat shoes resting on a pillow. The sofa itself was clad in a slipcover as baggy and gaudy as a muumuu; its pattern clashed badly with Mrs. Sweatt's skirt. A few spinstered straight-back chairs stood in the corner, wall-flowers.

The aunt tiptoed across the living room in an exaggerated way. I followed, trying not to imitate.

In a small back room, James sprawled across the bed on his stomach like any twelve-year-old. His legs were bent at the knees, and his feet waved in the air behind him. I realized I didn't know which ankle he'd broken. The latest pile of books I'd pawned off on his mother sat on the radiator, beneath a window with the shade pulled down below the sill. I immediately went to rescue them—heat isn't good for the glue—but their covers were perfectly cool. It was June; of course the heat wasn't on. I stood there, clutching the pile of books, then realized that it looked like I was reclaiming them, so I set them on a little table by the bed. That put me right next to James. I had no idea what to say.

"Well," I tried. "How have you been?"

His aunt answered for him from across the room, closing the door behind her. "He's been fine," she said. Her voice gave me a start, but a weird pleasure, too—it was a deep sticky voice, the kind a woman generally gets through sin of some sort.

James sat up, put his feet on the ground. His hair was flattened up in back, like a plant climbing an invisible wall. He blinked. I didn't know it then, but he was an inch taller than he'd been the last time we'd met.

"James," the aunt said. "Didn't you tell me that you had something to explain to the librarian?"

"*Tom Sawyer* got ruined, I'm sorry," he said in a rush.

"By what?" I asked. I couldn't figure out what could have ruined *Tom Sawyer*. Had someone told him the ending?

James leaned over and pulled open the drawer of the table by his bed; it caught on something, so he slipped his hand inside to press whatever it was down. I had to step aside to give him room. "It got dropped in a sink," he said, pulling a book out by the corner of its cover. I put my hands out to receive it, but he set it on the tabletop, next to the books from the radiator. *Tom Sawyer*, ruffled to twice its right size.

"I'm sorry," James said miserably.

"She doesn't care," said the aunt. "She has *lots* of books."

"Even a few more copies of *Tom Sawyer*," I said.

"I told you that's what she'd say," said the aunt.

"I'll pay for it," James said.

"No. Consider it a get-well present from the library."

All the time James put a hand on the cover, trying to close it. It sprang up under his palm again and again.

The aunt sat down next to him on the bed. She patted his knee.

"You know how boys are," she said to me. "He'd about vowed not to go back to the library over this."

He looked up at me, and his hair fell into his eyes, so he combed it with his fingers, both the front part and the part that stuck up in the back.

"Good heavens," I said. "You should see what some people do to books and don't even care."

"I told him," said the aunt.

"We've missed you at the library," I said. "I hope that's not the reason you haven't been by."

"No." He wiggled his ankle—the left one—as if to remind himself there had been another reason.

"Okay, Jim?" the aunt said.

"Yes. Look." He reached into the drawer again and pulled out a pack of cards, then, using only one hand, fanned them in the air, snapped shut the fan, fanned them again, made one stand up from the deck.

I couldn't decide whether I was supposed to pull the one card from the others. I wanted to. He looked at the cards, then using both hands, closed the deck.

"That's as far as I've got," he said.

"Not too shabby. You'll need a rabbit next."

The aunt laughed. "A rabbit? Sounds delicious."

"Yuck," said James.

I said, "I quite agree."

The aunt stood up and stretched. Her red-checked shirt pulled out of her jeans, and she tucked it back down absent-mindedly. "Rabbit stew," she said to James, and then, to me, "You'll have to come to dinner sometime, and make sure to bring—"

"Dessert," I said, before she could suggest *husband*, or *gentleman friend*. I pointed at a small seascape painting over the bed. The one gull looked as menacing as a zeppelin. "That's nice."

"My husband is an artist. Yes," she said, thinking it over. "I wouldn't turn down dessert."

I leaned on that cool radiator. "Should think about getting back. We'll see you at the library, James?"

"Yes." He scratched his chin with the pack of cards. "Goodbye."

She saw me out, stepping onto the porch with me, still careful of the sleeping Mrs. Sweatt.

"I'm Caroline Strickland, by the way. James is my brother's son. Make sure to come to dinner."

"Peggy Cort," I told her. "I will." I wondered if she was going to issue a more decisive invitation than that.

"Well, Peggy Cort." She took my hand and shook it like a salesman. She must have been about my age, mid-twenties.

"You're not an unpleasant woman." Then she went back into her house.

I stood there for a while, staring at the flowers, lily of the valley, *Convallaria majalis;* poppy, *Papaver orientale.* They seemed just right blooming there now. I repeated Caroline's parting sentence to myself, but couldn't remember where she'd put the emphasis. You're *not* an unpleasant woman. You're not an *unpleasant* woman.

I could hear Mrs. Sweatt inside the house waking up, asking in her twangy voice, now unstrung with sleep, *what time is it?*

Early, said Caroline, which of course means nothing to a sleeper.

Then Caroline started to sing. Perhaps she'd been waiting for Mrs. Sweatt to wake up all afternoon, so she could sing inside her house. I imagined her stepping out on the back porch to sing now and then, like a polite smoker. She had the voice of a dancer, I mean like Fred Astaire or Gene Kelly, someone who has such grace at another art that the grace suffuses their voice, which does not quite match the tune but instead strolls up to a note and stands right next to it, that slight difference so beautiful and heartbreaking that you never want to hear a professional sing again. Professionals remember all the words. Caroline's song was patched together with *something something something.*

Everyone Felt Sorry for the Beiderbeckes

I won't pretend that I was in love with James right away. He was only a boy, though one I liked quite a bit.

Well, now. Only this far into the story and already I'm lying. Juvenile magazines feature close-up photographs of things that are, like love, impossible to divine close up for the first time: a rose petal, a butterfly's wing, frost. Once you're told what they are, you can't believe you didn't see it instantly. So yes, I loved James straight off, though I didn't realize it then. I know that sounds terrible, the sort of thing that makes people think I'm crazy or worse.

But there was nothing scandalous about what I felt for James. I am not a scandalous person. No, that isn't true either. Given half a chance I am scandalous, later facts bear that out. But life afforded me few opportunities in those days. He was not even a teenager and more than half a foot taller than the average American man. I was more than twice his age and I already loved him.

There's a joke about that. A forty-year-old man (it's always a man) falls in love with a ten-year-old girl. He's four times her age. He waits five years; now he's forty-five and she's fifteen and he's only three times her age. Fifteen years later he's sixty, only double her age.

How long until she catches up completely?

I love that joke. It reads like a chart, like the grids that were eventually printed in medical journals, describing James's growth, at age ten, age twelve, steady intervals of time and quite nearly as steady in inches. Imagine it: my age on one side of a chart, James's on the other. How long until he catches up?

James and I met at a particularly happy time in his life. He was just six foot two, remarkably tall but not yet automatically noticed on the street. At school, yes: he was eleven, and this was the year that the tallest kids in the classes were girls, and the boys, innocent of adolescence, occupied the front row of class pictures, the far right-hand side of gym class line-ups. James always knew where he belonged in such indexing, but he wasn't strange. Out in the world he just seemed like a nice, naive, full-grown man.

In 1950, when I met James Carlson Sweatt, I was twenty-five years old, without any experience at love whatsoever. I don't mean beaux; I'd had those, stupid boys. In college I'd had friends and boyfriends, was invited to parties and asked to the movies. I wasn't objectionable, not then, but neither was I exceptional: after graduation, I never heard from a single college chum. In library school I had a few after-class-coffee friends, but that was it.

Then I moved to Brewsterville. Suddenly, I felt quite sure I would never hear an affectionate word from another human being in my life. Most days I spoke only to my librarian patrons, which is one reason I loved my work—it kept me from being one of those odd women discussed in books of odd people: *her neighbors saw her only as a shadow on the street; then she died, buried beneath newspapers, movie magazines, and diaries filled with imaginary conversations.*

Even with work, I was odd enough. Every morning I walked along the gravel path from my house to the sidewalk, thinking,

Is this who I am? A lonely person? I felt awkward as a teenager most days, as if Cape Cod were one big high school that I had enrolled in too late to understand any of the running jokes. My life was better in many ways than it had been in high school, I knew that. I worked harder, which was a blessing; my skin had turned up pleasant enough. I had been kissed.

But I still dreamed of kisses that wouldn't be delivered, and I knew they wouldn't be delivered, and I grew morose as I waited to be stood up by nobody in particular. I was aware that I didn't know anything about love; every morning I realized it again.

And then I met a tall boy.

If I were a different sort of woman, I would point to fate. I would claim that I understood the course of the rest of my life the minute James walked into my library. But if I were a different sort of woman, I wouldn't have needed to cling to the weekly polite visits of a tall boy, or to wonder what went on in a house with painted flowers on the side, dreaming of the day I might be allowed back in.

That, perhaps, is all you need to know. *I was not a different sort of woman.* Right there you have my life story, because my life is beside the point. Most lives are. Just as *Barlett's* is not interested in the librarian's quotations, *Who's Who* is not interested in the librarian's life. In a big library you will find dozens of biographical dictionaries: South American women writers, Scottish scientists of the eighteenth century, military men and psychologists and businesspeople; the important citizens of every country.

You will not find a volume marked, *Everybody Else*.

You will not find me in any reference source; your finger will slide along index after index, under Cort, under Librarians—American, but you won't find the slightest reference to me.

You might be tempted to ask, but I'll tell you: it's a colorless story, one that no one could possibly be interested in. By now it's outdated and probably riddled with lies. If somebody wrote the story of my life before James (and it would be a short book, repetitious and unillustrated), I would not buy it; I would not have it on my shelf. It would be a waste of the budget.

* * *

I was a librarian when I met him. That much is important. I had my library, which I loved and despised. All librarians, deep down, loathe their buildings. Something is always wrong—the counter is too high, the shelves too narrow, the delivery entrance too far from the offices. The hallway echoes. The light from windows bleaches books. In short, libraries are constructed by architects, not librarians. Do not trust an architect: he will always try to talk you into an atrium.

Space is the chief problem. Books are a bad family—there are those you love, and those you are indifferent to; idiots and mad cousins who you would banish except others enjoy their company; wrongheaded but fascinating eccentrics and dreamy geniuses; orphaned grandchildren; and endless brothers-in-law simply taking up space who you wish you could send straight to hell. Except you can't, for the most part. You must house them and make them comfortable and worry about them when they go on trips and there is never enough room.

My library was no exception. It had started its life in 1880 as a nice one-room building; almost immediately the collection was crowded. The town started to tack on additions: a skinny hall, a dusty reading room, two stories of stacks with frosted glass floors. These floors—an invention of the nineteenth century—were composed of panes cloudy as cataracts which allowed only close-up objects to show through. On the second floor you could see the glow of the lightbulbs that lit the first floor; on the first floor you could see the outline of people's feet by looking up. The panes of glass were always cracking and had to be replaced with wood. The shelving went right through the floors, and there were gaps where they met the glass panes, which meant that a man on the first floor could look up the skirt of a woman on the second, if he were so inclined, and at least once a month some man was.

The tile teared up at a hint of moisture; the slender-throated plumbing choked on the daintiest morsel. The roof leaked. There were staircases that led nowhere.

I came to the job fresh from library science school. Purgatory would have seemed quite an adequate set-up to me then; I would have happily issued cards to the not-quite-condemned and the not-yet-blessed and thought it a vast improvement over the dullness of catalog class. I loved that building when I first met it; I suppose I continued to love it the way a woman will love a husband who sticks around while she silently prays he will leave or die. Indeed, until 1950 the library occupied much of my heart and mind. When we were apart, I wondered what wrong-headed thing it would insist upon doing in my absence (bursting a pipe, inviting birds through broken windows); when we were together, I cursed it and made apologies for its behavior to visitors. Before I met James Carlson Sweatt, the library was my best comfort and company. I was a fool for that library.

We are fools for who will have us.

I did see other people. My patrons, for instance. Pharmacists are the same, I guess—you learn the dirty little secrets of what's wrong with your customers and what might possibly cure it: shy men who want to read about wars, any war at all; fading women who need a weekly romance. Plenty of people came in more than once a week. Mr. Mackintosh, a widower, fancied himself a writer and wanted me to read his stories. I read one; it was about a stripper. Mrs. Carson was on her fourth husband; I wondered when she had the time to read her best sellers. A nice couple brought in pictures of their dogs, fox-haired terriers, natty dressers—the dogs, I mean; not the couple. My landlord, Gary, a tragic man whose wife had left him eight years before, came to read magazines once a week.

I had my co-workers, too, who some days I forget. I see myself alone in the library, alone with the patrons. Pride does this. I remember myself alone with James when he was dying, too, although that isn't true either; there were always other visitors. At the library I worked with two other people: Astoria Peck and Darla Foster, both part-timers. Darla was a twenty-year-old who'd have been better suited to waitressing. I don't know why I hired her, other than the fact she was my sad landlord's daughter. Darla shelved the books, put the daily papers on the forked wooden spines that rested in metal stands, worked the front desk when I was busy. She had a rear end as big as an open dictionary and a bad attitude.

Astoria Peck handled most of the library's technical processes—repairing books or sending them out to a bindery, if they could be saved at all; cataloguing; billing. Like me, she was a librarian (that is, she had a master's in library science) and had for many years worked at the elementary school. Once she hit forty, she said, she got tired of the smell of children.

"They smell like bad cookies," she told me. "Go ahead, get a good whiff."

I demurred, which was never enough for Astoria. The next child through the door prompted her to nudge me—"Go ahead."

Astoria had been told once that she should go to Hollywood; she never did, but she also never forgot the suggestion, and wore her hair and makeup like a movie star. She was the type of person who relied very much on what other people told her about herself. She'd been informed, variously, that she was a card, an enigma, a heartless woman. Her mood depended on what was last said to her; it prevailed until the next assessment. Her husband told her she had beautiful legs, and she was happy; her niece told her she had big ears, and she was devastated.

"I have big ears," she told me mournfully. "I'm a big-eared woman."

Astoria and I were bound together by our terrible struggles with the library building and the troubles it caused with the town manager, who, when we wanted our book budget increased, said that he'd *been* to the library, and the shelves were *already* full. He'd look at a repair bill and say, "What did they fix that toilet with, gold?" Between the building, which was falling to pieces, and the town manager, who was solid rock, we were left to setting out buckets for leaks and fixing wobbly tables with books we were going to throw out anyhow, books that had not circulated in thirty years. For some reason, though, a table leg set down on a dust jacket seemed to patrons the highest recommendation; they wanted to take those books out, accused us of neglecting great works.

* * *

Mrs. Sweatt started coming to the library for herself, for romance novels and women's magazines. She nodded at me shyly, sneezed in the dust. You could hear her sneeze in the stacks from anywhere in the library; it sounded like a reproach.

"What is her name?" I asked Astoria. "She calls me Peggy, but she hasn't even told me what her Christian name is."

"That's it," Astoria said. "That's what everyone calls her. I guess when she and her husband got married, they called each other Mister and Missus—you know, like any honeymoon couple—and they just never got out of the habit. Then other people picked up on it."

"She's not from around here."

"No," said Astoria. "Heavens, no. Midwest somewhere. Came out on vacation with her parents, met Mr. Sweatt, stayed. He could have swept any girl off her feet, that one. Charming, a fast talker. Nobody could figure out what he saw in her."

"Well," I said.

"I mean, she was this sort of tragic character—even then she was, I'm not sure why—and Mr. Sweatt was a boisterous, friendly guy. A bad guy who made himself seem nice sometimes, or the other way around, you know the type?"

No, I said, I didn't.

"He left. About six years ago, maybe. Just disappeared out west. That's where ex-husbands go, right? There must be whole ranches of ex-husbands out there, leaning on corrals and drinking too much gin." She laughed. "And now here's poor Mrs. Sweatt. Drinking a little too much herself, actually."

"Oh."

"She thinks it's a secret. But listen to her purse when she walks by. Slosh, slosh."

"I don't listen to purses," I said. "Purses are a private matter."

Shy, sensitive-to-dust Mrs. Sweatt. Her arms and legs were plump, as if her heart did not want them to get too far away, and sometimes she seemed to limp. I thought her marriage must never have been happy; I couldn't imagine her enjoying the company of a boisterous man. And if you were boisterous, it would be hard not to torment Mrs. Sweatt, who did not have a sense of humor in the way most people do not have a sense of French.

In our town, we did not measure time in years, but in winters. Summers were debatable daylight; winters were definite, like night. In the dark privacy of winter Brewsterville's citizens were more likely to drink, weep, have affairs, tell off-color jokes, let themselves go.

Then summer came around again, and they ironed their best pants, sewed on buttons popped by eagerness or an extra five pounds, and got back to work.

It wasn't that nothing happened during tourist season, simply that summers were so crowded with quotidian incidents as to appear identical to one another. The tourists came in. Every year one took a heart attack in a restaurant; several were accused (rightly or wrongly) of shoplifting a souvenir ashtray from one of the souvenir ashtray emporiums; dozens tried to seduce coffee shop waitresses and succeeded or didn't, depending on the coffee shop; and an even hundred tried to get library cards good for one week, despite living in California, despite a remarkable lack of identification. And then the summer ended, and the tourists left, and it was as if the town itself had just returned from a vacation somewhere far off, having never sent a postcard to keep all of us up-to-date on its seasonal goings-on.

There was the winter of 1951, with the bad ice storm (unusual for us) during which, Astoria said, Marie at the post office got stranded and then pregnant with a boyfriend from Hyannis at the only inn open year round. James was twelve, and just under six foot four. The following winter, there was barely any snow at all, and the used bookstore closed up when the man who owned it shot himself—nobody could understand why, with the weather so pleasant for a change. James turned thirteen. Next, the winter of 1953. His growth was like weather, some years worse than others: he grew six inches between his thirteenth and fourteenth birthdays, and Brewsterville lost power four times in thunderstorms.

Though I wouldn't have admitted it, what I'd mostly known previously was what everyone did: his height. The tall boy, our town giant. I knew that height well, of course: Astoria had given me the details. When he was a baby, strangers thought he was retarded because he was so slow for his size. The hems on everything he wore were deep as most people's pockets, so they could be let out, and his pockets were twice as deep as his hems.

I'd been captivated by his height, and the heroic way he seemed to bear it. Now I learned he was interesting in many unconnected ways. I could write an encyclopedia on his enthusiasms and how they accumulated, complete with dates and cross-references.

"What's your hobby this week?" I'd ask.

"I'm thinking model building," he'd say. "But not from kits. I want to start from scratch, so I need books on battleships." Or, "Gardening." Or, "I want to make my own root beer. Are there recipes for things like that?"

He was fond of the sorts of books that I'd loved as a child, huge omnibuses of humor, pranks, or science experiments. A serious kid most of the time, he allowed himself to get silly at strange moments.

He came in one day wearing a plastic nose, ordered from the back of a magazine, underscored by the falsest moustache I'd ever seen. (All his life, he loved what you could get through the mail. Eventually he had dozens of degrees from correspondence schools and was a mail-order minister several times over.) The nose was beaky and sharp and coming loose at the edges. I said, "You look like the canary who swallowed the cat," and he laughed his moustache right off. Every now and then he'd approach the desk with a glass of water filled from the bubbler in the hall, and would ask me, in a reasonable tone of voice, to put my hands out or turn my back for a second. I explained to him that I wasn't born yesterday. Astoria, however, was a perfect pigeon, and I more than once had to rescue her: she'd set her hands, palms down, on the circulation desk, and James had balanced a glass filled with water on each, then whistled his way to the back of the library. James introduced me to my first joy buzzer, and Astoria to her first whoopie cushion. I knew better than to accept candy from him: I knew it would be rubber, or bitter, or explosive.

Nevertheless, I was the town librarian—less a woman than a piece of civic furniture, like a polling machine at town hall, or a particularly undistinguished WPA mural—and even those years had a sameness to them, uninvolved in gossip as I then was. I have had to consult one of those medical charts to see during which year he grew six inches. James was a library patron, then, a cherished one, but when I saw him on the street with his friends, a rare summer sunburn across his nose, or, in the fall, heading toward his house with a bag of groceries, or, in winter, pulling on a knit cap that his mother no doubt insisted on, I was only one of the many people who knew him: everyone knew him. There was no way for him to tell that I noticed the sunburn, that I could summon up Mrs. Sweatt's voice commanding him not to be foolish, not to catch cold.

My own life went on in this way. I woke up, cleaned my apartment, went to work, came home. I almost always had a book in my hand, to shelve or read or consider.

James's life went on, too. He grew. That was his life's work. He got the glasses he needed. His uncle found him a camera, and James carried it by the neck strap all around town. I saw him making his way down the street clicking pictures. The year-rounders were used to him, but tourists stopped and stared.

Summers made even me feel as if I were becoming famous. That is, people took my picture constantly. That is, I kept accidentally stepping into the frame as a tourist took a picture of something else. These are the two truths of tourists: they walk slowly, and they must record their slow progress down the street. I appear in family albums, in slide carousels, sometimes a blur and sometimes a sulky stranger. When I ate my lunch on a bench outside the library, they thought me particularly picturesque, and photographed me on purpose.

They loved James, of course, and asked to take his picture,

usually alongside a wife. He allowed it as long as they returned the favor. He really was becoming famous; usually they asked his name so they could write on the back of the snapshot. Mother, Niagara Falls, 1949. Minna, 1950. James Sweatt, Brewsterville, Cape Cod, 1954.

He never recorded the names of the tourists; what made one different from another? He read books on developing photographs. He became a Boy Scout, the world's biggest. He wrote a prize-winning essay on community service. He played basketball, of course, and was always described as the star. By this they meant, tall. Any number of the words used to describe James just meant tall.

Certainly things could have continued thus, and I would have completed my life never knowing the lack. Or rather, I would have kept my relationship as it was with James, finding him books and recognizing a lack and counting myself lucky for that. Lacking things was what I did; I might as well lack something interesting. I felt in those days quite set apart from the rest of the human race, who regularly got what they wanted and complained anyhow.

•

On September 3, 1955 (James was sixteen and seven foot six; those are the vital statistics), I was just locking up the library doors after work, doing my usual ritual: check my pocket for the keys, close one of the big oak doors; check my pocket again, in case I was imagining things; close the other; check my pocket. Six steps led up to the library's entrance. When I stood on the top stair, my head was roughly level with that of the statue of the town founder, which stood in the park across the street.

It was one of those days when the clouds ran past the sun as if they expected it to give chase: instead, Brewsterville's main street dimmed, then brightened, then dimmed again. A small elderly woman stood at the base of the statue, trying to decide whether to sit down on the green park bench. A teenage boy in bad need of a haircut helped her—did she want to sit down? Was she sure? His hand touched the back of her elbow. I wondered if they were relatives or strangers.

Then the clouds moved along, and the street turned gold, and so did the woman's hair. It was Mrs. Sweatt, that hair like stained glass; I could almost see the comb marks in it, like mullions. The teenage boy was Caroline Strickland, her own hair cut recently and too short.

Mrs. Sweatt was wearing some kind of strange athletic outfit: bloomers and a zip-up jacket. I considered fishing my keys out and going back into the library. Not that I wanted to avoid them in particular: I wanted to avoid everyone I knew, when I wasn't in the library, out of that special brand of shyness that borders on arrogance.

But then they sat down and looked up. Mrs. Sweatt pointed at me. "The lady from the library!" Caroline said, so loudly I assumed it was a greeting. There was nothing to do but walk down the stairs and across the street.

"Hello," I said. "My name's Peggy."

"Of course it is," said Caroline. She didn't bother to tell me her name again, though I remembered it. "We've been playing baseball."

"Softball," said Mrs. Sweatt.

"Right," said Caroline. "Actually, *I* wasn't playing, just Missus, James, and my husband. The nursing home—where Missus volunteers—against the Brewsterville Inn—which is where Oscar, my husband, works."

"Who won?"

"The Inn murdered us," Mrs. Sweatt said softly, as if reporting an actual, traumatic crime.

"But Missus has been practicing, and she was very good."

Mrs. Sweatt laughed. She gave Caroline a pat, and then the park bench behind her. And at that moment, I knew why her husband fell in love with her, why any man would. The languid, fond hand, and that sudden giggle—it was like a magician pulling coins from your ear and then handing them over, as if the two of you were equally responsible for the sudden small miracle of wealth.

"What Caroline means is, I caught the ball once."

"But that's hard!" said Caroline. "It's a big ball!"

"For all the good it did us. Jim hit our only home run."

"We're waiting for the menfolk right now," Caroline said. "We're going to Charley's for ice cream. You want to come?"

You can't imagine how this question astounded me. Did people really do this? See somebody on the street and take her away, as if communing with others of the human race were the simplest thing in the world?

I couldn't think of the answer, and so I offered a simple statement of fact: "I don't want to intrude."

"No intrusion," said Caroline. "Look, here they come."

I turned around to see James walking toward us, a car driving slowly next to him, as if it were his pet. At a corner they both stopped, and James leaned over and stuck his head in the car. Then he turned down the side street, and the car continued toward us.

The Stricklands' car was an enormous green Chevy, with a sun visor that made it look perturbed and dishonest, like a gambler. The man who stepped out somehow matched, big-faced and lantern-jawed, with hair so glossy black I wondered whether it was dyed. He was broad through the shoulders in an old-fashioned square-muscled way.

Mrs. Sweatt was standing up, looking upset. "Where did Jim go?" she asked the man.

"Some kids are having a barbecue, so he decided to stand up the old people." He smiled at me. "I'm Oscar Strickland."

"Peggy Cort," I said.

"Nice to meet—"

"He should ask *me* for permission," said Mrs. Sweatt.

Oscar shrugged. "Sorry. I didn't think you'd mind." But Mrs. Sweatt was looking wistfully at where James had disappeared.

"I invited Peggy to come with us," said Caroline.

"Am I invited for the ride even if I don't eat ice cream?" I asked.

Oscar looked shocked at such a sentiment. "No ice cream?"

I watched Caroline pinch him in the side.

"You're welcome to come," she said, "ice cream or no ice cream."

I rode in the back with Mrs. Sweatt, who looked out the

window with a great deal of purpose. Charley's was in Provincetown, on the skinny main street that ran parallel to the bay. The sun had set by the time we got there, and the air was by-the-sea-in-autumn cool. Mrs. Sweatt announced that she didn't want any ice cream either.

"This is Charley's!" said Oscar.

Mrs. Sweatt pulled her socks up and tugged at the cuffs of the bloomers. "I'm just going to walk to the beach," she said.

"Peggy, why don't you go with her?" said Caroline.

Mrs. Sweatt sighed audibly.

"Good idea," Oscar said. "We'll have our ice cream and catch up with you."

"I may be a while," said Mrs. Sweatt. "I want to sit in a little silence."

"You can sit in silence with Peggy. We'll have our ice cream. We'll give you time."

"Okay," Mrs. Sweatt said to me. "Come on."

I didn't want to go with her, of course, and yet was happy to: I've always found a certain sullenness comforting. So Mrs. Sweatt and I walked the block to the bay, to one of the stone walls that separated the backs of the shops from the start of the beach. Mrs. Sweatt climbed up to sit down, and I followed.

"So," I said. "James hit a home run."

Mrs. Sweatt was trying her best to sit in a little silence.

I hadn't dressed for a sea breeze, and I rubbed my goose-bumpy arms. "I didn't know he was an athlete."

"You should see him play basketball," said Mrs. Sweatt. "He sure doesn't get it from me."

"But you played today, too, right?"

She smiled. "I caught one lonely pop fly. Thus begins and ends my career in sports."

"What about James's father?" I asked. "Was he an athlete?"

Mrs. Sweatt played with some sand caught in the cracks of the wall, then looked toward the bay. Her bloomers buckled up into silly pleats across her lap. Finally she said, "Who?"

"Ah. You've forgotten him."

"No." She sighed. "I can't forget him. I don't even try."

It was like a line of a popular song—*I can't forget, I don't even try*—and she made it sound like the truest sentence there ever was.

"Shouldn't you try?" I said dubiously.

"For what? Then I'd remember trying, too." She started digging in her soft purse. "There's two ways to get rid of something that big: effort and erosion. I'm trying for the second." She brought out a dark brown medicine bottle and drank straight from it. Then she coughed.

"It's not working," I said.

"What?"

"The cough syrup. You coughed."

She looked at the bottle. "Vodka." She screwed the cap back on. "I'm on this medicine. To keep my weight down. It makes me nervous, so sometimes I take a little vodka to balance it out. You're lucky, you don't have to worry about your weight. Without my medicine, I'd start eating the ice cream and I—I just wouldn't *stop*. So this medicine makes me stop." She shook the bottle, then took another sip. "Disgusting."

It was as much as I'd ever heard Mrs. Sweatt say. I understood, now, why I'd been sent along—to keep her, if not from actually drinking, then from drinking alone.

"I never was a vodka drinker," I said.

"Me neither. But if I don't—I get nervous. I can't sleep." She offered me the bottle.

"No, thanks."

"I drink too much," she said.

"Do you?"

"So they say." She banged her heels against the seawall, thinking. She shook her bottle again, as if she were trying to conjure up more vodka, and examined its level. "I know people talk about me, I know what they say about me, I just try not to listen or behave too badly. I'd drink whiskey, but people can smell that." She laughed her magician's laugh, wistful and miraculous. "That's all I need, to have people in this town talk truth instead of rumors. Nobody is invisible"—at this she elbowed me lightly—"but I aim to be at least confusing."

"Whiskey," I said. "Now you have me wanting some."

She cut a look at me. "Really? You'd drink whiskey?"

"Sure," I said. I half expected her to pull a second bottle from her bag, but instead she jumped up. "Come on," she said. "They're dawdling. We have time." She slapped sand off the seat of her dark bloomers. "Come on," she said again.

She led me to a door with a stained-glass window that showed two pilgrims, heels kicked up, mugs in their hands. The edge of the bar was two steps from the door. Mrs. Sweatt waved at the bartender, whispered something, and held up two fingers. He nodded and delivered two shots of whiskey.

"It's cold out," said Mrs. Sweatt to me, "and bourbon's better than vodka, you're right." She took one dainty sip from her glass. "I used to be quite a drinker, when I was younger. Teenager. Sweet drinks."

"This was where?" I held the glass beneath my nose. I was not a drinker at all. The smell was incredible. I knew from my college experiences that I'd have to down it all at once—the first sip would put me off.

"Davenport. Iowa. Bix Beiderbecke was from there, too. That's about it."

"Who?"

"*Who?* Bix! Really? You don't know him? Something I know and you don't. He was a cornet player. Famous one. Before my time, but his family still lived there. Everyone felt sorry for the Beiderbeckes. Drink your whiskey. We should get back."

"I will. Why did they feel sorry?"

"Well, their *son*. A *jazz* musician. And he was a drug addict, too. I think that's what killed him; he died young, anyhow. Everyone felt so sorry for the Beiderbeckes. Like they feel sorry for me in Brewsterville."

"They don't—"

"They do," she said. She'd finished her whiskey in small furtive sips.

"Have another," I said. "This is all I'm having."

"Maybe I will." She looked appealingly at the bartender, who brought her a second. "No," she said. "They do. And it's just like with the Beiderbeckes. Bix was the most important thing to ever happen to Davenport. And Jim will be the most important thing to happen to Brewsterville. I'm not just saying that because I'm his mother. He'll be famous."

"I think so," I said. "A famous lawyer, maybe."

She looked at me as if I were the stupidest person in the world. "Oh, I'm not talking about what he'll *do*. I'm talking about him. He'll be the tallest man ever, that's why he'll be famous."

"He's young," I said. "He won't grow forever."

"You'll see," she said. "Drink."

I didn't want to. I investigated my glass, trying to seem thoughtful. "But your husband," I said. "He wasn't from Iowa."

She wrinkled her nose, then scratched it. Mrs. Sweatt was always itchy when questioned. "No. He was a Cape Cod boy. Cape Cod." She sighed. "Ruined me."

"The Cape or the boy?"

"Oh, I guess I can't pin it on the Cape," she said. "Drink your whiskey."

"Okay." I lifted the glass, paused, poured it in my mouth, and swallowed. I concentrated on whacking the empty glass on the bar, so I wouldn't shudder.

Mrs. Sweatt smiled completely for the first time in my presence; I saw that one of her lower teeth was entirely silver. "Wow," she said. She'd forgotten that in whiskey, as in many things, it's the amateurs who have to be showy.

It wasn't as cool as I'd expected outside; it had been the wind off the ocean that chilled us, and now we were a block inland. Mrs. Sweatt was back to her usual silence. I still could taste the whiskey on the edges of my tongue. I felt a trifle unbuckled.

From behind us, a voice said, with a conspicuous lack of French accent, "It's les girls!"

I turned. Oscar, of course.

"Les Brewsterville girls! Where you been, girls?"

Mrs. Sweatt wore a distracted, wistful look on her face, like the girl singer of a big band during a tragic ballad's instrumental solo.

"Walking," I told Oscar. "Only walking."

* * *

Even now, I remember Mrs. Sweatt as the embodiment of every sad love song ever written; she believed every musical statement of what love did to you when it went wrong, how it was like a poison without an antidote, how you'd never breathe right again. Most people feel that way only when the music plays; all her days, Mrs. Sweatt's heart was tuned to some radio frequency crammed with tragedy. Even that night in Provincetown (sitting on the sea wall, walking to the bar, drinking whiskey) she sounded like she was singing her own sad, particular lyrics: *Can't blame it on Cape Cod, guess I'll blame it on the boy.*

To others, perhaps, Mrs. Sweatt and I seemed similar: two youngish single women in a town of married couples. People in town probably pitied our singularity. We were old to be unmarried, and odd, surely matchless. But here's the difference: she was ruined by love—that's how she put it—while I was ruined by the lack of it. And the fact is when you're flooded with something, you're more likely to rot away, to disappear entirely, than if you dry up slowly. Ask the Egyptians, ask anyone.

The Adventures of Rocket Bride

A month after that night in Provincetown, James brought me a folded piece of ruled paper.

"It's from my aunt," he said.

The handwriting said *Peggy Cort* on the outside of the fold. It was improbably fancy handwriting for the unfancy paper—brown ink and the practiced thick-then-thin cursive of someone who'd been brought up to write thank-you notes promptly.

Inside were the words *dinner, friday, six pm, dessert if you're willing.*

All my life, dinner invitations moved me peculiarly. Dinner parties, like romance, always seemed to happen to someone else. I was a librarian approaching thirty, and people perhaps thought I was allergic.

I kept the catalog cards of withdrawn books for scrap at the desk. I picked one up to respond and glanced at the back. *A home cyclopedia, encompassing health, nutrition, and child rais-*

ing. That didn't seem right. I sorted through the pile, hoping ridiculously I'd find one of the cards for that ruined copy of *Tom Sawyer* James had kept, but of course I'd pulled them years before. Some long-gone patron had already taken them, jotted down something less important on the back of the title card, the author card, the shelf list. I settled for *A History of Rhode Island*.

Dear Mrs. Strickland: Yes please, I wrote. *And yes to dessert as well. P. Cort.* I folded it in half. The printing on the front of the card left no room for me to write her name as she'd written mine, so I slipped my note in a library envelope.

Mrs. Sweatt met me at the door. Instead of saying hello, she plucked the bakery box from my hands by the length of string that held it shut, then turned from me, as if she were a servant taught not to interact with the guests. I hadn't seen her at the library in the past few weeks, I realized, and in that short time she'd changed. Her face puffed out, as if she'd gained ten pounds only in her head; the rest of her looked bird-skinny.

"Hello," I said. I tried to make it sound meaningful.

She sighed, and lifted that newly heavy head, and looked at me, and said, "I've been sick."

Oscar Strickland was just behind Mrs. Sweatt; he shook my hand. "Hello, Miss Cort." He, too, seemed strangely shy; I'd remembered him as a jocular man, even loud.

"Please call me Peggy," I said.

Caroline came out of the kitchen, drying her hands on the back pockets of her jeans. "Why Peggy Cort," she said. "How nice."

"There's cake," said Mrs. Sweatt. She'd set the empty box on the table by the door and now peered into the little white cake that balanced on her upturned palms.

James did not have dinner with us; he was working on some homework at a friend's. I wondered whether he spent a lot of time avoiding the grown-ups—I wanted to pin his absence on something other than my presence, since I'd secretly hoped that the invitation was his doing. Well, I thought: James's house. I wanted to look at every object and invest it with him, to pick up a bottle off the plate rail that ran the edge of the dining room, unfold the quilt hanging off the back of a chair, saying, *James?* as if James were a relative so long missing I believed he'd somehow become the bottle, the quilt. But that was impossible. The knickknacks had clearly belonged to some significant but long-dead old lady; the furniture was mismatched and gummy with years of hasty polishings. Nothing reminded me of him. I sat at the dinner table in what I assumed was his chair.

They called Mrs. Sweatt simply Missus and treated her like a girl who might be ruining her chance for happiness at every turn. Eat your meatballs, Missus. Aren't you cutting off your circulation, sitting that way? Missus made the dinner; she embroidered the tablecloth, too; we're trying to get her to sell her work in town, but she won't. I felt like they were trying to arrange a marriage between the two of us.

"I hope you're feeling better," I told Mrs. Sweatt, wondering what she'd been sick with. Perhaps I'd try to look it up in my book of symptoms: swollen face, lethargy. The only affliction I knew so defined was desperate weeping.

She shrugged. "They tell me I'm supposed to."

"Missus is getting skinnier," said Caroline, "while I'm getting *fatter.*" She thumped her stomach.

"Don't hit the baby," said Mrs. Sweatt. "Caroline's going to have a baby. She treats it like a drum, but it's a baby."

"It isn't anything *yet,*" Caroline told me. "I'm barely pregnant."

"That's wonderful," I said.

Caroline nodded shyly.

Mrs. Sweatt drank milk from an enormous glass. At first I wondered whether there was any vodka in it; then I saw that she wasn't really drinking at all: every now and then she lifted the glass to her face, looked in, and set it back down, the milk level the same.

After dinner Caroline suggested a break before dessert, and Mrs. Sweatt started to clear the table. She moved very slowly, as if the table were a magnet and all the dishes steel. Several times she lifted a dish a few inches and put it right down.

"Do you need help?" I asked.

Mrs. Sweatt straightened the tablecloth and said, slowly, "You're a guest." Maybe she *was* drunk.

Caroline took me by the elbow. "Come see the house."

So Oscar and Caroline gave me a tour; I looked around greedily. It seemed much the same as it had the last time I'd been there, a motley, homely, dazzling collection of furnishings that seemed to have only the most tenuous relationship to one another. I imagined taking down books and vases, anything I pleased, even curtains, and inquiring, in a businesslike tone, how long I might keep them. There is nothing I can't make into a library in my brain, no objects I don't imagine borrowing or lending out. Not out of generosity—I am a librarian, and protective—but out of a sense of strange careful justice. Part of me believes all material things belong to all people.

It was a house easily taken over by objects. White thuggy appliances crowded the kitchen; a huge unmade bed took up almost the entire bedroom. The thrown-back messy blankets embarrassed me.

On the back wall of the shadowy basement, dozens of little pictures hung off a peg board: the ocean, wheat fields, a woman brushing her hair, a horse, and one large canvas that looked abstract but I suspected was merely bad. They were Oscar's; he was the artist of the seascape in James's room, of the little flowers on the side of the house. The paintings were damp and blurry and looked ready to overflow their frames, as though they'd been painted through tears.

"What medium do you prefer?" I asked.

"All of 'em. I'm thinking of getting into comic books." He walked to a table and picked up a piece of paper. It was a cartoon of a bride, with long blond hair, her veil flipped back and streaming behind her like a cape. The bodice of her dress was tight, cut low, and the deep line of her cleavage split in two and broke into curves over each breast. Flames shot out from the bottom of her skirt, a train of flames, and her face was full-lipped and big-eyed and small-nosed and smirking and unmistakably Mrs. Sweatt's. Mrs. Sweatt a month before, with her old cheekbones and cynicism.

"Rocket Bride," Oscar said. "My newest invention."

Rocket Bride, Oscar explained, had been abandoned by her groom at their wedding reception. In her grief she developed the ability to fly and now traveled the world, looking for her husband, but more *importantly*, stressed Oscar, fighting crime and injustice. She subdued criminals with her bouquet. She sometimes worked with her sidekick, Maid O' Honor. It was her wedding dress that supplied her superpowers, and she vowed not to take it off until she found her wayward groom.

"Do you pose?" I asked Caroline.

"He's never asked me," she said.

Oscar laughed. "For a comic book? I work from the imagination only. Not that you wouldn't make an excellent superhero," he said to Caroline.

"I haven't got any superpowers," she said.

"What will she do when she finds him?" I asked.

"Finds who?" asked Oscar.

I took the page from his hand. "Her husband. Will they settle down and live happily ever after?"

"Lord, no." He looked over my shoulder at Rocket Bride, put a finger on the crown of her head. I saw by the careful signature in the corner that he was the one who'd written my dinner invitation. He stretched his arm around me, set his hand on my shoulder. Then he frowned, and with his other hand carefully whisked away a few pink-and-gray eraser leavings from the edge of Rocket Bride's veil. "Never. Rocket Bride's not the forgiving kind. No," he said. "I think that husband should just pray he never gets found."

His hand was still on my shoulder.

I am not a person who likes to be touched casually, which means of course that I like it a great deal. Every little touch takes on great meaning—oh, I could catalog them all for you: the bus driver who offered his hand as I stepped down from his bus, his other hand hovering near but not touching the small of my back. My flirtatious college friend who could not keep her hands off of anyone, who flicked one restless finger on the back of my wrist, on my forearm. Handshakes. Because I am short, certain tall people cannot resist palming my head; one college boyfriend stroked my hair so often in the early days of our courtship that, crackling with static, I could have clung to the wall like a child's balloon.

My list would go on forever, and still it would be shorter than other people's, because those tentative friendly fingers make me stiffen, and by the time I realize I've done it and try to relax, the hands are gone. People get the idea. The better they know me, the less they touch me.

But Oscar did not know me at all. Did not notice the way I quietly jumped as his hand touched my shoulder blade. Did not take his hand away until he was ready to set Rocket Bride down again.

"I have lots of ideas," he said. "She's just the first. There's Fancy Boy, and the Mighty Midget, and, let's see, Radio Dog—"

Caroline shook her head. "Oscar dreams big."

"Why not?" said Oscar. "Doesn't cost anything. Here's another idea. Record players for cars. I can't get anybody to invest, but it's what the American public wants."

"It is?" I said.

"Well," said Caroline, "it's what Oscar wants."

I said, "But is this a nation of Oscars?"

He got a happy, planning look in his eyes. "A nation of Oscars," he said, as if he were wondering how to swing it.

"*There's* an idea," said Caroline.

"A nation of Oscars," he repeated, smiling fondly.

He would have loved that, I think. Some people like to think they are unique; I saw immediately Oscar did not. What better than walking into a crowd of himself, brillantined, back-slapping men who would congratulate themselves on the good fortune of being who they were. "I commend you on your taste," Oscar would say to Oscar. "You're my kind of man."

When we went back upstairs, Mrs. Sweatt was simultaneously smoking a cigarette and trying to put on a duffel coat. She was apparently unwilling to put down the cigarette and kept switching it from one hand to her mouth to the other hand, trying to avoid the cloth.

"Where you going, Missus?" Caroline asked.

She looked a little panicked, as if she'd been caught doing something she'd been warned against. "Just going for a walk."

"Missus," said Oscar. "You think that's a good idea?"

"Around the block," she said.

"Why don't you have dessert with us," said Caroline.

"A short walk," said Mrs. Sweatt. She had the cigarette in her mouth now, buttoning her coat, her eyes shut to avoid the smoke. She slipped the last toggle through the loop by her neck.

"Alice," said Caroline. "He said he'd be home by nine."

The sleeves of Mrs. Sweatt's coat covered her hands; the smoke threatened to cover her face. Her skirt was longer than the coat and bunched up in flowered folds around her calves. She stood still for a minute, considering, then silently went to the table and sat down and ground the cigarette out on the edge of a plate.

"Peggy, come to the kitchen with me," said Caroline. "Help me cut your beautiful cake."

Caroline turned on the faucet and washed her hands.

"An after-dinner walk doesn't sound so bad to me," I said, rubbing my stomach. "Nice to take the air after a meal."

"Missus doesn't want to walk," said Caroline. "She wants to spy."

In the dining room, Mrs. Sweatt sat rigidly on her chair. "It's cold outside."

Oscar looked through the window at a thermometer attached to the outside sill. "Forty-one. Not too bad. Missus, why don't you take off your coat."

She undid the toggles slowly, top to bottom, then slipped out of it one arm at a time. It flopped over the back of her chair.

"Here," said Oscar. "Let me help you." He stood up and walked behind her.

Mrs. Sweatt took hold of one of the sleeves of the coat as if it were the arm of a favored suitor. "I might go out after."

"Just stand up a minute."

She did, and Oscar pulled out the coat and draped it over the back of her chair. "That better?" he asked.

She nodded.

Oscar picked up the plate with the cigarette. "Missus has started smoking again."

"I picked it up from some friends in the hospital," she said.

Caroline passed around slices of cake. The white frosting was gritty with sugar.

"Why, it's chocolate," said Oscar. "Sort of a surprise. Eat your cake, Missus."

"I don't want to get fat," she said.

"You!" Caroline leaned back to display her tiny gut. "I myself feel like the *Titanic.*"

"Be careful of icebergs," said Mrs. Sweatt. "I have it on good authority that it's a terrible thing to sink."

Then the front door rattled, and James stepped in, his hair blown back by the wind, his cheeks tweaked pink by the cold. Mrs. Sweatt stood up. Her chair fell back in a dead swoon.

"Jim," she said. She went to him, tugged on the lapels of his coat as if she were getting him ready to go back out again. She was tiny next to him, tiny and voluptuous.

"How are you feeling, Mom?" He set his hand on her head. Well, maybe he had been avoiding her, but the loving concern on his face was so clear it pained me, and then I was disgusted with myself for envying a boy's love for his mother.

"I'm okay," she said. "Here." She helped him off with his coat. Her hands went all around him, patting his chest, reaching up to touch his shoulder, his cheek. It was as if she wanted to check whether he'd grown while out of her sight, the way some mothers check for cigarette smoke or whiskey breath—though of course, she was the one likely to smell of either. "Did you have a good time?" she asked. "Did you get supper?"

"Stuart's dad has a darkroom," said James.

"I *thought* so," she said. "You smell like chemicals. Go wash." But she wouldn't let him go. His glasses had fogged up in the sudden heat of the living room, but he didn't take them off to clear them, just stood still and let his mother straighten his shirt, feel his hands for chill, smooth his cuffs. Finally she took the glasses from his face—he had to bend down to let her reach—and wiped them on the bottom edge of her sweater.

She handed them back. "You go ahead now," she said as he put them back on. "Wash your hands."

"First come say hello," Caroline called to him. She got up to help Mrs. Sweatt's chair to its feet.

"Hello, James," I said.

"Hello, Miss Cort."

"You like photography?" I asked, though I knew he did.

"Yes. I need a new camera, though."

In the living room, Mrs. Sweatt lay back on the sofa. The little bit of her face I could see past the dining room's doorframe was dreamy, resolved into its former beautiful shape.

I wanted to offer him something. "We have books on pinhole cameras." That was just the sort of thing that interested him. "You can make one from a box."

"From a box?" he asked.

From a box, I heard Mrs. Sweatt say from the other room, but I could not tell whether she was echoing my statement or her son's question.

That night, when I got outside, when Oscar and Caroline and James had seen me to the door, Oscar touching my shoulder again, Caroline my elbow, James not touching any part of me—I remember all the careless fingers of my life, those that settle and those that don't—when the door was closed behind me and I was alone in the cold, I hugged myself, smiled to myself, whispered assurances in my own ears—those little things you do, alone, when you have just glimpsed part of an agreeable future. No doubts, no apprehension—those are for later, when the future has arrived and you have to deal with the particulars. This moment was the best time. Everything was possible and improbable and meant nothing at all to anyone but me.

I'd read a little about magic; it was something I'd liked as a child, too, not sleight of hand but spectacular escapes. I thought my size would be an advantage. Houdini knew how to dislocate his shoulders, but I was so small I was sure I wouldn't have to do that: my mere tininess would free me.

Now, I wanted to out-Houdini Houdini, but in reverse. I wanted not to escape, but to enter, to insinuate myself into the smallest places in that house, behind the oil burner, underneath the buffet, inside the oven. I wanted to get myself so caught they'd have to let me stay. Look, they'd say, how did she manage that? That space isn't big enough for anyone. Look at her: she's surely trapped.

Cures for Height

Caroline started coming to visit me at work. At first I tried to give her library service. "What kind of books do you like?" I asked, and she smiled and said, "Nothing for me, thank you." She carried some knitting in a bag and sat at the front table, as though it were somebody's living room; she showed absolutely no interest in the smallest resource of the library, apart from the furniture and the librarian.

She wanted to make conversation. "How's business?" she asked. At first I was terse. (Well, all my life I've been terse, but I mean especially.) In my role as a boss I constantly had to give Astoria meaningful looks when one of her pals lingered too long. It rarely worked; Astoria kept on talking, setting first her elbows, then her upper arms, and finally her impressive bosom upon the counter. Sometimes her voice got too loud; sometimes she whispered in a conspiratorial way. For years I'd tried to keep myself pure in this respect, talking solely about library issues to patrons, even James. That way my meaningful looks could be righteous, if ineffective.

But that was impossible with Caroline, and finally I thought, *forget it, Peggy*. Astoria would never change. Astoria got to talk. Why not me?

"Can't I do anything for you?" I asked Caroline.

"Nope."

Still, I pulled chairs around so she could put her feet up, even filled and delivered pointed paper cups from the dispenser near the bubbler. I took care of her in any little way I could.

Finally one week, she said, "I wish I could return the favor."

"Okay," I said. "Next time, you get me a glass of water."

"No." She was working on a bright red sweater, which she set on the table. The needles stuck out of it, like Raggedy Ann's geisha wig. "I mean, invite you over. But Missus—well, she's not feeling well, and she doesn't want visitors. When she's perked up, you'll have to come back to dinner."

I wasn't sure what to say to that. Had I said something to alienate Mrs. Sweatt at the Stricklands'? Going over everything that I'd said that night occupied me for several hours after work, a jury member reviewing the evidence. *Hello?* Perfectly blameless. *I hope you're feeling better. Do you need help?* Maybe there was something in my delivery that poisoned my intended politeness. Or maybe she objected to something I'd said to someone else, conversation that floated up through the registers from the basement with the heat, my offer of books on cameras to James. I looked in my mirror and said Hello to myself. It took several repetitions for me to decide I was being ridiculous.

Besides, Caroline came and knit, more pregnant every week, and James came to play tricks, tell bad jokes, and do research. That was more than enough consolation.

"Can you imagine," Astoria said to me, when James came in. "Being that tall."

"No," I said.

But I tried. I imagined staring down upon the heads of the world. I imagined never fitting anywhere. I tried to move my body the way James did, one slow piece at a time. But when I thought about these things, when I saw myself as the tallest woman in the world, it felt hollow. So did I. One day after closing I stood on the circulation desk, made myself eight feet tall, taller than James was at the time. A short, ridiculous person on a waist-high desk. The tops of the shelves, I saw, needed dusting.

I could not imagine myself tall, could only imagine being held in the air, suspended at an altitude of seven feet. An uncharted stretch of big body surrounded my usual shape; I tried to feel it. My legs dangled, my fingers curled where my elbows should be. Like one of those maps of lakes, where the deepest part of the water is blue, surrounded by echoes of lighter blue until the cartographer hits land. My body was only the bluest, deepest part of the lake. I could not fill out the rest of the territory.

"Something must have happened," said Astoria. "To his mother, I mean, when she was pregnant."

"Astoria," I said. "I don't think so."

"Frightened by a giraffe maybe." She giggled like a bad girl. "Or—frightened by a basketball team."

"Don't gossip," I said to her. "Especially if you're going to make things up."

"Peggy, you're too serious," she said. "In this life, you have to make things up."

"Why?"

"Because," she said. "Because—that's what life *is*. Making yourself believe the best things you can."

"The best things I can believe," I said, "are the things that happen to be true."

James took out books on astronomy, ornithology: sciences at once about tininess and height. He approached the desk with books he'd liked and asked for more—he knew it was easier to find more books with a good example in hand.

Then one day, in the first months of 1955—I remember looking over his head at some awful persistent Christmas decoration Astoria had stuck to the ceiling—he came to me without books. His height had become unwieldy; he reached out to touch walls as he walked, sometimes leaving marks way above where the other teenage boys smudged their hands. "I want books about people like me," he said.

I thought I knew what he was talking about, but I wanted to be cautious. "What exactly about you?" I asked. I made myself think of all the things he could have meant: Boy Scouts, basketball players. Never jump to conclusions when trying to answer a reference question. Interview the patron.

"Tall people," he said.

"Tall people? Just tall people in general?"

"Very tall people. Like *me*," he said, clearly exasperated with my playing dumb. "What they do."

"Okay," I told him. "Try the card catalog. Look in the big books on the table—see those books?" I pointed. "Those are books of subject headings for the card catalog. Look under words that you think describe your topic." James was used to me doing this: I gave directions but would not pull the books off the shelf for him. My job was to show people—even people I liked—how to use the library, not to use it for them. "Dig around," I said. "Try height, try stature. Then look in the catalog for books."

He nodded, leaned on the desk, and pushed off.

An hour later he headed out the door.

"Did you find what you needed?" I asked.

"There isn't anything," he said. "There was one book that sort of was about it, but I couldn't find it on the shelf."

"There's something," I told him. "Come back. We'll look for it together."

That night after closing, I hunted around myself. The only thing under *stature* was a book about growth and nutrition. I tried our two encyclopedias under height and found passing references. Not much.

In truth, my library was a small-town place, and this was a specialized topic. Still, I was certain I could find more. I got that familiar mania—there is information somewhere here, and I can find it, I have to. A good librarian is not so different from a prospector, her whole brain a divining rod. She walks to books and stands and wonders: here? Is the answer here? The same blind faith in finding, even when hopeless. If someone caught me when I was in the throes of tracking something elusive, I would have told them: but it's out there. I can feel it. God *wants* me to find it.

That night I wandered the reference department, eyed the bindings of the encyclopedias, dictionaries, atlases. James was so big I almost expected to locate him in the gazetteer. I set my hands upon our little card catalog, curled my fingers in the curved handles of the drawers. Then I went to the big volumes of subject headings.

Looking under *height* and *stature* turned up nothing; *anthropometry* was not quite right. Then I realized the word I was looking for: *Giant.*

Giant described him. *Giant*, I knew, would lead me to countless things—not just the word, located in indexes and catalogs and encyclopedias, but the idea of Giant, the knowledge that the people that James wanted to read about, people who could be described as like him, were not just tall but giants. I sat in a spindle-backed chair in the reference room, waiting for a minute. Then I checked the volume of the Library of Congress headings. *Giants. See also: dwarfs.*

We did not have a book, but I found several encyclopedia entries. Nowadays I could just photocopy; but that night I wrote down the page and volume numbers, thinking I could not bear to tell him the word to look under. Most of the very tall people mentioned in the encyclopedia had worked in the circus as professional giants, so I went to our books on the circus.

The photographs showed enormous people. Not just tall, though of course they were that, often with an ordinary person posed beside them. The tall people looked twice as big as the ambassador from the normal-sized, as if they were an entirely different race. The books described weak stomachs and legs and bones. Sometimes what made them tall showed in their faces: each feature looked like something disturbed in an avalanche, separate from the others, in danger of slipping off.

Anna Swann, the Nova Scotia Giantess, married Captain Bates, the Kentucky Giant. As a young woman at Barnum's Dime Museum in New York, Miss Swann had been in two fires; in the second she had to be lifted out by a crane. No ordinary over-the-shoulder rescue for a woman better than seven feet tall. She and her husband retired to Ohio, to a specially made house. Their church installed an extra-large pew.

Byrne, the Irish Giant, lived in fear of a certain doctor who lusted after his skeleton; he imagined the doctor's giant kettle ready to boil his bones.

Jack Earle was over seven feet tall, traveled with the circus for years; after his retirement he wrote poetry.

I took comfort in Anna Swann and her husband. They were solid-looking people. Respectable. They'd had two children, though neither survived. The book described them as *in love*, and you could believe that from the pictures: their complementary heights were just a lovely coincidence to their love affair. I found myself that late night a little jealous of Anna Swann and her handsome, bearded captain.

The books said that giants tended to exaggerate their heights for exhibition purposes. I did not know it then, but every person I read about was shorter than James grew to be.

The worst book was called *Medical Curiosities*. I say worst now. That is hindsight. The night I looked, I thought, in fact, that it was the best book—not because it was good or even accurate, but because it had the most pages on the subject I was researching. I found it under the subject heading *Abnormalities, human*. A terrible phrase, and one I knew I could not repeat to James. It was a late-nineteenth-century medical book, described two-headed people and parasitic twins and dwarfs. And giants. Not exactly information, but interesting: giants who had enormous or usual appetites; ones who grew throughout their lives or only after adolescence; professional giants and private citizens.

So I took that book, and the circus books, marked the pertinent places with the old catalog cards I used for scrap, and set them aside. Ready for him, so that he did not have to look in the index, or wander through the pages at all.

"Your tall friend is here," Astoria said to me the next week. I was in my office, reading reviews. "He's looking for you."

James waited for me at the circ desk. "You said we could—"

"I looked," I said. I'd stowed the books beneath the shelf. "Try these out."

He took them to the big table in the front room. Read them. He made the sturdy chair, the same chair I'd sat in the night before, seem tiny.

Afterward he came up to me.

"How were they?" I asked. "Would you like to take them home?"

He shook his head.

"No," he said. "Thanks."

"Nothing useful here at all?"

"No," he said.

I tried to catch his eye. "Close?"

"Close. I guess." He pointed at *Medical Curiosities*. "I guess that's close."

I picked up the book and opened it to where the marker was, but he'd moved it to another page. A line drawing of a double-bodied baby looked up at me. Horrible. I snapped the book shut.

"I meant medical books," he said. "But new ones. Ones that say what goes wrong. How to cure it."

"Cures," I said. "Oh." Cures for giants? No such thing. No cure for height. Only preventive medicine. I said it as a question. "Cures? For tall people?"

"Yes," he said.

All I wanted was for him to explain it to me. It seemed presumptuous to come to any conclusions myself. I knew what he was talking about. I did. But what he wanted, I couldn't help him with.

Darla, the shelver, came rattling up with her metal cart. "Shelve these?" she said, pointing at the books. The catalog cards I'd used stuck out from the pages; James had lined them up, like a pack of cards he'd shuffled into them. "Hi, Jim," she said.

"Hi." He squinted down at her.

She stared at me; I waited for her to get back to shelving.

"Peggy. Shelve them, or not?"

"Not yet," I said. She sighed and pushed the cart off.

James stood in silence on the other side of the desk. He looked ready to leave.

"You mean how to stop growing," I said.

"Yes." Now he looked at me. "Medicine, or operations, or something."

"I'm not sure we have anything here," I said. That was a lie. I knew we didn't. "A medical library somewhere, perhaps. Or a university library. But really—" I started pulling the bookmarks from the books. I tried to sound gentle. "Really, you should ask your doctor."

"I have," he said. "I've asked a lot of doctors."

He didn't care about Anna Swann, or the Irish Giant, or the Kentucky Giant. He'd said—I remembered—"Tall people. What they do." I assumed he meant: what tall people do. What sort of work, what sort of lives. Instead he'd meant: what doctors do for tall people.

He was a teenager who had grown into a solitary race. There was no Anna Swann for him, no Cape Cod Giantess. Only him, his shoulders carrying his head so far away from the heads of others that he had to sit down to have a private conversation with anyone, and often there wasn't a chair large enough to accommodate him. Only a boy whose body was a miracle to others. You could believe in God, looking at James. He looked at himself, and decided not to.

The Assumption of Mrs. Sweatt

I sometimes got into disagreements with patrons. They were rare. Despite my clumsiness with the outside world, I was the perfect public servant: deferential, dogged, oblivious to insults. Friendly but not overly familiar. It was one of the reasons I loved being a librarian: I got to conduct dozens of relationships simultaneously and successfully. I conformed myself always to the needs of the patrons (they certainly did not care about mine), told them they were right, called them Mr. and Mrs. and Miss when they did not bother to learn my smallest initial. Do you wonder why we're called public *servants*?

Every now and then, though, I would have a run-in with a patron who demanded something preposterous. Maybe they wanted me to immediately hand over a book so popular that others had been waiting months for it; maybe they wanted to supply a page-long shopping list of books so I could pull them off the shelves. Maybe they wanted not to be charged a penny for their enormous fines because they had been too busy to get to the library. (The most unmanageable patrons always told me how *busy* they were.) I'd say, politely, no. They'd say yes. I got firm; they got insulting. I'd start to explain my position in depth, they'd ask to see a manager—and then I'd bow my head (I *loved* this moment) and say, "I am Miss Cort, the director of the library." It was not a title I ever otherwise claimed.

I longed to say, Listen: in my library, as in the Kingdom of Heaven, the rude and busy are not rewarded. We honor manners, patience, good deeds, and grave misfortune only.

And one of two things happened: the patrons returned, and either thought I'd forgotten what had happened or had forgotten themselves, and were amazed when I politely, smilingly remembered them by name.

Or they never came back.

James and I had not argued, but I'd felt I'd done something much worse in so misunderstanding what he'd wanted, in giving him *Medical Curiosities*. I could forgive myself social clumsiness, my occasional crippling shyness, a sharp tongue at the wrong time. I could not forgive sloppy library work, and that is what I was guilty of: a patron—my best, most beloved patron—needed help in finding something, and I'd jumped to a conclusion and given him books that were worse than useless. He'd asked me a straightforward question and I had not come close to providing an answer.

But he returned the next Friday, with a different question. I still remember: he wanted to know what an anti-Pope was.

Maybe it was forgiveness, and maybe it was just teenage obliviousness, but the sight of James that afternoon seemed miraculous. *You came back,* I said to him as I sent him to the card catalog ("Look under Catholic Church—history") and he said, *Sure, Peggy, where else would I go?*

I watched him read that afternoon. He sat at the table in the front room—his favored spot, ever since his first visit. Looking over his shoulders, I could see his book through the edge of his glasses. The words slid in curves as he moved his head.

I wanted to stand there forever, see what he saw. Not possible, of course. He'd stand up and take those glasses with him. I could only see through them now, me standing and him sitting, hunched significantly over, because he needed a stronger prescription. His eyes were growing at a different rate from the rest of him and would not stay in focus.

Caroline had an easy pregnancy. I'd expected that she would. It was as if the new stomach that swelled in front of her were something she'd expected all her life, an addition that she'd been meaning for years to install. Some women move into their bellies when they're pregnant; it's everything they think of, it's what they move first and most carefully. Not Caroline. She lived in her whole easy body, barely changed her flat-footed gait.

I myself hardly noticed my physical self, which I considered a not-too-useful appendage. Only my feet demanded my attention. When I wore a bad pair of shoes on a busy day, my feet swelled, complained. I was forced to think of them, to picture getting home and slipping off my shoes, the way a starving man will torture and comfort himself with fantasies of food. Nothing to do—I could not pad around the library stocking-footed. My mouth answered questions, but I was stuck in my throbbing feet.

My feet were wide, wide, wide, and flat-footed, which was mostly a blessing—no arches to ache or fall. Nevertheless, by the time I was in my mid-twenties, they were an old person's feet, bunioned and calloused and noisome and shapeless and yellowed. Blue veins ran the length; my toes, forced into tiny places for years, huddled together for comfort. I didn't mind so much: it was as if I knew what I would look like as a senior citizen, from the ground up.

James caught me late one Friday at the library, a week after his return. (Though he hadn't actually been gone, I always thought of it that way, *his return.*) I'd taken off a shoe and put it on the counter, searching for the boulder I felt sure was somewhere around the toe. Probably it was just a piece of sand. This close to the ocean, you always have sand in your shoes, embedded in your carpet, even if you never go to the beach.

"Your shoes bother you?" he asked.

"Oh," I said. I shook out the shoe, dropped it to the floor, and stepped into it. I walked around to the front of the desk, trying to get the shoe jammed on; on top of everything, it was a little too small. "Always, I'm afraid. Usually. That's what happens when you're on your feet all day."

"What size do you wear?" he asked.

"Five and a half," I said, automatically shaving a full size off. "Women's. Different from men's."

"I know. I wear a man's thirty," he said. Then he saw the surprise on my face and laughed. "Five times bigger. More than five times." He stood beside me and steadied himself with his hand on my head. I didn't take it personally—he often steadied himself with the closest person; it was usually the handiest thing. Then he took his hand away.

"Look," he said. He'd lined up his foot with mine. They didn't even look like the same part of the body, his high black shoe next to my white pump.

"Your feet are wide," he said.

"Yes."

"So you wear a five and a half wide?"

"Five and a half, six wide."

"Which one?"

"Okay," I said. "You caught me in a vain lie. Six wide. Honest."

"Vanity is saying you wear smaller shoes than you really do?"

"Well," I said. I blushed. "For some of us, it is. Women, I mean."

Two weeks later he brought me a small cardboard box.

"I got these for you," he said.

Inside were a pair of sensible oxblood lace-ups. Old-lady shoes. The good tangy smell of leather floated up.

"James," I said. "You bought me shoes." I could not remember the last time someone had given me a gift, other than the occasional Christmas box of chocolates from a patron.

"Well, I got them," he said. "These are good for your feet. I just started working for a shoe store. They make all my shoes."

I tried to picture James sitting on a shoe saleman's slanty stool. He would not fit.

"You're selling shoes?" I asked.

"Sort of." He lifted one of the shoes out of the box and held it in his hand. "I'm going to do personal appearances. You know, show up. Look tall. And they'll make my shoes for free."

"No pay?"

"Shoes are expensive," he said. "My shoes are, anyhow." He looked back down at his feet. "Maybe I'll go to New York."

"This shoe store is in New York?"

He shook his head. "Hyannis. But there's an expo in New York in the spring." He pointed with the shoe in his hand at the shoes on my feet, navy blue snub-nosed pumps. "You shouldn't wear those," he said. "They're bad for your feet. These"—he handed me the shoe—"they have ankle support and arch support and everything. I talked to the shoe guy. I was just going to get you black, and he wanted to talk me into pink. I knew you wouldn't wear pink shoes."

"I wouldn't," I said. "That's true."

"So we compromised on red. Reddish brown, anyhow."

"They're wonderful," I said.

"Try them on. Might be a little stiff at first, but they'll wear in. The shoe guys break mine in for me with a machine, but they know exactly how my toes go. They've got a cast of my foot. A couple of casts. They've got one they're going to put in the window, and a shoe in my size that they're going to bronze and hang outside. I have to sit down now," he told me. "Try them on."

He went to one of the library's older chairs—the nineteenth-century furniture fit him best; the newer stuff was blocky and ungenerous—and dragged it close so he could watch me.

I knew, looking at the shoes, that they would be murder. True, they had ankle support. And arch support, but for someone as flat-footed as I was—and getting more flat-footed every year—that would hurt, not help. Most important was the missing half-size I had shaved off, out of vanity's sake. Now what difference would a half-size smaller foot have made to a sixteen-year-old boy, especially one who wore size thirty shoes?

They'd put a little broguing around the toes of the shoes—to make them feminine, no doubt. They reminded me of the sort of boots sullen young girls of the gay nineties wore. I picked one up.

Luckily, I could get my foot in. I was glad James had made me confess to the additional half-size. I bent down to lace it up, disappearing behind the circulation desk. The shoe had a bracing, athletic feel.

"Try them both," he said, straining to see me over the desk. "I can take them back for adjustments. Get them to stretch out parts."

I'd deliberately chosen the left shoe, since my left foot was slightly smaller than my right. But I put the other on, laced it up.

"Walk in them," James said. "Make sure they fit." He sounded like my mother, school-clothes shopping.

I took a few steps. It seemed like a miracle, and I the heroine of a fairy tale. They fit. They were rigid and, truth be told, unflattering, but what did I have that needed so badly to be flattered? I walked around the front of the desk and wiggled my toes for him.

"Okay?" he said.

"I love them."

"But do they *fit*?" asked James, ever practical.

"Of course," I said. "I couldn't love anything that didn't fit."

"Aunt Caroline says I shouldn't take advantage of the shoe store, but they told me I could have as many pairs of shoes as I want, just ask. I was going to get a pair for Mom, but I didn't."

I'd been admiring the shiny uncreased toes of my shoes. When I looked up at James, he was staring at my feet.

"Why not?"

"She only wears tennis shoes now, when she wears them at all. Mostly she just sleeps or stays on the sofa."

At first I wasn't sure I wanted to talk about Mrs. Sweatt. "How's she feeling these days?"

"Um. The same, I think. Aunt Caroline thinks better, but I don't. She doesn't get out much. You should come see her."

"Oh," I said.

"Oh, well. I don't blame you for not wanting to."

"It's not that. It's just—well, maybe when she feels better."

"Sure," said James. He smiled at me. "Whenever that is."

Though I loved my shoes (they are even now in their original box, worn once, immaculate), I did not love the fact of the shoe store. How was this different, I wondered, from Anna Swann in Barnum's museum? In those days I still imagined James could have a career other than Acting Tall, that being inspected by the curious was fine on a volunteer basis (in the summer he could not help it) but was not a sensible profession.

"So," I said to Caroline when she came to see me the next Monday. "James has a job."

"He does?" she said. She took her spot at the front table; it was quiet, so I went to join her. "How wonderful."

"You don't know about the shoe store?"

"Oh, *that*," she said. "I never really thought of that as a job. He's just going to be there twice a year, walk around."

"And perhaps go to New York for them?"

"Yes," she said. "He's looking forward to that."

"A lot of responsibility for a boy."

"Good for him," said Caroline. "And that way the shoes are free."

"When I was a girl," I said, "I didn't have to work for my shoes—"

Caroline took my hand across the library table. "When you were a girl," she said quietly, "you didn't wear size thirty shoes. Peggy, if I could buy them for him, I would. But being that tall is an expensive proposition. I can't tell you. It's not like we're rich people. I mean, we do our best, but shoes cost seventy-five dollars, and clothing as much or more. Mrs. Sweatt can't do a thing for him. I mean, she does plenty *for* him, they talk, she loves him—well, that's neither here nor there. If I could go to the shoe store, walk around for him, I would, I promise you." She laughed, laid one hand on her stomach. "Goodness knows I feel like the biggest woman in the world, but they're not offering free shoes to *me*."

At home that night, I looked at my shoes and thought of Mrs. Sweatt, napping on her sofa in her sneakers. All I had wanted was to become part of that family. And not even an important part: a trusted maid, perhaps, a cousin several times removed. But Mrs. Sweatt stamped her foot, told her sister-in-law never to invite me back. I loved seeing Caroline and James at my library, but I was still being simply a librarian.

I was a fool. Foolish to imagine making myself part of a family that was not mine; foolish to think that people thought of me as anything but the librarian, a plain, no-nonsense, uninteresting person. Foolish to imagine myself some Hans Christian Andersen princess in those damn shoes, possessor of the only feet to inhabit the magic oxfords, especially since by the end of that day my feet—as if they might really have been momentarily bewitched into submission by the shoes—assumed their true size, and cursed at me bitterly for shutting them up in those leather dungeons.

•

A knock on the door usually meant my brokenhearted landlord. Gary was a quiet, plain man, and his excuses for coming to my door did not make much sense. In winter, he wanted to check my thermostat; for what he never said. In summer, he wondered if it was too hot, though of course there was nothing he could do about that. Even when I met him outside, on my way to work, he tested the air with his arm as if he had not been outdoors all along, and guessed at the temperature.

Nobody ever loved a woman more than Gary loved his wife, everybody said, and this might be so. People in town were amazed when he, who was heartbroken and not very handy, converted the attic of their house into the apartment I moved into.

"He's getting over her," Astoria told me, just after I'd moved to town and started work at the library. "Otherwise he never would have been able to do it."

This proved not to be the case. Even my most casual conversation with him—at the house, at the library—was peppered with references to My wife, Cynthia. Finally I told him: I know her name now, you can just call her Cynthia. This seemed to both alarm and please him, as if I were laying claim simultaneously to his memories and the burden of them.

So when someone knocked on the door a few days later, I assumed it was him. It was winter and I didn't know what sort of conversation he might make. Instead, it was Caroline.

Messy people might wish their apartments clean when unexpected guests arrive. I wanted mine messy so I could do something, glance around nervously, shuffle newspapers to make room on the couch. If, upon my death, someone decided to turn my apartment into a museum, as Caroline did years later with James's cottage, they'd have to bring things in. History is all in how you display it, what's preserved: this is the lesson of Pompeii. Better to use the library, string velvet bank ropes in front of the tall stool behind the circulation desk, fan out my typed catalog cards in glass cases, frame the form letters to the thoughtless people who kept books too long and the hopeful people who returned them late but never paid the fines. In my apartment even the toothbrush was shut in the medicine cabinet. It was a toothbrush anyone might have owned. Everything was in its place, exactly, and there was nothing to occupy my worried hands.

Caroline sat down slowly on the sofa; I sat next to her and straightened the fringed throw that our weight had disturbed.

"What is it?" I asked.

"Well," Caroline said. Her bright lipstick hadn't quite made its way into the corners of her mouth. "Missus is . . . she had an accident."

"Oh, dear," I said. "What happened?"

"That, of course, is the question. Something went wrong with her pills. She took too many of them, I guess."

"On purpose?" I asked.

"Oh, maybe she forgot she'd taken it. We don't know. She'd had a drink or two. No," she said, suddenly sure. "Not on purpose." Then she took a deep breath and told me this story:

Something had gone wrong with Mrs. Sweatt's medication. That is, she took a quantity of sleeping pills—Caroline had been sure she'd thrown them all out—together with a quantity of vodka. In the middle of the night, as far as they could tell, she began to get sick and wandered—on purpose? thinking it was the bathroom?—into James's room. For some reason he elected not to wake Caroline and Oscar but to help his mother get some fresh air. Together they stepped outside onto the front step, which because it was January was icy, and because it was two-thirty A.M. had not been sanded and salted by Oscar—Caroline explained that her husband was always careful about such things. James slipped and fractured his shin; Mrs. Sweatt tumbled into the bushes. By the time James had gotten into the house and woken his aunt and uncle, his mother was unconscious.

Now James was in a hospital in Boston. The doctors said they were surprised it hadn't happened sooner—growing at such a rate guaranteed weakened bones, and almost any bone in his body was a candidate for breakage. Especially his legs, which grew faster than any other part of him.

"Oh," I said. "I'm so sorry. How is Mrs. Sweatt?"

"She's dead," Caroline said wonderingly—and she made it sound as if she were (like Mrs. Sweatt) merely repeating something I had said, as if I were the one with sudden tragic news.

"Good heavens," I said. "I'm so sorry. Poor Mrs. Sweatt."

"We wanted you to know—"

"—I appreciate it—"

"—we wanted you to know that we're not telling James. That she's dead. Not right off."

I looked at her. "How can you not?"

"We'll tell him when the excitement is over."

"It's not going to be over," I said. "His mother is dead." The Stricklands' extreme secrecy struck me as craven; they were as stingy with bad news as some people were with good.

"We've thought this over," said Caroline. "We really have, Peggy. James was trying to save his mother, if only for one night. How can we tell him he didn't?"

I didn't know.

"So maybe when he's a little better. When he's up and around. Just not today, and not tomorrow."

"Okay," I said. "I understand."

"You'll have to excuse me," Caroline said.

"Yes." I waited for her to get up. Instead, her eyes filled, and then tears rolled down her face. No other evidence of grief, just slow tears and an embarrassed smile. Then she set her wet turned-up hands on her considerable stomach, as if she intended to save her tears for some future use.

"We'll miss her," she said. Then she patted her face with the back of her hands.

"What will happen to James?" I asked.

"Oh, he'll stay with us," said Caroline. "He'll always stay with us."

"I know that," I said. "What did the doctors say?"

"They don't know. Get taller still, I guess. Bound to stop eventually."

"The doctors said that?"

"No. The doctors say he's healthy. They've said that all his life. For now, he's still growing." Caroline shook her head at this, as if his growth were some teenage notion he'd got ahold of, motorcycle riding or a wild girl. "That's all they'll say."

"What have you told him? About his mother, I mean."

"The truth," she said. "Just not all the way. She's tired, she's gone for a rest. James likes you," she said, and even given the circumstances, that trilled my heart. "Just be nice to him. I mean, I know you are."

"I am," I said. "I will." I went to put my hand over hers, but couldn't. "You'll need help," I told her. "Especially now that you don't have—"

"Yes. Well." She played with the fringe of the throw. "I just never saw it coming."

"Never saw what?"

"Mrs. Sweatt's problems," she said. "She seemed so happy to me. She had James, she had plenty to do. You'd never have known she was the least bit sad."

Not sad? To me she seemed the saddest person in the world, a woman completely perplexed by her life and its trappings. Being myself a sad person, I recognized that much. My own sadness isn't something I admit to people. If someone asked, yes, I think I might. If someone noticed and inquired, I would explain—I think I would explain—that I am a fundamentally sad person, a fundamentally unlovable person, a person who spends her life longing for a number of things she cannot bring herself to name or define. Some people can. Some people are small reference works of their own obsessions and desires, constantly cross-indexed and brimming with information. They do not wait to be consulted, they just supply.

Others of us—and I include Mrs. Sweatt—do not. We are the truly sad, I think; just as in some religions, those who pray alone, who do penance and charity work alone, are the truly pious. Like the truly pious, we can recognize one another. Mrs. Sweatt and I were lonely, independent mourners.

But she was beautiful, and I was not. This is a vital difference. She grows more beautiful in my memory, looks more like James. True enough she is small and curvy and he tall and thin, but they have the same hair—though hers is blonder, by the grace of nature or science—the same upturned nose, the same pink pillowy lips. Young faces, much more alike in my memory than they ever were when alive.

They are both dead now, and I can make them look however I want.

She was beautiful. That is a fact. So beautiful Oscar could take her face and turn her into a superheroine, into Rocket Bride, and think he was only drawing *a beautiful woman*, no one in particular. He gave Mrs. Sweatt, abandoned wife, powers that might have made her life bearable. Maybe not. Maybe they'd have been a burden, a constant reminder. Did Rocket Bride want simply to leave, her gown a netted heap on the ground? Say, forget it, I'm taking my honeymoon solo? Crime can take care of itself; injustice will have to continue unabated without my help. I will drink blue drinks and dance alone. I will love myself.

But you cannot fly away from people who have flown away from you; you cannot fly into your own arms. Mrs. Sweatt's husband had left her, James himself was growing away and away. Once you have been left you are always left; you cannot leave your leaving.

Mrs. Sweatt did not lift into the air like Rocket Bride, even though I liked to imagine she did. She died in the hospital, or on the way there, and that was only the end of the story. All night long she'd been dying on that gaudy flowered sofa, where she napped, where she waited for James to come home from school, where she spent her solitary nights. That sofa already missed the dip of her back, the way her legs were too short for her body. The way she hid those short legs with her full, high-waisted skirts.

I see her rocketing into the sky, not in a wedding dress but in one of those skirts, so big it blossoms up and haloes her. Not defiant, as Oscar had drawn her, but pensive, full of plans.

She is looking for an aerial view.

There she goes, into the thin air that wraps around the heads of statues, not the sludge near the ground that we usual people must make do with. Everyone stands up as she leaves, though she's flying away from us and can't see. She just knows. Do we miss her yet? Our heads are thrown back, mouths wide as bowls, ready for her to drop something into them. Maybe she'll write something in the sky with her vapor; maybe the vapor will use her up entirely. She levels off, inclines her head toward the ground. She's so far away she can see everything and everyone, she's made them all neighbors this way, her long-gone husband and the President of the United States and Orson Welles and she can't tell the difference between the people and the buildings, the Washington Monument is just a stop sign from this altitude. It's like she's turned everyone on earth into tacks on a child's map, each marking our own place. That far up she can see the slow curve of the earth. She sweeps closer, so she can see what we're wearing, the color in our cheeks. James is here, in this crowd of people watching her, and she can barnstorm him, run a hand over his head without disturbing anyone else. We don't even feel the breeze of her skirt as it flutters by, as she reaches down and touches his hair and his chin. Even now she straightens his collar, not on tiptoes this time. Only she can do this for him.

There's James below. Really, he doesn't look so tall, so unwieldy. He looks handsome and manageable. An aerial view is not the whole story, it's a gloss, an abstract, a beautiful, beautiful summary.

In the end, she died as most of us do, absolutely still, earthbound.

The Boy in the Bed

Mrs. Sweatt's body was sent to Iowa, to be buried in her family's plot. "We'd like to come to the funeral," Caroline had said when she called to make arrangements, thinking she'd send Oscar out, since she felt too pregnant to travel. But Mrs. Sweatt's mother said that wouldn't be necessary. Funerals were not a tradition their family observed.

That upset Caroline; it seemed heathen. But she couldn't hold a funeral herself, and she couldn't sway Mrs. Sweatt's family, and so the body was buried in Davenport, without ceremony.

"Terrible," said Caroline, and it was terrible. "But at least she's back in Iowa." She said this as though Mrs. Sweatt had just gone home to visit friends, stare at her old high school, have a drink in her favorite bad bar. As if being dead were like getting pregnant while unmarried, and Mrs. Sweatt had to disappear until the trauma was over.

"When you think about it," Caroline said, "Iowa is not such a bad place to be."

* * *

I talked my way back into the house that Saturday, by insisting that the only thing that would make me happy was doing the Stricklands' housework for them during their difficult time. This was a statement of fact.

Caroline was suddenly hugely pregnant, pink-cheeked and pretty. "Write to James, why dontcha," she said. "He'll be there awhile. At least a couple of weeks."

"I'm planning to go to Boston tomorrow," I said. "I figured I'd take the bus."

"Nice of you," she said. "He could use some company. Oscar will drive you to the bus station."

"Oh, that's not—"

"No. He will. Don't argue. Well, shall we sit?"

"How about laundry?" I said. My unoccupied hands made me nervous, as if I needed to prove that I was here for one purpose: housework. "There must be plenty to do."

"Most people I would tell no," she said. "But I know you won't be happy unless I say yes."

"That's right," I said.

There was plenty of laundry. Oscar's paint-spattered clothing, some of the cotton men's shirts Caroline wore instead of maternity smocks. Two shirts and a pair of pants belonging to James, which I set aside for hand washing to save wear since they were so expensive. It was the last of his laundry for a while; now that he was in the hospital, he'd dirty nothing. I didn't know where Mrs. Sweatt's clothing had gone.

"Have you been to see James?" I asked.

She shook her head. "I want to, but my doctor says stay put till the baby comes. Which should be at any moment. You don't know how to deliver a baby, do you?"

"Why? Are you feeling—"

"No. I just thought maybe you might have read a book on it," she said, as if baby-delivering were a knack, like refinishing furniture, that people picked up for the pleasure of doing. "I feel very *pregnant,* and I feel like I will be very pregnant forever." She sighed. "Luckily there's a cure for it."

"Has Oscar been to Boston?"

She leaned on the dryer. "Just once. He gets nervous. Thinks I'll go ahead and have the baby without him. Once the baby comes, everything will be easier."

"I admire your optimism," I said.

"I hate suspense," she said.

A line of socks waited for their matches on the top of the dryer.

"These poor socks have lost their spouses," said Caroline. She picked one up and talked to it. "Poor widowed sock."

"It's true," I said. "Socks mate for life. Socks and swans."

"But you can't just throw them out, can you? I always introduce them to another abandoned sock." She picked up two lone socks and began to roll them together.

"Still," I said, "they're never really happy."

"Oh, I don't know," said Caroline. She unrolled the socks and held up both to inspect them. "Wash them together enough, and they grow to look like each other. Just like an old married couple." Then she rolled them back up and threw them in the basket.

"A sock love story," I said. "I've never before thought of the laundry as romantic."

"Everything's romantic," she said. "But I suspect you're a cynic."

"No doubt."

"Peggy," she said. "Do you have a boyfriend?"

"No," I said. I snapped a pair of Oscar's pants so the wrinkles flew out, then began to fold.

"No possibilities?"

I folded clothing double-time to show that I did not care to talk about it.

"Hmm," she said. I didn't know what she was hmming about. "You should try it," she said.

"I'm afraid I'm not cut out for all that," I said.

"Well, who cut you out?" she said. "Cut yourself out again."

"Easy to make it sound so easy," I said. "But it isn't."

"A girl needs a husband, Peggy," she said.

"Well," I said. "I've always been a terrible failure at being a girl."

Caroline did not understand me. She was as beautiful as her sister-in-law but never seemed to put much effort into it; every attractive thing about her, from the way her clothes fit to the red lipstick that flattered her skin exactly, seemed like great good luck. She was a dry person, not in an unpleasant way: like a flower that had been pressed in a dictionary for years, lovely and saved but liable to fall to dust. Like a pressed flower, she was messy but steady, captured at some moment for good. Even her clothing was like that, thin pretty cotton that showed the faint tint of her skin beneath it. For all her messiness, her clothes never seemed dirty, as if they came away from meetings with her unimpressed.

Caroline pulled a cobwebbed chair out from a corner and lowered herself into it. "I don't know," she said.

"What don't you know?"

She stretched an arm, thinking. "I wish my family were here. I mean, Mrs. Sweatt is gone, poor Jim's in Boston. I even miss my brother, and I haven't missed my brother in years, not since he left Mrs. Sweatt. It's like I'm about to have even more family"—she put a hand on her stomach—"and all I can think is it isn't enough, I want *more*. Don't you ever get greedy for relatives?"

"You forget," I told her. "I'm a librarian. All I'm greedy for is peace and quiet."

Caroline wanted to find me a romance. Perhaps it was the action of a friend who was worried about me, of a soon-to-be mother who suddenly planned to take care of the world. Perhaps without Mrs. Sweatt, she needed a new person to take in hand. Perhaps she wanted to get me out of her hair.

I did think of love sometimes, for months at a time, to the exclusion of everything else. If I had love, I could concentrate on other things. If I had love, then my entire life would open up. Late at night I wouldn't have to dream of who would love me, and how; nor while shelving books; nor moments when I found myself not paying attention to what people were saying to me. Ordinary people, I thought—loved people—could devote themselves to good works, or other sins, or benign undemanding hobbies.

And then the feeling would pass. I would realize that I hadn't thought of such things for ages, that such hopeless dreams of romance were like a language I had made up to communicate with a childhood friend and, losing that friend, the verbs and nouns curdled to gobbledygook, evidence of a passion and belief I could not believe I'd ever taken seriously.

I had not had that feeling since I'd met James, and perhaps I was now, for the first time in my life, in love. If that were so, I was wrong: my thoughts were not freer, my life not more efficient. Not even more pleasant—like Caroline, I hated suspense, and suddenly it seemed suspense was the fabric of my life. What will happen next, what will I say next, what will be said to me?

*

James looked trussed as a turkey in his hospital bed. Actually, it was two beds, laid end to end, at a funny angle to the wall so they would fit. His broken leg was suspended from the ceiling.

"James," I said. I couldn't tell whether he was awake, and all of a sudden I realized I hadn't brought him anything. Not even library books, which would have cost me nothing.

"Yes?" He reached over to a chair by his head, found his glasses, and put them on. He'd outgrown even these; the wire earpieces stretched out from the edges of the lenses to embrace his ears.

"Oh," he said. "Miss Cort. How did you get here?"

"By bus," I said.

"That must have been nice. I thought you were a nurse." He gestured at me. "You're dressed in light colors. That's all I can see without—" He tapped one lens of his glasses; it flashed with the overhead light.

"How's the old leg?" I asked.

He said, "Broken." He was wearing a strange sort of hospital gown. Looking a little closer, I saw that it was two or more regular gowns sewn together.

The wall above his bed was feathered with get-well cards. I was about to walk closer to see—I'd been standing just inside the room—when someone knocked on my shoulder as if I were a door.

I stepped aside. The man who'd knocked was fat, with a moustache that covered his mouth.

"Hello, hello," he said. The moustache bobbed up and down.

"I have a visitor," James told the man.

"Yes, I know. Very nice. The aunt?" he said to me.

"No. A friend."

"Nice," he said. "Jim's told me all about you."

"You don't even know who she is yet!" James said.

The man bowed to me politely. "You are—" He tried to look as if he were racking his brain for my name, but I knew the look. Library patrons who pretended to know the title of a book so as not to seem stupid wore the same expression.

"Peggy Cort," I said.

"Of course!" He nodded. "I'm Dr. Bosley."

"We're busy," said James.

"Of course you are," said the doctor. He sat down in the only chair in the room, right by James's head. "I'm just here to see how you're feeling."

"Fine," said James. "Go away."

The man nodded, still sitting.

"Dr. Bosley is a psychologist," said James. "He always wants to know how I'm feeling. He never believes me."

Dr. Bosley laughed in a way he probably thought was jovial. "I believe you," he said. "Of course I believe you. Okay, okay. I'll see you later, Jim—" He stood up from the chair with a great effort. "And it was nice to meet you, friend."

"That man," I said when he'd left, "does not have enough friends." I went over and sat in the chair.

"I have to talk to him every day," said James. "I mean, I like visitors, but he drives me crazy."

James's lack of affection for the doctor pleased me; I liked to think, sometimes, that I was his only friend, though this wasn't true. I turned in the chair and looked at the cards. Most of them were from teenagers, kids in his classes.

"Who's come to see you?" I asked. Until that moment I seemed to have forgotten the enormous fact that Mrs. Sweatt was dead. I felt dread drop down through my body, from my forehead to my stomach.

"Uncle Oscar. A teacher drove up some kids from school. If I'm here long enough, Uncle Oscar says they'll bring the baby after it's born."

"How do you feel?" I asked.

"Lousy," he said. "I'm sorry. I mean, I shouldn't complain, but I feel lousy."

"Leg hurt?"

"No." He rubbed his hand on the metal at the side of the first bed. "That's the problem. I don't feel anything in my legs at all. I didn't even know I broke it at first, I tried to walk on it."

He was moving out of that body in steps.

Then suddenly he looked at me, directly in the eyes. This was new. Usually, like his mother, he concentrated on some other part of a face, perhaps because faces were frequently so far downhill.

"I hate it here," he said.

"I know you do." I tried to keep his gaze, and for a moment I thought I couldn't possibly, that looking straight into his eyes was a weight I could carry only for seconds without resting. Then I realized all I had to do was do it, and it was easy. "How long will you be here?" I asked.

"I don't know, they won't tell me. They're going to give me braces," he said. "They're going to give me a cane."

"Until your leg heals?"

"Forever," he said. "I want to go to college."

I nodded.

"I want to be a lawyer," he said. "I want to leave Massachusetts. I mean, just once."

"You will," I said. "You'll go to New York, for that shoe convention."

"*How?*" Now he looked up at the ceiling.

"What do you mean, how?"

"Car? Don't fit. Bus? Less room. They had to take me all the way here from Hyannis in an ambulance, and even then it was crowded. Forget about airplanes." He closed his eyes, clenched his jaw. "It's been ages since I've been in a car. I stopped getting in them because I thought, well, they're not all that comfortable. But I was just thinking: even if I tried now, no way for me to fit. It's like I outgrew cars without even noticing."

"That can't be true," I said.

"It is true. When you guys went to Provincetown for ice cream, don't you think I wanted to go? I couldn't cram myself into the Chevy for that long."

"We'll find a car for you," I said.

"I'm outgrowing everything. I'm outgrowing my house. I can't go anywhere by myself."

"James." What would I say to him? "We'll figure things out."

"I know," he answered, though by his voice it was clear he knew no such thing.

The psychologist stopped me as I left James's room.

"Where's the mother?" he asked.

"I'm not sure," I said. "You should ask Mr. or Mrs. Strickland."

"I've asked Mr. Strickland. He's vague. Is she in the state? Her son would like to see her."

"He's told you that?"

"Jim is a complicated young man," he said.

I rubbed my forehead. "I don't think she'll be able to come see him."

"I see," said the psychologist. "You folks are an odd family. Well, if she's available"—he said this in a way that made me sure he knew the truth—"she should come. And if she can't, Jim should know that too. He is understandably a little blue over his state."

"Blue?" I said. "That's your professional opinion?"

"Understandably blue," he repeated. "With all that's happened to him, and will happen."

"What will happen to him?" I asked.

Dr. Bosley blinked, then smiled shyly. "He'll die," he said.

"What?" I'd only wondered about the cane, the braces.

"Amazing he's lived this long, in some ways. I mean, not that he's about to die—the leg is healing pretty well, he'll be up and about—but in the next few years, chances are."

"Of what?"

"Of himself," said the doctor. "The family knows it, Jim knows it. Sorry. Thought you did too. Giants don't live long. The good Lord knew what He was doing when He constructed the human body; when something goes wrong, well—basically, there's such a thing as being the right size."

This was all news to me. They all knew, and nobody had told me, and I hadn't done my research. I could have gone to a medical library, found articles. Everybody knew.

"Nothing to be done?" I said.

"Some things. Make his life easier. Get a car and take out the passenger's seat, and he can ride in the back—a pretty big car will give him some space. Think about an addition to the house built to his scale. He's likely to fall again, navigating small spaces. He needs as much room as possible, an environment that is more to his proportions."

"But for him, the growing."

"They don't know enough yet," he said. "You could talk to one of the medical doctors, as I have, and they'll tell you the same thing. There's so much we don't know."

I thought about staying in Boston for a few days. My parents lived here; I could see them. I'd grown up in Boston, my childhood unfurnished by religion or siblings. My parents were frugal and did not even give me a middle name. My parents were in love with each other, and that is a blow that no child can recover from. I walked around the city of my youth for a while, suddenly a little nervous. I held on tight to my pocketbook.

Would they let me stay at the hospital, pull up a chair and nap, a vigil? Perhaps they only let you do that if the patient was about to die. But he was a boy in a bed—in two beds—in a big city, far from his family.

Still, I could not make myself ask anybody at the hospital,

and I could not make myself call my parents, who, whenever I suggested a visit, made themselves sound busy. Now that I had moved out, I became just like any would-be visitor: an inconvenience not to be tolerated. They would happily meet me in a restaurant, and for a moment I thought I'd call and suggest that. But the last bus back to Hyannis was in an hour, and Oscar had already agreed to meet me, and so I went to the station, bought a magazine, and waited.

On the bus ride home, I faulted myself. I should have known to stay, I thought. I should not be a coward. My love for James until this day had always been troublesome. I didn't think I was any good at it. No good at talking to people in general and sometimes him in particular. He could make me feel uncomfortable, because I did not always understand him. I did not understand myself when in his presence.

The rest of the world fell in love, and the physics baffled me. I could see it happen—God knows, all around, I saw falling couples—but I did not understand the emotional gravity that allowed their descent.

And then, like Newton, I felt it smack me over the head.

Those people had made a decision, and then they fell; they did not find themselves hip deep in love and wonder how they got there. For years I'd waited for someone to love me: that was the permission I needed to fall in love myself, as though I were a pin sunk deep in a purse, waiting for a magnet to prove me metal. When that did not happen, I'd thought of myself as *unlovable*.

But now, with James lonely in his hospital room, I realized that waiting like that was hopeless. I could wait forever and he might never know to love me back and I would live and then die with a tiny awful feeling that could have been love, had it ever seen light or oxygen.

Well, I'd change that. I would love him. It would be easy as keeping his gaze, easy as saying, This is what to do. I would perfect my love for him, never care what others thought of me, or even what he was thinking of me. It was *this* I'd waited for all my life: a love that would make me useful, a love that would occupy all my time.

Well, who cut you out? Caroline had said when I told her I wasn't cut out for a boyfriend. I would, now; I would redesign myself.

I knew that day on the bus home that I was giving up things, old habits, future friends. That day I renounced everything, even my love for Caroline and Oscar—because I knew I would lose that; in certain ways I would now be at odds with them. I burned each of my possibilities in my head, those I recognized and those I didn't.

Perhaps I was a princess from a fairy tale. Sometimes, when your lover does not step from the woods to save you—because how many of us are rescuable, how many would look at some fool in a pair of tights and a pageboy and say, Of course—sometimes you have to marry your tower, your tiny room. You must take great interest in everything, a spinning wheel, a perfect single bed, the sound of someone breathing on the *other* side of the door. Once I had thought that the library was my tower, but that wasn't true. My love for James was the dark room I moved into that day.

It's where I still live.

I did not love him like a brother. I did not love him like a son. And though I loved him because of his body, it wasn't his body I loved, not the body of some man I dreamed would hold me, a body containing secrets that would somehow transform my own. Some will hear this and say, librarian, spinster: clearly there's a block, clearly there are problems here. But I've thought about this enough, and I've dreamed of other men's bodies that way, and I know the difference.

Perhaps it was because James's body was unavailable, belonging to himself and no one else, or perhaps because, though I knew it, his body was still always unimaginable. Unimaginably that large, unimaginably refusing to stop, unimaginably killing him just with its growth.

I did not imagine.

I loved him in a way that I have never and will never love anyone ever again, in a way I suspect—Peggy, always greedy—few people love, or have been loved. I loved him because he was young and dying and needed me. I loved not only his height, but his careful way with any hobby, his earnestness, his strange sense of humor that always surprised me. I loved him because I wanted to save him, and because I could not. I loved him because I wanted to be enough for him, and I was not.

I loved him because I discovered that day, after years of practice, I had a talent for it.

Part
Two

Careless Love

When I was in college in Philadelphia, I had my first job in a library. I sat behind the reference desk late nights, after the librarians had gone home, and tried to help students. I wasn't good at it yet. A library is an exosomatic memory—what they nowadays call an out-of-the-body experience, though I believe most experiences are. Books remember all the things you cannot contain. I didn't understand that at first. I wanted to remember only facts, not how to reach them; I was a tourist who hated travel.

Afternoons, I trailed the librarians, trying to pick up tips. Some casually listed off names of sources the second a question was asked; they might not even stand up to talk to the patron. If the student still looked confused, the librarian would say, curtly, *index*. Impossible to tell whether there was any pleasure to it. Others loved every query. They were the ones who knew the most: not just facts—though they did—but the organization of every book, where you'd find bibliographies, where you'd turn up empty. They knew the subtlest treasures of national biographies and climatological tables and censuses.

I stayed at the job when I went to get my master's. My memories of library science school—and they are fading, thankfully—are of an alphabetized wilderness. Book leaves flapping in the afternoon, fine dusty mists rising from them. Equatorial heat. The toes of a dozen pairs of sensible shoes squeaking beneath desks. The teacher passing out the syllabus, the room filled with the soft click of hand-held hole-punchers, a three-syllabled call, then the shush of hands over desks scooping up paper dots.

Our professors told us that order was important. This is true; I love order. But they never explained why. Order was for order's sake, they said, and the other students nodded seriously: for them precision was a religion taken up at late age that would keep you from sin and keep you from Hell and everybody who didn't understand this was damned. Presumably, two years of graduate study was far cheaper than the psychoanalysis it would have taken to get over whatever it was their mothers had done to them.

But a library is a gorgeous language that you will never speak fluently. You will try every day of your life. Order is a certain clumsy grammar, a mnemonic device. Order just means: try to use verbs. Consider the tense. The poetry will follow.

The school's motto should have been, *Neatness Counts*.

I did well in library school. I am, in many ways, small-minded.

Still, behind the reference desk I frequently felt like an idiot. I didn't recognize the names of certain cabinet members, or the currency of some unfamiliar country, or a great Scandinavian author. There were times I couldn't even make sense of a problem, never mind find the solution. Some evenings I sat and thought up reference questions that only I could answer. Something about a newspaper article I'd read that afternoon, or all the known facts about one of my favorite painters. A student would approach me, shy and pessimistic, and when I gave them the exact answer, more information than they'd thought possible, when I said, "Rosa Bonheur . . . ," oh, they'd melt, they'd thank me and tell their friends: see that woman? She knows everything.

In my life I have spent hours constructing questions from just the right person, in just the right tone of voice: *Have you ever known anyone who's committed suicide? What celebrity would you marry if you could? Who was the first boy you ever kissed, and what do you remember about that boy?*

And then the best part, the part where I answer, carefully, at length, because there's someone who wants to know.

Truthfully, this is the fabric of all my fantasies: love shown not by a kiss or a wild look or a careful hand but by a willingness for research. I don't dream of someone who understands me immediately, who seems to have known me my whole life, who says, *I know, me too.* I want someone keen to learn my own strange organization, amazed at what's revealed; someone who asks, *and then what, and then what?*

But you can't spend your life hoping that people will ask you the right questions. You must learn to love and answer the questions they already ask. Otherwise you're dreaming of visiting Venice by driving to Boise, Idaho.

That year—the year that James turned seventeen, 1956—everything changed. Caroline had her baby, a girl, and they named her Alice Sweatt Strickland. I met her when she and Caroline came home from the hospital; I'd never known a baby so young. She was damp and stunned-looking, as if she couldn't believe everyone had been expecting her to come ashore for months: she herself never imagined such things—February, Cape Cod, all these looming faces, and dry land—were even vaguely possible. *Not really*, her expression said, *not this.*

We started work on a cottage behind the Stricklands' house for James, with funds raised through the town, my doing: jars by cash registers in stores, a pancake breakfast, collections at basketball games. I'd asked a contractor about building an addition to the house, but he said it wasn't possible: too much weight on a not-too-sturdy building. Besides, he said, it would have looked terrible. Plenty of room behind the house, though, and I liked the idea, because I thought a cottage would belong absolutely to James, and therefore also to me.

We got businesses to donate furnishings, everything specially made: a huge armchair made by a man in Dennisport who just wanted the pleasure of building it; a bed from a mattress factory in Tiverton, in exchange for bragging rights. Their slogan was: for the longest night's sleep you ever had.

My doing, my doing, my doing. Oscar and Caroline were alarmed, I think, slightly grateful, quite bewildered.

"Slow down!" Oscar said when I breathlessly listed the things I thought James would need in his cottage. I spoke more slowly.

"No," said Oscar. "Slow down everything. You'll wear yourself out."

"I have plenty of energy," I said.

"You'll wear me out, then."

But I couldn't stop. I bought a hot plate, a little radio, a record player. I convinced a local carpenter to make a desk and end tables. I got the permits for building, painted the walls myself. Every night after work, I went to the cottage. At first just to walk around outside, and then, as it took shape, to sit inside on the floor and try to see what else it needed. In many ways it was not a proper house—no bathroom (we didn't have the money; he'd have to go to the front house); no basement; no kitchen; no closet until I pointed out the lack. But there were high ceilings without eaves and a door that was wide and tall with a threshold plumb to the floor and no treacherous steps. Nothing for him to trip on. I'd thought at first that there'd be two rooms, because the idea of spending the whole day in one small place seemed depressing, but the contractor said that a single room allowed for the most space. Caroline sewed curtains to match those in the front house; Oscar painted the trim green, with a few trompe l'oeil jokes—ants on the sills, one long rose across the sash of each window. They wouldn't have fooled anybody's eye.

Nights I sat on the floor and listened to the sounds that made their way from the front house to the back: the baby crying, the chatter of dinner plates in the sink. It was spring, and their windows were up, and I opened the front door of the cottage so I could hear Caroline's lovely, odd voice singing to the baby, their whole house a radio. Never lullabies, just love songs: *The Tennessee Waltz, After You've Gone, Careless Love.* One night I heard all of a song about a woman who'd killed her lover and was pleading for the electric chair—*Judge, Judge, please Mr. Judge*—a morbid song for a baby, but it seemed to work: I heard Caroline finish and then Oscar's awed voice saying, after a pause, *she's asleep.*

My years of simple living and careful saving meant I had enough money to buy a car, as well as all the knickknacks I stocked the cottage with. Oscar had a friend with a huge used Nash who sold it cheap. The front seat was divided in half, and each side would fold back to meet the backseat, forming (it was pointed out to me by the leering mechanic who looked it over) a bed, single or double depending. I figured we could fold down the passenger's seat, and James could sit in the back, with his legs in the front.

I was not much of a driver, having grown up and gone to school in cities, so I drove around town for practice. The Nash was the first car I'd ever owned, the first car I'd ever driven to amount to anything. It made me feel as though I were a Victorian lady who'd finally been allowed to wear bloomers—I could go anywhere, I realized, I could just start driving. But the only place I wanted to go was Boston, to visit James.

And so I did. Every Sunday for four months I drove the two hours to Boston, checking my rearview, the speedometer, the gas gauge, the odometer. One of the reasons I'd never had an interest in a car before was certainly fear; so much could go wrong. But those simple controls were as reassuring to me as footnotes. They explained, they quantified. If I had gas, if I drove at a sensible clip, if I noted the car directly behind me and the one passing me on the left and kept all of these things in mind, surely everything would be fine.

When James finally came home from the hospital—after four long months of healing and therapy and visits from friends, weekly visits from me—he lived somewhere new. He had a new relative, Caroline and Oscar's daughter, Alice Sweatt Strickland. And he had me.

* * *

"How is it?" I asked. He walked slowly into the cottage, leaning on the cane. The town would hold a welcome home party for him that night at the high school auditorium; they'd wanted to greet him at the cottage—they thought having made and eaten pancakes meant they deserved full credit for the building—but I'd dissuaded them. Let him get settled, I said. James was not quite graceful with his new cane, with the braces I could hear squeak with each step. Oscar stepped across the threshold, followed by Caroline with the baby.

He reached over to the lamp on the closest table and snapped it on. The tables were the faultiest pieces of furniture: the carpenter had made them regular-size with extralong spindly legs.

James sat down on the bed and let the cane fall to the floor.

"It's incredible," he said.

"Look," I said. "Here's a closet. And you should try out the desk—if it isn't high enough we can raise it." I turned the faucets of the little sink on the back wall, as if I had not tried them every night for a month. "Works," I said.

"Well, sport," said Oscar. "What do you think?"

"It's good," said James. He stood up with a great deal of effort; I saw that we'd have to raise the bed on blocks. It hadn't occurred to me that the bed would have to be high, as well as big. He walked along the perimeter of the room, leaning on the walls.

"Don't you need your cane?" I asked.

He shook his head.

"We couldn't afford a bathroom," said Oscar apologetically. "But we figure that way we get to see you every now and then."

"Wouldn't want you to forget us," said Caroline. "You'll come over for meals, too." She walked with James to the window. "See the rose?" she said. I didn't know whether she was talking to James or the baby.

"It's pretty," said James.

Everything was suddenly pretty: the June light coming through the window, the filmy curtains that, I noticed, matched Caroline's skirt.

Caroline cupped the baby's head in her hand.

"Oscar?" she said. He walked to them, and they stood there for a moment, looking out the window.

"Jim," said Oscar. "Your mother—"

"My mother is dead," said James.

I wonder now whether they really meant to tell him then. Perhaps Oscar was about to say, *Your mother is proud of you*, or, *Your mother called this afternoon*. I didn't even know whether James had known all along, or whether he'd just figured it out. I'd spent so long wishing they would tell him that I'd never imagined how it would happen.

James looked at Caroline, leaned on the wall for support, and put his hands out for the baby. Caroline lifted Alice to his arms.

Alice—higher in the air than she'd ever been—opened her eyes, looked at James. Caroline put her hand on his hip. "She misses you," she said.

"She doesn't know me yet." He put his nose to the baby's stomach.

"Your mother misses you, I mean."

"My mother's dead," James repeated.

Caroline moved her hand in a slow circle on his hip. The baby made a noise as if she were about to cry, but she didn't. "That doesn't mean she doesn't miss you," said Caroline. "Because she does."

Did she think that would do? Did she think, *now it's over, now he knows and we don't have to pretend*. I did, I admit it. *That was easy*, I thought.

James said to the baby, "When were you going to tell me?" We were silent. Maybe we thought the baby would answer. She opened her mouth, but it was only to yawn.

"We meant to—" Oscar said.

"When?" said James. "When you figured I'd forgotten about her?" He was still looking at the baby, and Caroline put her hands out.

"Don't drop—" she said. James lifted Alice higher, as if it hadn't crossed his mind before, but maybe he would. Maybe he would drop the baby. Instead, he swung her around and set her in her mother's arms.

"How long have you known?" asked Oscar.

James folded his arms across his chest. "How long has she been dead?"

"You've known all along?"

"How long has she been dead? Because I don't know." He reached into his pocket and pulled out an envelope. "No such patient," he read. "I wrote this to her two months ago, got it back two weeks later. So then I called, and they said nobody named Alice Sweatt was ever there. So. She's been dead for—"

"Four months and thirteen days," said Caroline.

"And you don't even miss her."

"Oh, Jim," said Caroline. "You don't know how much."

"I don't know if I even believe that." He walked to the bed as fast as he could, which was not fast at all. I thought, he wants to throw himself down on the bed angrily, and he can't even do that. Instead he sat on the edge and put his face in his hands.

Caroline shook her head. "Peggy?" she said. She handed the baby to me. Alice was an awkward bundle. She still wasn't crying, and I waited for her to. I thought that's what babies did. They cried. I looked into her face, a five-month-old face, and waited for it to pleat and redden. I guess I wanted someone to cry.

I got my wish. Caroline inhaled deeply, as if she knew what she was going to do would be an effort. She knew it would be the last clear, easy breath she'd take in a while. "It's like this," she said in an improbably careful voice, and then, suddenly, she was weeping.

Oscar said, "Caro—"

"I'm *sorry,*" she said angrily. She shook her useless hands as if they were full of something she wanted to get rid of. She brought them to her face, let them grab her shoulders, hit her thighs.

James looked terrified. Boys never see grown women cry. Or perhaps he had—what did I know of his life when I wasn't around? Perhaps his mother cried every day she lived. Perhaps the secret of her perfect skin was gentle tears, applied first thing in the morning and just before bed.

But what Caroline was doing was not an everyday occurrence. It was something hoarded, a fortune stuffed under a mattress that has inexplicably managed to gather interest as fast as any bank account. She flung herself into the big armchair, then slid to the floor. Her pretty face was bright red.

Oscar tried to help her up, but she wouldn't let him—she elbowed him away and continued to weep. I didn't know why she was crying, and I wanted to know, I wanted it explained. I wanted her to say: this is guilt, this is delayed grief, this is postpartum depression mixed with a lot of other things. I hadn't ever seen anyone cry like this in all my life. It was like she was poisoned and crying was the only way to get the poison out.

"I'm sorry," said James.

"No!" Caroline stood up and stumbled to the bed. She sat next to James. She leaned into him. He put his arms around her.

I rocked the baby a little in my arms. "Hush," I said to her, though she wasn't crying. I didn't say it loud enough for anyone else to hear. I whispered, "Everything will be fine."

"We should have . . ." Caroline said to James. She couldn't get the rest of the sentence out.

"Yes," he said. "You should have."

There was nothing else to say. No. There were dozens of things to say, but I didn't know what they were, or how to say them. Oscar sat on the ground at his wife and nephew's feet. James was crying a little too, tears without effort, as if his aunt, who still wept beneath his arm—silently now—had done the hard part.

"I'm sorry," I said. It was something we all felt obligated to say.

"You didn't know," said James.

I looked at him, then at Caroline. All along I'd thought he'd known that I was every bit as guilty as Caroline and Oscar—more, perhaps. I was James's friend.

When I didn't say anything, Caroline said, "No, it's true. She didn't know."

Sometimes we need people to lie for us. That lie was a gift I shouldn't have accepted: inappropriate and unethical and much too generous. But I did; I took it silently; I nodded.

That night was James's welcome-home assembly at the high school. Caroline and Oscar had been consistent in their lie—everyone in Brewsterville believed that Mrs. Sweatt was alive though ailing in a New Hampshire hospital.

The town, one person at a time, came up to James to greet him, touch some enchanted faulty part of him. And James thanked them, then broke the news, and consequently their hearts: *My mother has died*. And the town, one person at a time, left him to his grief, griefstruck themselves.

There was a program at the end of the evening; James walked across the stage to shake the principal's hand. I sat in the audience with Oscar and the baby; Caroline sat on the stage with James. She'd asked me to join them.

"No," I said. "I hate the idea of an audience staring up at me."

James seemed old every day of his life, but never as old as that night. There was the cane, and the braces, and the careful, shuffling walk of an old man whose legs have outworn their usefulness. Caroline walked alongside him, her hand up at his elbow. She looked old, too.

"There's Mama," Oscar said to the baby. He squinted. "She should be wearing a slip." He was right. The outline of Caroline's skinny legs was clear behind the fabric.

The principal shook hands with James for a long time; you could tell he wanted something to give to James, a proclamation or a key to the city or a diploma. Something about James made you want to offer things up. But all the red-faced principal had to offer was his comparatively small hand, so, when that wasn't enough, he offered the other one, sandwiched James's own hand between them. They stood there awhile, James holding on to his cane, the principal holding on to James.

The Bachelor's Cottage

It hadn't occurred to me that now I would have to announce myself at the cottage until my hand was on the high doorknob; I had walked from work, as I had for several months, to see the inside and wonder what was left to do. Nothing now, I supposed. It was the Sunday afternoon after the high school assembly. We hadn't installed a bell, so I knocked.

"Come in," James called.

I opened the door. He'd already rearranged a few things—the bed was in the opposite corner, beneath a window. Doilies had been plucked off the armchair and lay like a stack of flapjacks on the desk.

"Settling in?" I asked.

"Have a seat," he said. I took the chair nearest the wall; James was sitting in his big armchair. "It's weird," he said, rubbing the chair's arms. Without antimacassars, I thought, the upholstery would be black in a week.

"What is?"

James looked around the room. "I have a house. I feel like I've been gone for five years."

"Well, a lot has happened."

And then we just looked at each other. We were strangers, after all; at least, we'd never been alone in a small space like this. We had talked at the hospital, where there was plenty to talk about—James told me about his physical therapy, the terrible psychologist, his visitors—any of which might interrupt our conversation. In turn, I had caught him up on the news of this world: the weather, the renovations on town hall, Oscar's newest schemes. Now he'd returned and I had no news.

I reached into my pocket. "I got you a new pack of cards," I said, tossing them.

He caught them in one hand.

"You're still doing magic, aren't you?"

"Well, I haven't for a while." He undid the lace of the cellophane and opened the box. "Maybe I should start again." He began shuffling.

"Let's see a trick."

"Let me practice a little." The cards clattered, then shushed into a bridge. "What do you want to see?"

"I don't know. I don't know card tricks. I like them, though."

He shuffled. Then he looked through the cards. "Wait," he said. "Don't look at this part. Okay, now you can look. Come a little closer, I need some audience participation." I dragged my chair up to the foot of the armchair.

He spread the cards into a fan. "Draw a card. Don't show it to me, but remember what it is. Now stick it in the deck. Anywhere, that's fine. Now." He shuffled the cards a different way, letting them waterfall from one hand into the other. "Is this your card?"

The seven of clubs. Yes, it was.

"That's great—"

"Wait," he said. Then he ripped the card up and stuck it in the pocket of his shirt. Then he tapped the pocket with the corner of the pack. "Okay," he said. "Reach into my pocket." He leaned over, so the pocket fell away from his body. Inside was an intact card. I reached for it carefully. The seven of clubs.

"Wait a minute," I said. "How did you do that?" I sat back on my chair.

"A magician never divulges secrets."

"No," I said. "Tell me!"

"Look it up," he said, laughing. "I'll give you a hint: you can find the answer in the Brewsterville Library."

I handed the card back to him. "I was a big magic fan as a girl."

"But not card tricks."

"I didn't have the patience. I didn't *do* magic at all, I just read about it. I wanted to be an escape artist."

James started shuffling again. "Yeah? *You?* Like Houdini?"

"Just like Houdini. I wanted to escape from milk jugs and glass booths."

He laughed. "Can't picture it. Why?"

"Oh," I said. "I don't know. I never thought about it much. I guess: escaping was very dramatic, but with a happy ending. Like with the movies. I never liked comedies, because they were too silly, but I couldn't bear tragedies because such terrible things happened at the end. And suddenly appearing after everybody has decided you were dead, that seemed like a tragedy with a happy ending."

James started examining the face of each card, as though they were snapshots of loved ones. "Houdini had a thing about death. Didn't he want to talk to dead people? At séances?"

"He wanted to believe he could, but he decided that he couldn't, that nobody could. All that reading about magic, but you never wanted to be Houdini?"

James held the cards in one hand, tapped them against his chest, as if that were the start of another magic trick. "No," he said. "Maybe I'm not that ambitious."

"But you learned the card tricks," I said. "I wanted to be Houdini, I just didn't want to do the work. Or maybe I knew I couldn't. It would have been too difficult to learn how to escape."

"But that's the thing of it," said James. "It wasn't escaping that was hard. I mean, he made it look harder than it was. He took just long enough to make the audience think he was dead.

That was the real trick. Not that he *was* alive, because he was alive at the start and nobody was so impressed, right? The trick was he made people think he was dead."

"Yes," I said. "I think you're right."

"Maybe that's why he could never talk to dead people. Dead people didn't *want* to talk to him, because he only pretended to be what they already were." James had an amused, pensive look on his face.

"Do you think that anyone can?" I asked.

"What?"

"Talk to the dead."

"Here's what I think, and lately I've been going over this. I think there's definitely life after death."

"You do?"

"*Definitely*. But the reason that there's no real proof is that dead people—or spirits, or whatever—are different from us. Don't you think?"

"I don't know, James," I said.

"I mean, not only do they live somewhere else—which means I guess a different language—but they believe different things. I think—" He sighed. "I thought I figured this out. Give me a minute. I think Heaven, whatever you call it, is a different religion. A really strict, different religion. As time-consuming as a serious orthodox earth religion. And that people in Heaven are just naturally not going to talk to people who aren't part of their religion. I mean, they don't need to convert people, that's for sure."

"Does everybody who dies join the same religion?"

"Yes," said James. "You have to. And there's no point in being religious before you die, because whatever you learn, it's all wrong. It's like really religious people have had this hunch, but they've jumped to the wrong conclusion. It's not what you should do, it's what you will do. You'll convert sooner or later anyhow."

"What about God?" I asked, though I'm not sure I wanted to know the answer. I was fairly sure he was an atheist, but it seemed a young man should have faith in the wonders of the world. On the other hand, I wanted us to have things in common.

"No such thing," said James.

"But—"

"There's no God. There's just dead people."

"So." But I couldn't figure out what the rest of the sentence should be. The windows were all open, and the long curtains were blown back, like the capes of magicians who had just left the room. Finally I tried, "Your mother—"

"Peggy," he said. "Do you think my mother killed herself?"

I shrugged.

"She didn't," James insisted. "I would have known." Then he said, "I was a lot of trouble for her."

"No," I said, though I wasn't sure what I was disagreeing with.

"You don't think I'm a lot of trouble?" He smiled.

"Look," I said. He had his hand on the arm of the chair; I stood up, and I put my hand on his. This was that rarest thing in my life, an unpremeditated move toward another person. Once I'd done it, however, I felt awkward. "Your mother loved you more than anything."

"Maybe," he said. I couldn't tell what he was thinking. His skin was pale, scrubbed by the fluorescent lights of his hospital room, and he'd picked up a habit of his mother's: he bit his lip, though he made it seem thoughtful, not nervous.

"No. It's true. Everyone could see it."

"Mothers love their kids. It's a rule."

"Not all of them. And not the way your mother loved you." His hand was still under mine. I wanted to check my watch. This wasn't the sort of thing I usually did, putting my hand on someone else's, and I wasn't sure how long was comforting without being unseemly. "I've known a lot of mothers. Most of them don't hold a patch to yours."

"What about your mother?" he asked.

"My mother? No," I said. "She didn't."

"Didn't what? Didn't hold a patch or didn't love you?"

I took my hand from his and scratched my ear. "My mother," I said. "My mother is a good woman."

His hand, free from mine, bounced on the chair's arm. He opened his mouth to say something, but then changed his mind.

"I don't know what happened to your mother," I said. "But I know it had nothing to do with you."

"She didn't kill herself," he said.

"Good."

"No, she didn't," he said, as if I'd disagreed. "She would have told me. That's one thing about her, different from everybody else around here. She was lousy with secrets. She couldn't keep them for a minute."

"I didn't know that," I said.

"From me," he said. "She told me everything. I mean, about her life, about my father. I knew when she had heartburn. I knew every last thing about those old ladies at the nursing home. Nobody will ever tell me the kinds of things Mom told me."

"Somebody will," I said, because it sounded like something he wanted. I almost said, *I will*, but I didn't think I had it in me to honor that promise, not then. Worse, I didn't think I was the one he had in mind.

"*Nobody* will," he said again. "I knew everything she did all day. I knew when she was *menstruating*." He stumbled over this last word, and I could tell he'd probably never said it aloud before; we both blushed. "I knew that she took sleeping pills. She took diet pills, too. I didn't want her to. If I knew all that, don't you think she would have told me something so big?"

I nodded, for his sake. But I was a grown woman and knew any grown woman was crammed full of secrets—you couldn't open her like a medicine cabinet and read the indications.

"She would have," he said. "She wouldn't have let me talk her out of it, but she would have told me. She believed in putting all her eggs in one basket. I was her basket." He rested his chin in one hand. "That's one thing I used to be."

We heard somebody coming up the gravel path.

"Hello," Caroline called. Then she knocked. Then she said, "Hello?"

"Yes?" said James.

She stuck her head in. "I've run away," she said. "Can I come in?"

"Sure," said James. "You didn't run away far."

"Actually, Uncle Oscar's giving Alice her bath. Then it's dinnertime. Peggy, you're more than welcome."

"No thank you," I said. I was fairly dizzy with the afternoon's conversation, wanted to get home, lie down, think about it.

Caroline sat down on the floor and leaned against the wall. Her skirt draped between her knees, a flowered V. "Don't let me interrupt you. Go ahead with whatever you were talking about."

"I was just practicing card tricks on Peggy," said James.

"Oh," said Caroline. "That's all?"

"That's it," said James.

"Were you fooled, Peggy?"

"Utterly."

It was clear that Caroline wanted us to talk more. Clear, too, that Caroline was somebody that James would keep secrets from—that he would, in fact, withhold things that would not ordinarily be secrets, just for the pleasure of withholding them. This was because Caroline so desperately wanted to hear them. You never tell your secrets to people who want to know, I understood that much.

"Nice afternoon?" Caroline asked me.

"Yes," I said. Impossible not to follow James's terse lead.

Caroline let her head fall back to the stucco wall and stamped one foot. "You are the two most reserved people I ever met."

"Reserved?" James said.

"Like a book," I said. "A best seller waiting for the people who have asked for it."

"Like a table in a restaurant," said James.

"Like a sauce."

"A sauce?"

"Yes," I said. "When you cook, sometimes you have to reserve some of the sauce for the end of the recipe."

"No," said Caroline. "Not like any of that. *Reserved*. And I

don't think it's such a great thing, if you want to know the truth."

"Reserved," I said. "Like the *best* table in the restaurant."

Caroline didn't think that was funny. "But the table is reserved by somebody, for somebody. The sauce is reserved *by* the cook, for the meat. The book is reserved *by* Peggy, for someone she knows wants to read it. The table doesn't reserve itself, just in case the party of its dreams comes in, right? You guys, you're holding on to yourselves, for—well, who for?"

"Who for what?" James said quietly.

"Who are you saving yourselves for?"

"Myself," said James.

"Well, that's about as ridiculous as the book holding on to itself for itself. What's the point? Here's what I think: you can't save yourself. Somebody has to do it for you. I don't mean rescue, I mean: hold on. I mean: reserve. What if you save yourself for marriage—"

James laughed and looked down.

"—yeah, save yourself in all the different ways, you don't tell anybody your secrets and you don't sleep with anybody, and then you don't get married. What happens then?"

"Not everybody has to get married," I said.

"Of *course* not!" said Caroline. "You're not listening! If you save yourself for marriage, and then you don't get married, then what you saved isn't worth anything. It's like Confederate money. You're bankrupt, you have nowhere to spend it."

"Someone," said James. We waited for the rest of the sentence, but that was it. Finally, he elaborated. "I'm saving myself for Someone."

"But who?" said Caroline.

James didn't answer.

Caroline was right, and she was wrong. People are not tables in a nightclub up by the entertainment. Tables empty, they start fresh several times a night, seven nights a week, a clean cloth snapped across and fresh candles stuck in holders. If only one party could be seated at a table for years and years, well, the maître d' might have different thoughts. He might keep that best table, reset it every day, waiting for Greta Garbo, the president, his future unmet undreamed-of inlaws.

And me? Now I understood. I was saving myself for James. *Myself* meant only my secrets. Any other commodities (my youth, my virginity, any brand of innocence or hope) I'd years ago lost, a gambler who didn't understand the game. My secrets were all I'd saved, all these years, the only thing I hadn't and wouldn't cash in on just anyone. If you poured out yourself to anyone who might for a moment listen, on just a usual day—it struck me as cheap, the way some girls' mothers used the word. I was saving what was left of myself for James.

•

That summer, Mrs. Sweatt died all over again, to nobody's surprise. She'd died in January and stayed in limbo through Easter, into June, but still, death and resurrection didn't seem so farfetched. Not that Mrs. Sweatt rose from the dead. She didn't. Her death was just brand new in a way it never had been. I thought of James and his theories of Heaven. Mrs. Sweatt, who died twice, was born again, converted again into the religion of the dead.

Dying seemed a shame. Still, if we'd picked a time for her to die, we'd done a good job. The town was never so alive as in late June, early July, when summer and tourists still seemed like a pretty good idea, what with more money, fair weather, new faces—it wasn't till August that you wondered what sort of blockhead had dreamed summer up. Years hence, when James thought of his mother—those annual remembrances when mourning and regret become what you do for the day, out of loving habit—the weather would be sweet, the shop windows in bloom, the breeze off the bay full of kind meaning.

Suddenly, after having gone underground, to Iowa, to New Hampshire, wherever it was we thought she'd gone, Mrs. Sweatt was back. She was everywhere. Not just in stories, though there were plenty of those. Waltzing at her wedding with all the guests, because her new husband, after six cocktails, insisted on doing the Alley Cat using only his a priori knowledge of the dance, angling on the dance floor peppy or slow depending on the music, while Mrs. Sweatt wanted to be hospitable; besides, she'd taken lessons. Reading her *True Love* magazines and crying at those unfortunate women, more unfortunate than her because now the whole country knew their heartaches. Cooking her midwestern cuisine, which meant opening a can of something and pouring it over something else: meat cooked in Coca-Cola, cake mix sweetened with half a can of frozen lemonade, apples poached in red soda pop. "Use cherry, not strawberry," she'd advised Caroline. "Strawberry is too bright."

She showed up in photographs, too, mined from albums and boxes and envelopes, now set on the mantelpiece and tucked into mirror frames. It didn't seem like she'd ever shied away from the camera. Her high school graduation portrait as Caroline's bridesmaid, six years old on the boulevard at some Western amusement park. And in James's pictures, too, where she was prettiest. You could tell which ones he'd taken; in them she was smiling at her son, not the camera, and the fond reproach on her face was unmistakable.

Maybe the kids who started showing up at the cottage were there to offer comfort to someone who had suffered a loss—though their visits were awfully loud for sympathy calls. By August, the place was full of high school kids, some who knew James well and some who'd never spoken to him. The few boys who'd toughed out the Scouts to make eagle—boys you'd expect to be polite—were the ones most likely to laugh too loud and smell of smoke mixed with chlorine from the swimming pool. It was a mean, petty smell.

They always came in groups. I watched them tour the cottage sometimes, each teenager clearly thinking that if only it were him—if only his parents agreed to build him a house in the backyard—his life would be perfect.

I stopped by the cottage every day after work. I brought books, small gifts—cookies from the bakery, or a marbled composition book, or a new pack of cards. James sometimes spent hours shuffling; when you talked to him, you got used to the steady noise of the deck meeting itself. His hands seemed to double over themselves to manage it. He shuffled several packs at a time.

"That's quite a nervous habit you have there," I said.

"Not nervous." He cut the cards several times. "Trying to keep my fingers limber."

Work piled up at the library. I was as thorough as I could be during the day, but I'd stopped staying late evenings to read reviews and do the statistics and balance the budget.

"Are you having an affair?" Astoria asked me.

I looked at her. "Would I tell you if I were?" I said. But then I saw the delight in her face and had to own up. No, no affair, no intrigue. Just helping some friends. I wondered who she thought the affair would be with.

Soon others came to the cottage. I'd forgotten what an odd place it was, the high ceilings, the oversize furniture. On one side of the room the builders had set windows into the wall in two rows, because specially made proportional windows were too expensive, but the ordinary number of ordinary windows would have looked as strange and dismal as submarine portholes. People loved to sit in the big armchair, let their legs dangle off the edge. Teachers came, and neighbors. Astoria asked me if I'd take her with me one day.

"Why do you need to come with me?" I asked.

"You know me, Peggy. I'm not so good with idle chitchat."

"Astoria. You do nothing all day but chitchat idly."

She twisted her wedding ring around. "I'm not so good with sick people. With sick young people, I mean. I get sad easily."

"He's not sick," I said. "He's tall, and you can't catch that."

"I'm just curious. I just want to see."

"See what?" When she wouldn't answer, I said, "I can't stop you from visiting, but do it yourself. We're not here to satisfy your curiosity."

For a while there were almost always a few kids loitering when I arrived. They brought records for the player; sometimes they even danced in the middle of the room, in the pleased, measured way you dance for someone else's benefit. James sat in his chair; a visitor balanced on the arm, which was big enough to be a chair itself. I tried to like the music. Mostly I lurked by the door, feeling like the oldest person in the world.

Some nights I could not bear all that youth and possibility: I'd hear laughter through the door, and I'd turn around and leave.

One night as I came up the walk, I saw through the window a boy and girl dancing—or should I say, embracing while revolving in tandem. The music was slow treacle. Boys sat on the floor or the bed, looking up at the couple every now and then, not talking. Other people's happiness is always a fascinating bore. It sucks the oxygen out of the room; you're left gasping, greedy, amazed by a deficit in yourself you hadn't ever noticed.

The song was just ending as I walked in; the couple parted, and the girl clapped her hands three times, as though she believed she would hurt the singer's feelings if she did not acknowledge him.

The boy looked at his watch, then at the girl.

"I know," she said.

She had dark wavy hair pulled back in a ponytail, and her tight sweater rode up in creases above her bustline. Her lipstick was a bit smudged; I located some of it on the boy's cheek.

"We have to go," he said to James.

"Us, too," said one of the boys on the bed.

"Okay," said James. "Tomorrow?"

The dancing boy pulled his record off the player. "It's Friday," he said. "There's a dance in Brewster. You should come, Jimmy."

"Oh," said James. He kicked at his cane, which he'd set down at the foot of the chair. "I'm not much for dancing."

"I'll dance with you," said the girl. She obviously thought that this promise—not even the dance itself, but the promise of a dance—would solve anything, and she was the type of girl who might convince a boy it could. *I will save you from being a wallflower*, she'd say, *I will cure your life*, and a boy, looking at her face, the line of delicate beauty marks on her neck, would think he was the only boy who'd ever been promised such a thing.

"Maybe the next dance," said James. "When my leg is better."

"Swear you'll dance with me sometime," said the girl.

"I swear."

She looked at me and smiled. I was happy to see there was something a little wrong with her teeth, a faint chalky discoloration.

"Good night," she said, and then she walked out, followed by first her dance partner, then the whole line of boys who had watched them.

"You have a lot of friends," I said to James.

"I don't really know some of them. I know Ben—" He patted the arm of the chair to indicate the heavy boy who'd been sitting there. "And I know Stella."

"She's pretty," I said, which was what I said as soon as I could about any pretty girl. I wanted people to know I saw it, too.

He nodded, then kicked the cane up with his foot and caught it. He twirled it in one hand; his card exercises were paying off. "I can't dance," he said.

"Neither can I."

"You *could*," he said. He spun the cane faster, and I could tell he wished he'd thought to try this trick while Stella was in the room. Then he missed, and the cane fell to the floor. "Maybe in a while I can. When the braces come off."

"The braces are coming off?" I asked.

"They might," he said, the way you say things that you have made yourself believe, other evidence to the contrary. "I mean, I won't ever be a *dancer*." He moved his feet across the floor nervously, knocking into the cane. "But that. What they were doing. I could dance like that, maybe. Slowly. If I had someone to lean on."

"Maybe so," I said. No girl in the world was tall enough for James to lean on. That girl was just a usual height; taller than me, but not tall. I handed James the book I had under my arm. "*William the Conqueror*," I said. "It's a new one."

She knew he couldn't dance. He could barely walk.

Still, she was one person who could offer him things I could not. Let's face it: a girl his own age.

When I was in eighth grade, there was a girl all the boys called Hickey Vickie. Whether she'd realized at a young age that the neat rhyme made the practice inevitable, or whether it was a coincidence, she was a master at this teenage art, and boys proudly wore her work. Some advanced girls delivered orderly hickeys, circumspect enough to be mistaken for some other adolescent skin problem. Vickie was the Rocky Graziano of kisses; necks left her mouth nothing short of mauled.

I was what is known as a late bloomer—though I am not sure I've bloomed yet—and years away from the crude puberty that would visit me late my senior year of high school. I didn't understand. I knew what a hickey was, technically, but I'd seen movies and believed that passionate kisses were strictly a mouth-to-mouth transaction. Occasionally a leading man would tenderly apply his lips to a forehead or cheek, but his lady would only close her eyes, clearly unbitten.

No amount of prepubescent contemplation could explain it. I did my best. I tried to imagine a situation in which I would be willing to receive (delivering was out of the question) a kiss on the neck at all, never mind a forceful, capillary-busting buss. And though I was able—had long been able, as a matter of fact—to imagine myself with some handsome man who curled his fingers beneath my chin, tilting my lips toward him, these pictures might well have been movies themselves, so devoid were they of any physical nuance. I knew what a kiss looked like, but I had no idea of what one felt like and, being an unimaginative child (as I am now an unimaginative woman), was unable or unwilling to speculate.

Which did not stop me from picturing those kisses. I needed them. I hoarded them. Still, I would not have confessed them, even to girlfriends who, assaulted already by puberty, confessed to much more. In eighth grade it seemed that puberty was a campaign whose soldiers could not find me—I was down the hall and around the corner, or already in a nook in the library, while puberty, like polio, struck the kids who hung around in crowds by the swimming pool or punch bowl. By the time puberty located me, I was sixteen and so frightened of boys I'd given up my dreams of kisses. I'm not sure what I was afraid of. It wasn't exactly sex, which I'd read up on, eager to understand my still-dreaming and sometimes treacherous friends. Maybe it was too much contemplation, maybe I was finally certain that, left alone with me, a boy would surely try to sink his teeth into my neck.

Now, with James, I was in eighth grade again, curious, not yet frightened. I longed for something physical, but what that would be I could not feature; could not even speculate.

There is his hand on the tabletop.

There are his shoes, still warm from his feet, worn down on either side from where the brace buckles around.

There is his chair, and look, he's still in it.

There, behind me, retreating, is his window, and his light is on, he's still awake, just as he was thirty seconds ago when I closed the door.

It's sex you're thinking of, Peggy, people will say, you are being naive on purpose or by nature, but anyone else can see it plainly.

Well, perhaps. But those seeing people, those who have in their lives fallen in love without impediment, cannot understand. Nowadays sex is the guest you should always expect, because it's supposed to knock down your door without an invitation: you might as well be prepared. If you haven't set a place at the table, you are called naive or repressed.

But sometimes, honestly, the mind makes calibrations, but not for sex, because sex is not coming to you, sex is down the street wrecking your neighbor's house, sex has—for any number of reasons—washed its hands of you, even if you are not done with it, even if the breakup is not mutual. In which case, if you are lucky and you work very hard, you learn not only to be satisfied by other things, you start to long for them. And you don't feel starved; you find your hungers are simply different, as if you've dropped your Western upbringing for a childhood in a country where ice cream was unheard of, available only in books.

And so I stared at the hand on the tabletop, wanting it to come toward me even if I wasn't sure for what. I wanted to stick my own feet in his recently occupied shoes to sop up that warmth. I wanted to turn back at night, open the door and say, *I think I'll stay awhile*—not the way they do in movies; no meaning or implied unspeakable verb, just to stay, just to be there, just to stay.

James's ambition—besides dancing—was to attend one of the twice-yearly shoe conventions in New York. Perhaps he thought of New York as a city of size, avenues and skyscrapers and noise. Would the tallest boy in the world be such a sight on those streets? Wouldn't he be able to walk them, plenty to look up at, thinking, this place is so *big*? All his life he'd taken pleasure in the smallest tricks: sleight of hand, a camera, what made one bird different from another. He looked for a patch of red beneath a wing, or made a visitor wonder where a card had gone to, or shrank the world into a snapshot.

Finally, though, these things were small, in theory and in fact, and they were no longer enough. He could not shrink himself by loving smallness, though he tried; perhaps he could manage it by courting things even larger than himself. His books on magic taught him that you can convince people of anything if you just direct their attention where you want it, distract them from the matter at hand. Plenty of distraction in Manhattan.

He wrote away for train schedules.

"We could drive," I said. I still hadn't convinced James to get in the Nash with me. After all those years of avoiding them, cars made him nervous. They seemed an easy way to break a bone.

"I like trains," he said.

He bought a map of Manhattan and stuck it to the wall by his bed. I brought him books about the city's history, the stories of O. Henry, *Knickerbocker Tales*.

"I had a dream about New York City," he said sometimes.

"What about it?"

"I was there," he said. "That's all." I waited for him to say, You were there, too. But he didn't.

As the summer progressed, something changed. He still spoke of New York, but it was something he'd see in years, not months. He scorned his physical therapy.

"No point," he said. "I can't feel it working."

"Well, you wouldn't," I said. If he didn't feel his legs, how would he feel improvement? "The doctors know best."

"The doctors don't live with it."

The only place he ever went was the front house, and then only to eat, to take advantage of their more extensive plumbing. In the fall he'd be a junior at the high school, but he decided not to go back.

"You could just go some of the time," said Caroline. "They won't care. Show up when you feel like it."

"No," he said. "If I can't do it right I don't want to do it at all."

"Right?" she said. "What's right? They'll be glad to see you whenever you show up. You always do well. Isn't that right enough?"

"I don't want to."

"Jim—"

"I don't want to fall," he said. "Those floors are slick. I can do the work at home."

When he wanted to quiet us, he talked about his health, and we thought, at least he's being sensible. This was something we—Caroline and I—had in common: a passion for the practicals. Yes, that's right, he could fall, he could break a leg or worse. Sometimes we worked hard to believe it, because otherwise we'd fret too much. Best to stay home.

Best to hold court in his own house, imagine himself a bachelor with a dance floor and a juke. If he fell at school, he'd be helpless in front of everyone he knew; at home he sat in his chair, did the schoolwork a tutor brought over, and waited for three o'clock, when his friends came by and Caroline brought refreshments and maybe—not that he cared or anything—maybe Stella would show up, too. Because she did show up sometimes, and danced, or flirted, or combed her hair. Her boyfriend, whose name was Sean, didn't seem to mind that she flirted with every single boy there, and I wanted to take him aside, say, Doesn't this bother you? Don't you worry?

All those boys—fat and thin and tall and cross-eyed—had lipstick on their cheeks, little Stella kisses. Maybe she kissed them hello, or maybe she let her lips brush against them when they were dancing, because she danced with all of them. But only the one boy ever got to hold her when the music was over, when she'd clapped for the song and settled herself on the sofa we'd recently moved in. He was the handsomest boy, no doubt.

Some days I wondered why James tolerated me, a comparatively old woman of thirty-one, when he had those teenagers. Other days I knew why: he felt, if not older than the kids, at least significantly different. Maybe those days—the days he seemed sadder, the days he'd talk so long I wouldn't leave for hours—were the times he remembered that he was going to die sooner than they were.

I have forgiven myself for the fact that I liked his sad days best. That was when he was happiest to see me. He liked the fact I was around so often that he did not have to lie about a bad mood. He'd become accustomed to me. I don't know exactly when that happened—at the hospital? Afterward? Those days I could think that Stella and her visits and her pretty hair and tight sweaters could not make him happy. Those days he needed me most.

Where He Was

In newspaper articles that came toward the end of his life, when James had attained some measure of fame, they'd note: "He eats no more than the average growing boy." People always wanted to know his appetite, his shoe size, how many yards of material it took to make one of his shirts. *How much does it cost to run such a concern*, they wondered, as though they'd plan to be as tall themselves if only it weren't such an expense.

To build the World's Largest anything requires money, usually in advance. James's entrepreneurial body constructed itself without backing, and then threatened to bankrupt him in any number of ways. Including, of course, the coarsest, most literal way. The town had been generous with donations to build and outfit the cottage, but we could not set the collection cans out every time he outgrew a pair of pants, every time a shoe or shirt size lapsed into obsolescence. For a while Caroline tried to make his clothing, just as she made some of her own. Her talent was with delicate fabric: she hid the messy seams of her dresses and the odd bell-shapes of her skirts with too much cloth and loud unruly prints. The materials for a boy's clothing—denim, tweed, oxford cloth—confounded her fingers.

James knew he needed money, not only for himself and Oscar and Caroline but for Alice, his cousin. She was a year old now, a petulant child, with Oscar's round face and Caroline's pink cheeks. She ruled the front house with her chubby fist; I thought her voice alarmingly loud for a baby's. I'd have predicted that the Stricklands would be casual, even negligent parents, but they fussed over Alice from the time she formally woke them up at five A.M. until her bedtime, and then almost hourly after that, each time she demanded their attention.

"When do they start sleeping through the night?" I asked Caroline.

"College," she said.

Alice was one of the reasons I stopped spending time in the front house. Frankly, I was tired of looking at her, and whenever I was there, I was obligated to.

"Look at Alice!" Caroline would say, and I would think, I have seen your child suck her toes a dozen times and once would have sufficed. I have heard the question, "Alice, what are you eating?" a thousand times, answered these ways: dirt, a piece of cereal, tin foil, and whatever-it-is-it's-gone-now. She wasn't exactly a Broadway musical.

I tried to ask Caroline politely. "Don't you get bored sometimes? Don't you want to go to a movie or read a book?"

"Nooo," Caroline said. Alice lifted herself to her feet, dropped to her bottom, considered crying, rejected the idea, and pulled herself to her feet again. "If I had nothing else to do I could watch her all day."

"Huh," I said. Alice bit into a plastic squeaky pig. Then she did it again.

"You wouldn't get bored if she was yours," Caroline said. "She'd be better than any novel."

"Babies," I said, "have no plot."

James, on the other hand, loved Alice. When he was depressed, he spoke of her as his heir, and sometimes I thought it was her existence that depressed him, made him think about his death. He'd realized he wasn't the last generation. Seventeen years old was too young to realize that.

He wanted to accomplish something, and because he was a teenager, he figured the way to do it was to earn money. Sometimes it was for Alice's college education, sometimes his own. Sometimes it was for the trip to New York City that he still dreamed of.

I wondered what my job was, pessimism or optimism. When he spoke of New York, he seemed to see himself everywhere, doing everything—in Broadway theaters, climbing the Statue of Liberty. I'd been inside the Statue of Liberty; despite her exterior size, she was not a generous hostess, and James could not possibly have fit on her spiral staircase, nor would he be able to climb all those stairs. I didn't know whether to indulge his dreams or quietly remind him of his facts.

I chose indulgence; it was easier for both of us. When he wondered whether Alice would remember him when she grew older, I said, of course: they'd know each other all their lives.

I knew that he would die, but I never thought—or almost never thought—of James as someone who was *dying*. His death would shatter me. That was clear. I did not see how accepting his dying now would make his eventual death easier to bear: I knew my devastation would be so total there would be no leavening for it. His death was a thought that occurred to me, just as my finances were something I worried about, once a month, in the middle of the night, and then put off for another month.

So I argued for him to keep things in mind, practical, possible things. The shoe store people, for instance. They'd started to offer more: not just shoes but money. They reminded him of the expositions in New York. They'd give him money up front.

"Soon," he said. "I'm just not ready yet."

It would take something other than my daily nagging. So one night, a night I knew would be good for it, I waited outside the cottage, and when the kids left and said their good nights, I called her over.

"Stella," I said. "May I ask you a question?"

She stepped closer. A clear, warm April night, and Stella wore a thin sweater with cap sleeves: her upper arms were plump. Pretty, too.

"I was wondering," I said. I beckoned her around the house, so that James could not see us through his window. "I was wondering if you'd be willing to invite James out for a walk."

I'd asked her this question in my head several times. Sometimes I heard her answer, "You mean, like a date? No, I don't think so." Sometimes she asked why, and I explained, made an elegant case that she agreed to. Sometimes she said scathing things, said, "You don't think I have something better to do than take a walk with Mount Everest?"

What Stella actually said was, "Sure."

I waited for her to ask me why. But she didn't, didn't even raise her eyebrows, wanting me to tell her more. Perhaps she simply understood herself as something that people would request.

"It's that he's not getting much exercise," I said. "We try and coax him, but I thought if you asked if he'd like to take a walk, just as a friend, that might seem a little more attractive."

"Sure," she said again. She smiled. I tried to make it a mean smile. "You want me to ask him now?"

"No," I said. "Next time you visit."

"Okay. I'll ask him tomorrow after school."

"If it's no bother—"

"Nope. I like Jim. Happy to do it."

"Terrific. If the weather still holds."

"Well, sure."

She wasn't a bad girl, despite my best hopes. She was a bored girl, slightly nervous, smarter than I wanted her to be. Although I admit it wouldn't be hard for her to be smarter; I wanted her stupid. She was a girl who boys loved, and she loved their love of her. In fact, she was like Mrs. Sweatt, come back young and brunette and before all her bad luck. I had no doubt that James's mother had been just this sort of girl, though midwestern, nicer, not so obvious. If Stella made James happy—and clearly she did—who was I to complain?

I hated her.

The weather held. So I stood behind the circulation desk about the time school let out and gazed through the window. There was only that one main strip in our town; chances were they'd walk down it. Three o'clock, then three-thirty, then four. And then, finally, I saw them.

If his legs gave him much trouble, you wouldn't have known. He did lean on his cane, and they did walk slowly, but they were chatting. Stella laughed, then said something, and James laughed.

There was once a boy I'd liked a little, one of the kids I hung around with in college. I always knew where he was in a room. At a party, in a classroom, at the movies or a lecture, I'd be doing something else, talking or watching or sitting waiting for the next thing to happen, and I always knew where he was, could feel the fact of him on the back of my head or on my cheek or right through a person talking to me. At the movies I heard when he laughed and when he didn't; when he leaned over to the person next to him and made them laugh. I could think, *I'm keeping track of you, doesn't that count for something?* and I never paid attention to anything so diligently as his body as it ordered another drink at the bar or asked somebody else to dance. One late night, as he passed by, I leaned forward and kissed the boy I was talking to. It was not a kiss for my own benefit or for the recipient, but for the green-eyed tweed-clad boy who was now talking to somebody else entirely. You should never kiss for somebody else's benefit—proper kissing is a selfish undertaking—but I was too young to know that.

The fact is, I always knew where James was, too. He was in his cottage, and I was with him or I wasn't. At breakfast or dinner he was at the house; Caroline brought a lunch over. And maybe I'd built the cottage to keep track of him, so I counted; maybe I wanted him to know that I knew where he was.

You understand why I had to follow them.

Astoria agreed to take over the desk; I told her I had to walk some papers down to town hall. By the time I got out the door, they were two blocks ahead. Easy to spot James on a street this small and skinny. I wondered: should I happen into them? No, because I knew James might not be happy to see me, not when he was taking the air with Stella, and I could not bear to see him not happy to see me. I kept them in sight. I window-shopped. I tied my shoes. I walked a block, then waited. I was ready to duck into a shop when they turned around, and then I could shadow them as far as the library. By then, they'd be almost home anyhow.

Suddenly they turned down a side street. I hadn't expected that; nothing was down that street. I walked faster. James still might fall or get tired—he was walking farther than he'd walked in months, and he'd scorned the physical therapy, and he should know better than to forget that. When I got to the side street, they'd gone. I'd lost them.

I leaned against a street sign, a little winded from my trot. I didn't get enough exercise myself. Foolish, foolish, I thought, but I didn't know whether I was bawling myself out for losing them or for following in the first place.

I turned back down the main street. You've learned your lesson, I told myself: even if you wanted to be a spy you haven't the knack for it, and an incompetent spy is soon unemployed. I walked past the library and went to town hall anyhow, just for verisimilitude's sake. I stood inside the lobby a minute, then headed back for work.

They were just coming up on the library themselves. Now he was walking with difficulty, hesitant steps. Stella's hand fluttered up to his elbow, the one that didn't hold the cane. They parted in front of the library; James started up the stairs. At first I couldn't tell what he was doing, exactly, and then I realized: he was walking up sideways. He set his right foot a couple of steps up, then his left foot on the step below. Then again. His feet had gotten so big he could not fit them any other way. I had no idea when this had happened: it had been ages since I'd seen him climb stairs.

I began to walk briskly, in a businesslike way, the gait of somebody who *had* just been to town hall, who knew nothing about teenagers and their afternoon constitutionals.

He was sitting on the wide bench inside the front room of the library.

"Peggy!" Astoria said as I stepped inside. "Look at the stranger who's come to see us."

"What do you know? Decided to get a little air?"

He nodded, smiling.

"What brought you here?" I said.

"Decided it was time to get out," he said. I could not tell whether his cheeks were rosy with health or exertion. Unfair of the body, I thought, to make a man dying of a heart attack look just like a man who has finished his daily improving run.

"How was it?" I sat down next to him. I wanted to know what made Stella look so worried at the end of the walk. "Worth the trip?"

He shrugged. Then he said, "Yeah. You're right. I shouldn't spend all day inside. I almost forgot what this sorry old town looks like."

Well, I thought, it worked. Still, I wanted him to mention Stella, I wanted to be able to put to use the feigned surprise I'd practiced all the way up the street.

There were two things I hadn't expected: Stella was a good girl, and she honestly liked James. Several times a week she dropped by the cottage early in the afternoon, before the rest of the teenagers, and suggested a walk. Sometimes they dropped by the library—I imagined Stella suggested this, to show me she was serious about her assignment—sometimes they just passed the big windows by the circulation desk. Should I take her aside and explain that I'd only meant one walk, one time, not this extended engagement? No, of course not; not even I could be that dumb or mean.

She still had her boyfriend, the skinny and handsome Sean, who arrived with the other boys nearly every day. James rarely mentioned Stella, that's how much he liked her. I don't know whether he watched Stella and Sean leave at dinnertime, hand in hand, hating both of them, or just him, or, briefly, just her; or whether the pleasure of her solitary company a few times a week was enough for him to think that she couldn't care for this Sean, this dull American boy of dull Irish parents.

Some afternoons I arrived at the cottage to see Stella and her Swains—what a name for a 1940s band!—arranged around the room. And like a good, shy bandleader, there was Stella in the corner, each Swain absorbed in whatever he was doing and simultaneously paying her the most rigorous, imperceptible attention. The studied negligence of the Swains! They didn't just listen to music and dance; they played cards or did homework. One boy sat cross-legged on the floor with a book on a knee, another leaned writing against the doorjamb, stopping every now and then to shake down the ink of his ballpoint pen. "You get the answer to number eight? No? Did you, Stell?"

Normally these were kids who'd come to the library, whispering questions and answers, bottles of Coke hidden beneath jackets. Here they didn't have to whisper, and their soda bottles stood on every surface, leaving kiss marks on the wood.

When I came in, only Stella and Sean and James would say hello. I got to know the other boys slowly: chubby Benny, whose eyes were so sunken they looked like bruised thumbprints in his face. Sullen Frank, who stuttered darkly. Eric, a good friend of James's, a small kid with a brush cut who I knew from his visits to the library to take out books on sports. When Eric walked, he did not move the upper half of his body at all—passing by the circulation desk, he looked as if he were on wheels. He also could not speak in words, but offered nervous polite sounds—not the rude grunting noise other nontalking boys used, just pure open vowels.

"Hello, Eric," I said.

"Ah," said Eric.

"How's school?"

"Oh," Eric said, halfway between *good* and *I don't know yet*.

And from across the room, Stella would call out, "Hi, Miss Cort!" I'd give her a jaunty, uncaring wave. She could break Frank's heart, and Benny's and Eric's, but mine was safe.

Or mostly; sometimes even I was charmed. She was the object of so many glances, stares, careful appraisals, compliments that when she looked at you it was as if she reflected all that dazzling attention upon you. She did it without talking: she looked at you directly, a small touch of cynicism to her smile. It was the cynicism, strangely, that made it appear she was paying attention; it made you feel like her co-conspirator.

James started asking me about my car.

"I can fit, right?" he said.

"Yes. Sure."

"You wouldn't mind giving me a ride somewhere?"

"Say the word. Where do you want to go?"

"I dunno."

"We could take it to the shoe store, you know."

He made a face. "I was thinking somewhere closer. The beach, maybe."

"Okay."

"And maybe I could bring a friend."

"Oh," I said. "Sure."

"Another person could fit, right? In the backseat? A small person?"

I smiled. "Yes," I said. "A small person could. Eric?"

"No. Stella maybe."

"Stella would fit," I said, as if I'd just measured the backseat for Stella's measurements.

"So. You wouldn't mind? Like maybe Sunday, when you weren't working."

"James," said I, the chaperone, unwitting and unwilling cupid, "of course not."

So I did a little research, asked about beaches. I even bought the fixings for a picnic lunch. James himself could not have been as nervous as I was; the whole week felt like one terrible endless day without break, with Sunday, twilight, promised at the end, Stella ascendant.

Except they took a walk together that Friday, the last Friday of the school year, and Stella told James—who, she said, was her best friend in the world—this: that Sean had proposed, and she had accepted, and that in two months they would move together to Virginia, where Sean would work for his uncle and Stella would, despite everything, finish high school. In Virginia, in some small town, she would be the prettiest housewife in the twelfth grade, and Sean the only husband at the senior prom.

I was afraid that he'd stop walking, now that Stella was planning for her wedding. But he didn't; he walked by himself. I got used to seeing him at a distance. No, that wasn't true—I was used to that already. Was it because of his size that I was so unused to putting myself in the frame? Did I think I wouldn't fit?

No. That was how I always saw myself; that is, how I didn't see myself. I have felt out-of-frame all my life. At best, even as I say this, I am the court painter who, after years of painting the royal family, can no longer resist slipping a bit of herself in the frame. Look, there's Peggy, her forearm, the toe of her shoe, her frozen unrecognizable face in a swollen mirror on the farthest wall of the room. It doesn't matter who I am looking at: they are royalty, compared to me.

James was the only one who ever drew me in at all. In the evenings when we talked, after the teenagers had gone off and there was room, he was the one who made me feel looked at instead of just looking.

Now James walked alone. James with his cane went down the street, stopped at the end. James inspected the bay from the town pier. James browsed in no stores, endured no conversation, took out not a single book from my library. He returned to the cottage, where the boys were sometimes already waiting outside.

And three weeks later he came in to see me at work, holding a cream envelope with a card inside. "I'd like to go to Stella's wedding," he said. "I asked; you're invited too, if you'll drive me."

I smiled at the poor bargain of that invitation. But I agreed.

I had never wanted to be one of those girls in love with boys who would not have me. Unrequited love—plain desperate aboveboard boy-chasing—turned you into a salesperson, and what you were selling was something he didn't want, couldn't use, would never miss. Unrequited love was deciding to be useless, and I could never abide uselessness.

Neither could James. He understood. In such situations, you do one of two things—you either walk away and deny yourself, or you do sneaky things to get what you need. You attend weddings, you go for walks. You say, *yes. Yes, you're my best friend, too.*

Stella Ascendant

We drove up Route 6A to Wellfleet. Late June light flattens and brightens Cape Cod into a postcard. All reds seem like the same red: the flung-back shutters on the identical cottages that line the road; the lassos of neon that spell *Motel*; a red-bottomed buoy that has washed up on the beach; a sign that promises lobster with a picture of a lobster. All blues the same, sky, convertibles, James's eyes. The sand, gold where the wind has combed it; his hair, the same. The sea gull in front of a cloud, the cloud, his oxford cloth shirt, all three washed just enough for a hint of gray.

And me and my big black car and what felt, increasingly, like my big black heart, as unwieldy and peculiar as my car. Maybe as hard, too: that car could have crumpled anything with its unstoppable, undentable bumper. Reserved, Caroline had said, and despite my best intentions, she was right: my torso an unorganized cabinet of secrets I was saving for a later date. They knocked into each other, they bruised and then calloused.

I'd pictured us driving along, talking, perhaps listening to the radio to music that James dialed up. Which shows you I hadn't thought it through: in the car I couldn't see James or his hair and eyes that matched the passing scenery. That they matched is something I know now; I might not have realized it then. He sat in the backseat and had rolled down the back window; every now and then he'd say something I couldn't hear (my window was rolled down, too), and I'd turn my head and, at the same time, by accident, the wheel; the car would swerve. "LATER!" James would yell as I straightened the car and blushed at the cars that honked at us. We did this three times.

"I have four left wheels," I said to James, but he couldn't hear me.

We drove up to the church early. It took James a while to disentangle himself from the Nash. It seemed obvious to enter from the front, but how to exit was less clear.

"Here we are," I said.

"Good Luck Cottages," said James. "We passed those a while back."

"I saw them. Run-down places. Probably Luck is the only good thing they can promise."

When I'd heard the service would be in a Catholic church, I'd imagined something like Our Lady's, which was down the street from my girlhood home. I'd snuck inside one afternoon; it was as spindly and impossible and arched as a split pepper. Even though all eyes in the paintings looked away from me—they were trained toward Jesus, or up toward God—I'd felt accused and frightened.

But St. Catherine's was plain and white, pretty stained-glass windows set into the doors. Maybe because it was so many people's summer church the builders thought it proper to dress it like a vacationer: sweet and only informally gaudy. When we went inside, an usher took us to the front pew, the family spot. Stella had thought this out; she knew the front was the only place James would fit. He took the aisle; I sat next to him, and eventually an unspeaking grandmother of some sort took the seat next to me.

James wore a necktie that Caroline had sewn for him; I recognized the print from one of her fall skirts. I wore a blue dress and a silly hat of feathers balanced on top of my head; Astoria had lent it to me. It was designed to cling to a hairdo without interfering, and so when I'd clipped it onto my uncoifed head that morning, my hair pinned up, more pins in the hat to affix it, the thing looked like a stuffed bird nailed to a tree branch. By now, having been knocked about by the wind through the car window, its grip was loose. I tried to fix it.

As entertainment, the wedding wasn't much. The principals kept their backs to us. The priest mumbled and flubbed Stella's name. I wanted some sort of dramatic ceremony, with wailing or hysterical laughter. James beside me was silent. Then the priest said something, the happy couple kissed, and it was over without bloodshed or tears.

Despite everything, I never felt jealous at weddings. I longed for love, yes, but I never saw that love was in greater supply at weddings than in butcher shops or department stores. The sight of a couple furtively holding hands beneath a restaurant table was more likely to remind me of the hopelessness of my life than any number of ladies dressed in giant christening gowns reciting words to become joined to a man in a rented suit. I do not like public ceremony, not graduations, not weddings; not pep rallies, nor church. Perhaps I simply do not understand trying to share one emotion (love, relief, faith, pep) with a quantity of strangers.

The reception was in a restaurant down the street, close enough to walk. Once there, James found a cluster of kids from school, who'd been seated in less prime spots near the back of the church and so were among the first to leave. I recognized Eric from the cottage, but the rest were an assortment of lean boys and sweet girls (girls! I hadn't imagined that Stella knew, or would acknowledge the existence of, any girls) whom I had never met. That Stella had other friends—that she had, in fact, a life outside of the cottage—never occurred to me.

Food was served in a willy-nilly buffet. I decided I would rather be alone than be one adult among teenagers and said good-bye to James. I took a seat at a table on the other side of the room. There was no seating plan, which meant that Stella was more civilized than I'd thought: seating plans, in my opinion, are a form of social incarceration.

"What the hell is that?" a woman next to me said as the band set up by the door. She was forty, maybe, a blonde in coral lipstick that looked like a medicine meant to prevent infection. I followed her gaze, sure that it would end at a musician carrying an instrument she could not identify. Instead she was looking at James, returning from the men's room.

I started to answer her; her date, a man in thick glasses, did instead: "Jesus Christ. How tall is that?"

They had been drinking beer in bottles, which amplified their amazement.

"That's James Sweatt," I told them. "He goes to school with Stella."

"He's a *freak*!" exclaimed the man, as if what I said was impossible, that the sight James presented, his jacket off and his tie loosened, could not possibly know Stella, go to school, walk the floor of the dark wood restaurant in Wellfleet.

"He's tall," I said casually. But the woman shook her head. *Well, he shouldn't be,* she seemed to say.

By then the bandleader had stepped to the microphone to make some announcements, and Sean and Stella, the train of her wedding dress drawn up like a curtain so she could dance, took to the floor for an inane song by, according to the bandleader, "Mr. Irwin, um, Berlin, ladies and gentlemen." ("A doll I can carry / the girl that I marry will be. . . .") The people who sat next to me eventually forgot James, but I didn't forget them: I wanted to be a movie thug who could pick them up by their shirtfronts and shake them like maracas. Even they would not know whether they were trembling from fear or physics.

Instead, I drank coffee till I was the one shaking. Stella took the middle of the floor, and the bandleader called for all unmarried women to take the floor around her. I thought I saw James look for me, but his gaze skittered past.

"You should go up," said the despicable woman next to me. Did I look so unmarried?

"No." I smiled. "My husband wouldn't like it."

The drummer rolled his sticks low, and then hit the cymbal as Stella turned her back and pitched her bouquet into the arms of the plumpest bridesmaid, a dour girl in her peach-colored dress who caught the package with a sigh, as if this were what she was used to all her life, picking up after careless Stella.

Then the floor in front of the band filled with dancing couples. When I looked across them, James was talking to Eric and a girl even smaller than Eric. James drank a beer, smoked a cigarette. Maybe he was taking up all his mother's old bad habits. He looked like an adult. Then Eric and his date excused themselves as the band started a new, apparently meaningful song. Stella approached, asked James a question while holding his hand. He shook his head, and she went away. I waited until he finished the cigarette, then went over to him.

"You going to dance?" I asked.

"Doubt it. You?"

"Nobody's asked me."

"Ah," he said. "I'm more popular than you. Somebody asked me."

"So why don't you?"

"I can't dance."

"Look at that dance floor," I said. "Look closely at the men. Most of them can't dance, but all of them *are* dancing."

He watched them for a while. "Well," he said. He picked up the beer. I sat down in the chair next to him. "Let me put it this way. I don't aim to make a spectacle of myself."

"You—"

He laughed. "Peggy, listen, imagine it. Me dancing. You don't think that would be a spectacle?"

The song ended, and some couples drifted back to the table. James didn't make a move to introduce me. In fact, he turned his back toward me and spoke to them in conspiratorial tones. Teenagers.

A man with a belly and a bow tie approached and asked me to dance. "I'm Uncle Fisher," he said by way of introduction, which seemed to be enough. He was around forty, with black hair, good-looking enough if you squinted. On the dance floor he asked me whose side I belonged to, and when I said, "Bride's," he answered, "Ah. She's a pip."

I smiled. "And what side are you on?"

"Nobody's," he said. "I'm totally impartial."

He was a good dancer; I'd forgotten how easy it was to dance with a man who really knew how. Suddenly he said, "Excuse me," and reached for my hat, which he plucked from my head. The bobby pins clattered to the ground and my hair fell to my shoulders, as if my whole hairdo were a breakaway movie prop designed for this moment. "Much better," he said. He stuck the hat in his jacket pocket. "Now I can concentrate."

"I'm not much for hats," I said. "It was a loaner."

"Oh, don't blame yourself," said Uncle Fisher. "Never blame yourself. It was the hat's fault entirely. Where are you from?"

"Brewsterville."

"Pretty," he said, and I blushed.

"Whose uncle are you?"

"Everybody's. I'm the universal uncle."

There was something about meeting a man away from my life that made things easier; I could almost flirt. Somehow I felt he could not see my flaws. Nothing mattered. I hoped the hateful couple would see me; I couldn't decide whether I preferred them to think that Uncle Fisher was my husband or my paramour.

"You're just jealous of my hat," I said. "It's a fine hat."

"It's a sin against nature." He hummed something. "You're not married," he said.

"That obvious?"

"Well, I'm everybody's uncle, and that means I've been to an awful lot of weddings. Single women are easy to spot—they're the ones who are surprised when asked to dance."

"Are you married?"

"No, no. I believe marriage is a spectator sport. You're a fine dancer, Peggy. Where do you dance in Brewsterville?"

"I don't."

"Well then, you should come to Wellfleet more often. I'll take you dancing."

"Where?"

"There's a wedding almost every week. You should come visit me."

Between James acting impossible, and my not knowing anyone else in the room, and the effortless way he made me dance, I could entertain the idea. The notion that some afternoon I could get in my car and crash a wedding with Uncle Fisher seemed quite possible, as the band swung into another song and he did not even start to surrender me to the chairs that lined the room.

I said, "Sure."

"You won't," said Uncle Fisher sadly. "I'd like to believe you'd come, but you won't."

"I might," I said. But his doubting it made me certain: I wouldn't. I would step from his arms and forget him.

Which I did, at least sort of. But for weeks after this—longer, really, but with frightening regularity for those first few weeks—I would think of Fisher, with his dark hair and soft body. I could see myself in my car, going to visit him, and wonder, why not just up and go to Wellfleet? Would I know where to find him? Would he be at another wedding, dancing with someone who looked good in a hat? I would calm myself down, I would acknowledge that it couldn't be anything personal—after all, he didn't even know me. He asked me to dance before he'd heard me speak. For instance: he didn't know how I felt about that sullen, bespectacled, irreligious teenager who, as we danced, drank a beer, played with his cane, and longed for the bride.

Later I would think of Uncle Fisher again, a guilty pleasure. He was someone outside of my life who might possibly think of me. A possibility. Some people live in a world of such things. Think of Stella—couldn't she have had anyone she wanted? Don't you think even now, with two grown kids and a husband who drinks too much (and I don't know where Stella is this winter, I only know what I saw that night: Sean drinking and embracing his friends, Stella dancing with everyone, old men, five-year-olds, female cousins), mightn't she think of all the things she could have chosen?

As for myself, I can't, I don't. I am happy with my life, largely because it *is* my life. How many regrets can I have? I didn't turn much down. Indeed, perhaps on the dance floor I saw the future, knew I'd stay with James forever. Before it was just what I did: I stayed with James; each morning I woke up knowing that it was a day I would devote to him in some small or large way. I was offered so little explicitly in my life, and I accepted nearly every explicit offer. Uncle Fisher was one. A small choice, but a particular one. And I turned him down.

When the second song ended, I sat down on the other side of the room from James and talked to Uncle Fisher.

James approached us. He squinted at Uncle Fisher.

"I want to go home now."

"In a minute," I said.

"Peggy," he said. "I don't feel well. I want to leave."

I stood and shook Uncle Fisher's hand and then gave it a fond pat. "Thank you for the dance. Okay," I said to James. "Let's go."

In the parking lot I said, "Did you have a good time?"

He shrugged. "Let's *go,*" he said.

"Why yes Peggy I did. And did you have a good time? Why, yes James, I had a good time too."

"Oh, is that why you came," he said. "I thought you were just supposed to drive me. I didn't know you wanted to have a *good time.*"

He looked absolutely disgusted, I couldn't tell over what.

"I didn't know you objected to me having one," I said. "I thought I was doing you a favor, giving up the better part of one of my days off to drive you to a social event where I wouldn't know anybody. I'm sorry. Perhaps next time I'll wait in the hall, and you can come get me when you're ready to leave."

I couldn't tell if we were arguing like husband and wife or mother and son; I wanted to rectify that. "I'm happy to drive you anywhere, James. You know that. But I'm not your mother. I'm doing it as a *friend*, and so you better treat me like one."

We walked to the Nash in silence. Then he said, "I want to drive." I heard this as, *I want to die*. He rubbed the fender and repeated it.

I answered, not unsympathetically, "You're drunk."

"No I'm not."

"You don't know how to drive."

"You can teach me. I only had one beer. Oh, two, I guess. I mean, you wouldn't even have to teach me, I took driver's ed, the classroom part, so basically I know how. The driver's seat flips down the other side, right? It's perfect."

I looked at him. I had my hand in my purse, my fingers sliding along the serrated edge of the key.

"I'm insane," I said.

"No! You're not! I'll be really careful, we won't even go on the highway."

"Okay. First: which one's the brake and which one's the gas?"

He set his hands in front of him, palms to the ground. He closed his eyes. "Brake." He depressed his left hand. "Gas. Gearshift." His right hand closed to a fist, up toward the imaginary steering wheel. "Ignition." His left hand came up. "Lights. Windshield wipers." Then he flipped his left hand up, stuck it out, flipped it down. "Right. Left. Stop."

"You promise to keep your eyes open if I let you drive?"

He opened them, nodded. I flung the keys, and he caught them in a snatch.

"Your reflexes are good. That was the last test. Let's go."

I folded the driver's seat down. Even he needed a pillow behind him to drive; luckily, so did I, and I tucked it behind him, then got into the backseat so that we were sitting next to each other. I was miles from reaching the radio.

He was a good driver, improbably good for someone who'd never driven, but maybe I was just in a suddenly fine mood. I was surprised by my willingness to let him drive; proud, even. As soon as he got used to the way the car jumped when given too much gas or brake, it didn't jump anymore. I pointed out his tendency to rush traffic lights and stop signs.

"What the heck," I said. "You might as well drive all the way home."

"On the highway?" he said.

"It's the middle of the night. There isn't any traffic, and actually it's easier to drive on the highway. There's less to avoid hitting."

"I'm ready to go to the shoe store," he said casually. "You can call them."

"Oh. Good. What changed your mind?"

"It's time," he said. We finally found Route 6A, and pulled on.

"I want a cigarette," James announced. He pulled out a crumpled pack from his shirt pocket and looked at me, wanting, I supposed, to gauge my disapproval. I tried not to show any. "Could you get one for me?" he said. "And light it?" So I stuck a cigarette in my mouth, while he unrolled the backseat window by his elbow.

"How often do you smoke?" I asked. He took the cigarette from me, put that hand on the steering wheel, and looked at the watch on his other hand. I'd forgotten what a complicated process juggling the wheel is in the first few days of driving.

"Well," he said. "Every morning this month."

"Really."

He laughed. "It's one A.M. July first. I'm only telling the truth. Not that much. Almost never."

"Me neither," I said, and I lit a cigarette for myself.

"You, too?"

"Occasionally," I answered, though it had been since college. I touched my hair, realized Astoria's lurid hat was still in Uncle Fisher's pocket. Somehow I suspected that if I told the story right, she'd understand. And then I rolled down my back window, too, and we smoked our cigarettes and when we were finished we tossed them out, and they flew behind us like Stella's bouquet, except that no plump bridesmaid anchored down by satin shoes and a tulle petticoat caught them. Only the highway, which took care of us in this and other ways on the ride home, our windows still unwound, James still at the wheel.

But before we got to Brewsterville, he said, not looking at me, "Peggy. Have you ever been in love?"

Ah, he was a romantic, like his aunt. I stared out the windshield, wondering what to answer.

"No," I said finally. "Have you?"

"Hmmm. I don't know. Maybe. Not sure."

I locked and unlocked the car door. "Who?"

"Who?" he said, and then he must have realized he was stalling. "Who-who. Who indeed." He sighed. "I think I used to be in love with Stella."

"Used to be," I said. "Not anymore?"

"No."

"What cured you?"

He laughed. "The cure for this terrible ailment was. Well, I don't know what it was. I guess I talked myself out of it. I guess unrequited love is a bed of nails I don't want to spend my life lying on."

"That bad."

"No. At first it's the mere feat of it, you know? The fact that you're doing it, the adrenaline gets you through. But after that—"

"After that, you start to feel the nails."

"Yup."

"You ever tell her?"

"Fat chance. She has guys telling her they love her all day long. She told me so. Now, if I said I loved her, would she tell me things like that? Anyhow, that's how I feel today."

Just a crush, I thought, but I didn't say it. I'd heard enough of the music the teenagers played to know that saying such a thing would turn me into A Hated Grown-up.

"So you never had a boyfriend." He said this as a statement of fact.

"Yes, I have," I said. "In my wicked past. A few." Then I regretted it, because if I'd said no, it would have made our lives more alike. I looked for things that made us seem alike. But I would have been lying; it had been a while, but I'd had boy-friends.

"You had a wicked past?" he said. He smiled, clearly not believing it.

"Semi-wicked," I said. "Absolutely saintly compared to most."

"Tell me about it. Did you break his heart, or did he break yours?"

"It isn't interesting."

"I want to hear about your past," he said.

"My past," I told him, "is a series of practical jokes carried out by bored and nasty-minded boys."

"Oh," he said. It wasn't the answer he'd wanted.

But for some reason I couldn't help but elaborate. "Every now and then, I get offered a chair, and I think, nope, not going to fall for this again, but of course I do, and when I go to sit down, it's been pulled out from under me."

"But your heart was never broken," said James.

"Not my heart," I said. "I never landed on my heart."

Meet the Tallest Boy in the World

With the money the shoe store advanced, James commissioned a new pair of pants and a shirt. The Portuguese tailor from the next town came to the cottage to take his measurements.

"Yes," he said, looking at James. "This is the biggest challenge of my career." His accent gave the words a jaunty pessimism. But he did good work, though he called several times to make sure that he'd got it right, that the collar would really have to be that expansive, the legs that long. "I saw him but I forget. Remind me again."

The shoe store people were beside themselves. They took out ads in several local papers, geared toward children and their parents. MEET THE WORLD'S TALLEST BOY, 10AM–12PM, HYANNIS SHOES.

I offered to let him drive, but he said he was too distracted. Not distracted enough, however, that he could not criticize with his newfound knowledge of the road. I was a careful driver. Still I could hear him sputter in the back.

We got there at nine, an hour before the store opened, so that James could get settled and get his feet measured for a new pair of shoes; the old ones, he said, were hard to get on in the morning. That was the only way he could tell he'd outgrown them: the difficulty in getting them on first thing, off at night. Sometimes he slept in his shoes, he told me. Between the size of his feet and the distance they were from his arms, it was easier that way.

"Get Oscar to come over," I said.

"Too much trouble."

They'd decorated the front of the store with balloons, streamers. A huge shoe took up most of the window display; just like James's, though made years before, so smaller. A middle-aged man in a suit leaned on the short brick wall that held up the shop windows.

"Jim," he said, standing up, holding out his hand. "Hugh Peters. President of the chain." True enough, he was wearing beautiful shoes, rich and red as porterhouse steaks. "Glad we finally coaxed you out here."

"Nice to meet you, sir."

You could see Hugh Peters trying his best not to notice James's height. He shook his head and laughed. "How tall are you, exactly?"

"It's been a while since I've checked," said James. He smoothed his new shirt.

"About?"

"Eight feet two, last time I was measured."

"But still growing?"

"So far," said James.

"So you must be the tallest in the world by now. I mean, *nobody's* eight feet tall. Am I right? *Basketball* players aren't eight feet tall."

"I don't know," said James. "I don't follow basketball."

"Well, come on in," said Hugh Peters.

The shoe store had two doors: regular-sized and child-sized, right next to each other. "Play your cards right," Hugh Peters said, "and we'll put in another one for you."

It looked just like the shoe stores of my youth: boxes stacked along the walls like a puzzle whose point was to extract what you wanted without disturbing the whole pile; slanted stools; gray metal slide measures. Up front there were chrome chairs with shiny red vinyl seats; halfway back, in the children's section, were identical chairs half the size. From the front the chairs looked like some botched trick of perspective. A wicker basket in the back held prizes for children who'd been good, and probably for those who hadn't. No customers yet.

"What's that?" James asked, pointing at a piece of machinery in the back.

"Fluoroscope," said Hugh Peters. "Like an X ray. Helps us look at the bones of growing feet, figure out what'll fit 'em best."

We stood there. James looked around for a wall to lean on or a chair without arms. But the walls were jumbled up with their boxes, and we were standing by the banks of extrasmall chairs.

"Would you like to sit down?" I asked him, loud enough for Hugh Peters to overhear.

"Oh," Peters said. "Well. Didn't think of that. Those chairs—" He pointed at the adult chairs near the front. "No good?"

James shook his head. "The arms will get in the way."

"Let me look out back."

He called over a salesman, and together they went to the storeroom. The salesman came back wheeling an oak desk chair, took a look at James, then wheeled it back.

"Maybe this wasn't such a hot idea," James said to me.

"They'll find something."

Then Hugh Peters and the salesman came out carrying a desk that matched the chair. Peters had taken off his suit jacket, had flipped his red necktie over one shoulder. The blotter slipped off the top and hit the floor.

"I hope, that this, is fine." They set the desk down. Peters adjusted his tie, then wiped his shining forehead. "Should be tall enough, right?"

James sat on the edge. "Fine."

"Well, let's see. I think we'll get a pretty big crowd. We've done radio, we've done the papers. Town's talking about it.

Kids mostly, and parents. So all we need you to do is sit and chat. Mention what you like about the shoes. How they treating you, our shoes?"

"They're good," said James.

"They don't pinch, right? Give you good support?"

"Very good support."

"Okay, mention that."

"I will." James nodded.

"Good support for growing feet—and who'd know better than you, right?"

"Let's take a gander at your dogs, Jim." The salesman knelt down. "Let's see," he said, looking at the brace that buckled beneath the sole of the shoe, "how does this work?" Then he figured it out, undid it. The brace swung back with a creak. He unlaced James's high stiff shoe and slipped it off.

Even I could smell it: terrible, acrid. James's sock was soaked through at the toe. The salesman made a face.

"Wow," he said. He held on to James's heel a moment, at a dry spot. Then he said, "Maybe you want to wash your feet, Jim. There's a sink out back, in the men's room."

James looked down at his foot. "Okay. Put the shoe back on?" The man did. "Tie it, too, will you?" The man clearly wanted to get away from that foot as quickly as he could, but he obeyed.

James stood; the unfastened brace clattered against itself. I followed him to the men's room, which would have been cramped for a regular-size person.

"Do you want some help?"

"Be quicker that way." He wedged himself in and sat on the closed lid of the toilet, leaned against the wall.

I knelt down; I had to open the door to give the back half of me room. "Hand 'er over," I said, and he scooted the foot in my direction. I unlaced the shoe—the salesman had fixed a knot instead of a bow—and slipped it off.

I'd been mad at the salesman at first for what seemed like rudeness, but this close I understood that it must have taken all he had to be that polite. It was what you might expect something dead to smell like, complicated and searing. I tried not to cough.

Then I slipped off his sock and saw that what I had thought was just sweat, just the usual bad manners of boyhood biology, was blood and fluid. His foot was meaty, rubbed wrong by the shoe and by itself. Some places the skin was white, other places pink. Up by his heel his skin was so dry it looked like it would flake off at a touch. The whole thing was cold. His toes were worst: the nails curled around their own toes, or knifed their neighbors, tore them up.

"Jesus Christ," I heard somebody say. It was the salesman, looking over my shoulder. "Doesn't that hurt?"

"We'll be with you in a minute," I said. "We're taking care of it." I got up and turned on the sink, soaked some paper towels through. I pumped some soap from the dispenser into my palm and then let the water flow over it into the sink.

I said, "Are your feet always like this?"

"Sometimes," said James. His voice was low, and when I looked up he was close to tears. "I can't feel them," he said. "How can I know if I don't feel them?"

"It's okay," I said. "We'll clean them up." I picked up the wad of paper towels and knelt again.

"I can't help it. I can't help it if I don't know."

"James," I said. I held on to his foot. "Just calm down and everything will be fine." I doubted this. The foot looked infected, and suddenly I realized there was a good chance the other would be just as bad, if not worse. I stuck my head out of the bathroom. "Hey," I said to the salesman, who was talking to Hugh Peters. "Do you have a bowl, and perhaps a towel, a cloth one?"

"Let me look," he said.

The paper towels fell to messy pieces as I swabbed at James's foot. "That's better," I said, because it was, anything was better. "What you chiefly need is a pedicure. In the meantime, maybe we should go home."

"No," he said. "I told them I'd be here."

I thought, But I bet they don't want you here now. Of course they didn't, and that made me want to stay. I wanted to fix the whole thing, but the whole thing was so bad. How could this have happened? We kept him fed, got him books, we sent him on a walk with a pretty girl, we worried and we fussed and we never thought about his feet. Never occurred to us that someone who could not feel his feet would have problems with them: weren't all foot problems pain?

"Let's give it a chance," he said. "They advertised and everything. They've already paid me some, and they're going to pay more."

"Here you go," said the salesman. He handed me a grimy towel and a roasting pan. "Borrowed them from the restaurant next door."

I said to James, "Let's get you clean." I filled the pan and lifted it, wobbling, to the floor. "Pick up your foot and set it here." I rolled up his pant leg so that it wouldn't slop in the water. It was a man's calf now, thin but with hair scattered over the skin.

"I have to do this," he said. "I can't have come all this way just to leave."

"Oh, honey," I said. I put my hand in the water. I laced my fingers between his toes, those sticky toes, sharp with their uncut nails. "I don't even know if I can get your shoe back on."

"Give it a chance, huh? We won't get my feet measured, but I can still meet the kids."

We kept still a minute, me holding on to his foot, him wedged back on that toilet, one arm draped over the sink. Shouldn't he get to a doctor, get those feet checked out? The water in the roasting pan was getting cold. I wanted to dry his foot, but the restaurant towel was filthy.

Well, we'd have to improvise something. We were used to it. Ordinary-size people, they don't know: their lives have been rehearsed and rehearsed by every single person who ever lived before them, inventions and improvements and unimportant notions each generation, each year. In 600 B.C. somebody did something that makes your life easier today; in 1217, 1892. Somebody like James had to ad-lib any little thing: how to sit, how to travel.

I looked at him. "How long?"

"Half an hour," he said. "Hour tops. And in the future," he said, "we'll know."

"Know what?"

"Know to be careful," he said, but all I could think of was all the other things that could go wrong.

So I cleaned the other foot, which was bad, but not quite as. Blotted them dry with paper towels, chased down drops of moisture between his toes, in the cracks of neglected skin at his heels. The shoe store carried foot powder, and they donated a can to the cause. I got the shoes back on, without the socks, and told him to sit on the desk and stay put—avoid walking at all costs.

And in fact we stayed two hours. We agreed with the shoe salesman that there was no point in measuring him for shoes—"His feet are all swollen out of size right now anyhow," he said, "you can just measure them for me when you get home"—so James sat on the desktop and waited for the customers. Children ran in, their mothers following with the rolled-up newspaper page: **Meet the world's tallest boy!**

"I figured he must be," said Hugh Peters. "Now I think he must be the tallest man, too."

The children were amazed by him. "You must be very old," one said. James handed out presents from the wicker basket. He talked to mothers. One was holding a fat baby. "Ninety-ninth percentile for height and weight," she said, joggling him. You could tell it was something she usually said with pride, but this time her voice was tinged with apprehension.

Hugh Peters tapped me on the shoulder. "Cup of coffee?" he asked. I shook my head. "Come back and talk to me a second, anyhow."

He took me to the storeroom and sat down on a wobbly salesman's chair. "Nice kid," he said. "Here, let me write you the check for the rest of his fee."

"Got a lot of customers," I said.

"Yeah. Advertising pays off."

"Sorry it took so long to lure him out here. Now that he sees it's easy—he's having a great time with those kids—next time won't be so hard."

Hugh Peters nodded seriously.

"And I was wondering," I said, and why was I so bold? Two pleasant hours in a shoe store, and I was ready to ask for, I was ready to *demand* the moon. "What about the exposition in New York?"

"Oh," said Hugh Peters. "I don't think that's such a good idea."

"Why not?"

"He seems pretty fragile, don't you think?"

"Not as fragile as he looks."

"I just don't want him to overextend himself."

"I appreciate your concern—"

"Miss Cort," said Peters. Now he looked me in the eye; I hadn't realized he'd been avoiding that. "We're a *shoe* company. He doesn't walk well. He has foot problems."

"Foot problems one day," I said.

"It isn't good advertising. We can work something out, certainly, with making his shoes and whatnot, we'd still like to use his name. But the exposition, no, I think we'll have to turn that possibility down."

"I'm sorry," I said.

"I'm a businessman," he said, then he sighed. It wasn't a businesslike sigh. "He's a nice man, nice boy, but what can I do? He's got those braces. I didn't know about the braces. If he falls, where does that leave us? You understand?"

"Yes," I said. "I do."

"You'll tell him? Because it'll be better out of your mouth. Tell him what you like, what you think will make it okay. Make me a villain, if that's easier. I am sorry."

Out in the shop James had his foot under the fluoroscope. Through the shoe leather and skin, you could see the jumbled-up bones, gray and aquatic-looking. He wiggled his ghostly toes for the children.

Hugh Peters left me to drive home James, who'd thought the day was a success. I'd insisted that we stop by his doctor's on the way home, and was already filled with shame that I hadn't insisted on medical attention right away. "That wasn't so bad," said James, and for him that was a statement of starry-eyed optimism. "I'm thinking, Peggy, maybe I'll go into sales."

"I thought you wanted to be a lawyer."

"Law school takes forever. Next time I come out, I figure I'll prepare more."

"Well," I said. "That might be a while."

He didn't hear me. He was remembering the ring of the cash register as the mothers bought their children shoes, a sound that James could think he caused. He did cause it, I'm quite sure. The salesman would hand the customer the change, and the customer turned to James and thanked *him*, not the salesman, not the president of the company.

The doctor scrubbed his feet down and prescribed a salve. A mild infection, not too bad. But the doctor was angry.

"Who's in charge of these things?"

"Me," James said quietly. "I just didn't feel it."

"Well then, you need help," said the doctor. "If you can't tell when something's gone this wrong, enlist somebody who can. No reason for this sort of thing to happen."

He clipped James's toenails, too. "Come here," he told me. "Watch. Somebody else should know how to do this."

Of course I should have told James straight off about what Hugh Peters had said. James's life was constantly forged for him: your mother is alive, you'll be employed forever, you will never die, you should look forward to everything.

"Maybe New York in the spring," he said. "I need to get in better shape."

"Maybe so," I said.

The curious thing is that within weeks of that shoe store visit, James began to get letters. They started close to home—the Boston papers wanted to visit, then *Time* magazine. A letter of inquiry from the circus. A doctor from the Midwest, a specialist in gigantism, sent an article he'd written.

How had we previously kept him a secret, I wondered. Why did it take so long to find us? I don't know to this day what started it—whether Hugh Peters, feeling bad, had called up the circus, looking for another job for James, or the parents had told people, who told more people. Every day there were more letters. Soon people knocked on the door of the cottage. If I was there, I turned them away, but daytimes, when he was bored anyway, he invited them in to talk.

I made up a Do Not Disturb sign and told James to make good use of it. Saturdays, before I went to the cottage, I went to other libraries to look for James's reading material—he had long since exhausted mine. Soon I was driving to Boston on a regular basis, wandering through some other librarian's stacks like a regular, obsessed patron.

Time magazine featured him in an article titled "Strong and Big," along with a boy from Rhode Island who could lift 1,165 pounds attached to a bar across his thighs. When James turned nineteen, *Time* noted it in its "Milestones" column. It was as if he finally saw the pleasure in being that tall. Not that he loved it all the time, but a certain amount of attention and fuss was an acceptable dividend on all the energy it took to be the Tallest Man in the World. Caroline and Oscar and I felt bad. We'd struggled so long to make him *not* feel tall, worked so hard to believe that excess height was just a little quirk, a port-wine birthmark, a limp. Suddenly I began noticing his height myself. He was spectacular.

More letters. James worked up quite a correspondence with strangers, and I told him he'd have to hire a secretary to keep track of them all.

"I remember them," he said. "I remember everybody."

By the spring, he was famous.

Delaware Who?

Oscar was a good man and, before he became a father, an unworried one. I would have said that was his main character flaw: an unwillingness to worry. As soon as there was a problem, he would try to find an ingenious solution. A belt fixed with a bent nail, faulty locks repaired with folded paper. When a solution was not possible, he tried to turn the difficulty into advantage.

But then Alice was born, and the world suddenly seemed full of possible harm. He saw that a baby was a magnet for inappropriate objects. Bent tetanic nails could find their way to bare feet, folded paper sought the warmth of a baby's mouth. All his brilliant inventions turned to weapons aimed at his daughter. Even his nephew in the back house, even James seemed an advertisement for things that went wrong.

In the basement, Oscar still fiddled with his comic books, had in fact borrowed from my library (which had borrowed it from another, more cosmopolitan library in Boston) a book on drawing the things, and so he pasted up and used faint pencil for guide marks and wrote careful block-lettered dialogue in squared-off balloons that floated over his characters. Except that his characters rarely said anything. Unlike Oscar, unlike anyone in Brewsterville, they simply acted, no announcements or negotiation. One becaped man punched his enemies in the jaw without benefit of the smallest *kerpow* or *kaboom*. Another swam in the bay that granted his powers (he had none in the ocean itself), under water for miles, not even a soft thought bubble carbonating the water above his head.

And, of course, Rocket Bride. She threw rosebud grenades at single criminals; when confronted by a gang of thieves, she cast her veil over them, and they struggled against one another like minnows beneath it. When she took them thus wrapped to the police station, she let them file out singly, looking for the face of her missing husband, that one bad man who knew everything about her: secret identity, dreamed-up names for future children, ring size, how she looked in a bathing suit, best friends. She might find him in any group of no-goodniks.

Rocket Bride was inclined to overlook mistakes. Sometimes, if a crook was very small or very young, she'd let him go. She treated the worst of them with understanding; you knew that she brought down evil for its own good. Even when a thug lay at the back of an alley, his tweed-capped head surrounded by birds, or stars, or any swarming celestial indication of concussion, Rocket Bride saw and smiled sadly. This was any mother's son, any wife's misplaced no-good lovable husband. This man, in his cap and gray jacket (always with three fastened buttons) is not so bad: somewhere, there is a good woman waiting to take him back.

And the same for every woman who schemed against Rocket Bride—despite the villainess's tight black outfit (always black and tight, because Rocket Bride was bell-shaped and pale, and Oscar had perfected only one female face)—that bad girl was forgiven, too. Rocket Bride's strength was righteous anger, but her weakness was The Extenuating Circumstance, which, unlike kryptonite, was everywhere.

I always thought she looked less like a superheroine than a

medieval saint. Like any saint, she was caught at the moment of her martyrdom. Not run through with swords, not offering her eyes or heart or tongue on a tray, no bloody miraculous wound; instead, she was tragically physically intact, martyred as she was by heartbreak.

And then Rocket Bride, still husbandless, acquired a baby. Oscar showed me the panel, Rocket Bride and Rocket Girl, both in what were wedding dresses or christening gowns.

"Who's the proud father?" I asked.

"There isn't one. I figure, Superman has X-ray vision, nobody gave it to him. Rocket Girl is part of Rocket Bride's superpowers."

The baby nestled in her Rocket Mama's arms. Whether Oscar was thinking of the one historical precedent and His powerful mother, I didn't know. But I did see that Rocket Girl looked like Alice, with her blond sugary hair and slightly squinty eyes, and I knew that this was part of Oscar's dream, to put Alice in such a place that, with help, she could soar into the ether away from harm. She was a baby; he knew she couldn't do it without help. With her new responsibilities Rocket Bride avoided almost all confrontations.

"Tell me," Oscar asked me once. "What do you think caused Jim's height?"

"His pituitary gland," I said. "You know that as well as I do."

"But what caused *that*? There has to be a book that explains those things."

"No, not yet," I said.

Now the shady genetic side to his wife's family bothered Oscar. He hadn't thought to worry about it until his child arrived, and while he was inclined to blame Mrs. Sweatt for the inheritance that had turned James into what he called, "The Rockefeller of Height," who knew? Could have been Caroline's brother, could be his wife—and therefore his daughter—had some of the same genes.

Oscar watched Alice, waiting for her to get big. Maybe it wouldn't be all of her. Maybe just one leg, or an organ, or most likely her head; one little isthmus would start to balloon and fill like all of James. I saw Oscar with his hands on either side of Alice's head, as if he could discern growth by touch, as if he could hold it back with his loving strength. Had Oscar lived in another country, he would have been the first father to advocate foot- and head-binding. Get to the root of the problem and stop it.

"Oscar," I said. "Alice is fine. By the time James was her age, he was already growing."

"I know." Still, it seemed possible to him, her head expanding without the permission of the rest of her body. Like the comic books of the time, maybe, which he read: babies exposed to radiation who grew not only large but scaly and bug-eyed. One day he might wake up to find himself the father of the Turtle Girl of Cape Cod. Jimmy Olsen was always getting in scrapes like that, and when he did, he never recognized Superman.

The summer tourists didn't help. If Alice were around, they'd say, "Is this his little sister? She big for her age? She gonna be a giantess?"

"No," Oscar would say. "She's just an ordinary height. And she's his cousin, not sister."

"But still growing," a tourist would say, smiling, making it sound like a dark prediction.

Even though Oscar hated it, the visitors kept coming. All day long people showed up at the cottage. The locals would knock shyly. The tourists knocked raucously or not at all. They ignored my Do Not Disturb sign.

"Is this the place—" they'd say, opening the door. "Whoops! Guess it must be."

Mostly they didn't have questions, unless, of course, it was whether there were any souvenirs to be had.

"This is someone's *house*," I told them. "It is not a tourist trap."

"You could make some money," they said. "Think about it."

Most of the tourists were meltingly the same: families with one, two, or three children; portions of church tours (the tours themselves always had the sense not to come all at once, or else did not know about us); couples of which one member was an eager reader of the newsmagazines that occasionally profiled James as if he were a celebrity. They took his picture, had me take his picture with them, and sometimes sent a print when they'd returned home, as if he, too, would want a memento of the meeting.

A few of the visitors I remember with more clarity. A classics professor who'd come into the library, wanting to read town records (he'd mistakenly believed that one of his forebears had passed through Brewsterville), followed me after work and presented James with an ancient pen and pencil set, inscribed with the name of a bank. A middle-aged lady with dyed-black hair, a wide painted mouth, and an artificial beauty mark told stories of being a silent movie starlet; there was something Egyptian about her, and her ears were unfashionably pierced and hung with thick gold hoops. I did not believe her stories of the Sisters Gish and Mister Griffith, but when she died a year later, the Boston *Globe* carried her obituary with a photograph: the same black hair and dark lips, the same beauty mark more artfully applied, the gold earrings, and a cheroot brandished between her tiny fingers. The copy below said that records were so unclear, she might have been fifty-nine, sixty-nine, or eighty at the time of her death.

One tall man seemed both delighted and depressed by James's size. "I'm six foot ten myself, and I felt outta place all my life. But then again, I ain't as handsome as you," he told James, and in fact he wasn't: his features were thick and flat, like callouses, his voice sounded as though it came from a cave. He seemed like the friendliest, saddest monster I ever met. (By then I could diagnose it: acromegaly, the condition that results when the pituitary gland continues to produce even when the body has stopped growing in altitude. James, who never stopped growing, therefore never suffered.) This man had quit his job and was moving to California. To be an actor? we asked. Close, he said, professional wrestler; he'd met a man who'd promised him a job. "Lots of money in it," he told James.

The visitors—both tourists and people from town—bore gifts, told their friends, wrote back. Their visits were formal, natives come to gawk at a tree that has grown in a strange holy shape. They brought things they thought he would like: big-print books (he was nearsighted, that was all), round serving platters to use as dinner plates, unabridged dictionaries. Assuming any large thing would please him, make him feel normal-sized, they offered up huge slices of fudge and casseroles cooked in Dutch ovens.

James took up painting that summer. Oscar had encouraged him to give it a try, and now that people were likely to drop by the cottage, it seemed only right to look busy. That way James could set down the brush and invite them graciously in. He started with paint-by-number sets, then moved on to watercolors, he explained, because he liked their easy, curvaceous effect. I didn't know what this meant. At first he did nothing but ocean scenes, though he never went to the beach, sand being too tricky a surface for his feet; they were naive, trusting feet, assumed every surface was flat and unmoving. After a while he started painting interiors of his cottage.

"What happened to the ocean?" Oscar asked him. "For my money, it's a lot more interesting than your chair. Centuries of artists agree with me."

"I did the ocean till I figured out what I was doing," James answered. "No matter what, I could always get it to look like the ocean. Now that I've got the hang of it, I'm moving on to harder things."

"The ocean's hard," said Oscar, his feelings hurt. "Ask Turner. Ask Winslow Homer."

But James didn't catch his tone. He said, "The ocean just came too easy for me."

I offered to be James's secretary, to sort through his letters, but he wanted to do that himself. Every day he got at least one piece of correspondence; if it was someone who'd written before, who'd received an answer, it would be addressed to *James Sweatt, 9 Winthrop St Back*. The *Back* guaranteed that the mailman would bring the letters directly to the cottage, where Oscar had installed a box, instead of depositing them at the front house for the Stricklands to sort and carry.

"How do you keep up with this?" I asked.

"I manage."

I began sorting through the day's mail, which I'd gotten from the mailbox. "Oregon, Illinois—"

"Peggy! Don't look at my mail, please. It's private."

"I'm not reading it. I'm only looking at the envelopes."

"Well, stop," he said. But I had my hand on a postcard. I didn't read the body of it, and I didn't have time to look at the postmark, but it was clearly signed, *your father*, C. *Sweatt*.

I stacked the pile neatly, shuffled Mr. Sweatt to the center of the deck. "I've stopped," I said, but I stared at the top envelope, the one with the Oregon postmark.

"They all from strangers?" I asked at last.

"Mostly," he said. "Here, give them to me." He set them down on the corner of the desk and turned back to what he was writing.

"Aren't you going to read them?" I wanted to be there when James finally got word of his father; I wanted to know what Mr. Sweatt had to say for himself.

"Eventually."

I sat down. I stared at his back. He finished his letter, folded it, put it in an envelope. Then he began another.

"James," I said.

"What?"

"Why don't you look at your mail."

"I will."

"*James*."

"*Peggy*," he said, exasperated.

"There's a card from your father."

So he picked up the stack, not looking at me, and flipped through. I tried to see whether he lingered at the postcard, but his back was turned to me and I couldn't tell.

"Yes," he said finally. "You're right."

"What does he say?"

James sighed. "The usual." He turned to me, held the postcard up to the light for a second, as if it were instead a sealed letter he was not supposed to read. Then he opened a desk drawer and dropped it in. "I'll put it with the rest."

"The rest?" I said.

He turned to me. "He's been writing me awhile now. Don't tell Aunt Caroline. They're not speaking."

I waited for some explanation.

"Where is your father?"

"Different places."

Now I sighed. I said aloud, to myself, "Take a hint, Peggy."

James smiled. "Yes," he said. "Then it's unanimous. Please. *Por favor.*"

For a favor, yes, I did take a hint, I didn't ask. The most I was allowed—we agreed on this without discussion—was to inquire whether Mr. Sweatt had recently written. The answer was usually no. And though of course I would have loved to have read those misguided missives, I also understood: James needed whatever little personal life he could get, and his correspondence was pretty much it. This included whatever the hated mysterious Mr. Sweatt had to say, wherever he was, and why he did not sign that postcard *love*, or Dad, why he was so stingy he felt his first initial was enough for his son. This was the only information I had on him, and it fascinated me. James would not tell me anything else, and I would not ask.

•

One woman visited every day of her vacation. Her husband had come the first day, James told me, but after that she arrived alone. One night when I dropped over after work she was sitting there, in the chair I favored.

"Hiya," she said to me.

She was a young woman with skinny freckled arms and bad skin. For a second I thought she was a leftover school friend. Most of the teenagers had graduated from school that May and had already moved to the first cities of their new lives. But I looked closer at the woman and saw she was older than that, in her twenties. She smiled wide; her teeth looked like a pack of cards in midshuffle.

"Hi, Peggy," said James. "This is Patty Flood."

"We've been talking all afternoon," she said. "My husband, he's off at the beach. He loves the ocean, but we live out in

Montana and he never gets to see it. Me, I could care less. A lot of water, salty, what's the big deal?"

I shrugged. "We like it," I said.

"Oh, I *like* the ocean too," she said quickly. "It's beautiful. I just already know it's there, don't have to check on it every day. The ocean doesn't make conversation. That's what I like better than the beach. *People.*"

"You don't have those in Montana?" I said.

"Not enough of them," she said. "So, are you out here on vacation?"

"No," I said. I hated being mistaken for a tourist. "I live here."

"Lucky you," she said. "But lucky me, too. Montana's beautiful. The whole country's beautiful, each part in its own way."

Patty Flood and her good mood were starting to get on my nerves. Her mood was so good it was almost a physical thing, a monkey on a leash that she let leap all over the furniture, delighting only its owner. "But the best part of the trip," she said, looking at James, "is meeting this young man! You are about the most interesting person I ever met. Don't you think?" she asked me.

I smiled at James, who looked pained. "Of course," I said.

Somebody knocked at the door. "More visitors!" said Patty Flood, as if she'd moved in as hostess. But it was only Oscar.

"Dinner's ready, Jim," he said.

Patty Flood didn't budge. "Hey, Oscar," she said. "Remember me?"

"I remember you, Patty," he said. "It's only been since yesterday."

"Well," said Patty. "You guys are eating dinner, huh?"

"Yes," said Oscar. Still it took Patty a while to will herself to her feet, gather her purse, and walk out the door.

"Montana?" Oscar said, after Patty Flood finally left. "Nobody lives in *Montana.*"

Oscar was a good New Englander, of course: once upon a time we were all of the country, and suddenly two hundred years later there's this coarse swollen thing stuck to our back calling itself the United States.

"Delaware who?" Oscar would ask, confronted by history.

If you grow up around here you start to believe that somehow all American history previous to 1776 occurred in Massachusetts. If someone had asked me, at age eight, to name the thirteen colonies, I would have started, "Boston, Plymouth, Salem, Lexington, Concord . . ."

"That woman's here every day," Oscar said to me. "I don't know how Jim can stand her."

"She's lonely," said James.

"She's got her husband. Tell her to bother him."

"Oh, *Don*," James said, disgusted. "He just makes her lonelier."

"Some people are like that," I said, knowing that was true but unsure of whether I was one of them.

"Most people are," said James.

I ran into Patty Flood the next afternoon when I was outside on my park bench, eating some tragic sandwich I'd assembled from odds and ends out of my fridge—sliced apple, some cheese, pickle relish. Single people eat sadly—they cobble together things left from shopping trips based on dreams of all the meals they'd fix for themselves, all the ways they'd treat themselves to something grand; those dreams, for me, died by the next day and, despite my best hopes, I wanted only canned hash and apples. Dogged by practicality, I had to use everything I'd bought anyhow.

"Hey!" said Patty Flood. She sat down next to me. Her dress was white, with yellow and red polka dots. She looked like a well-dressed clown.

I nodded at her and bit into my sandwich.

"I was just going to go see Jim," she said. "You wanna come with?"

"I have to go back to work."

"Right." She laughed. "When I'm on vacation I think the whole world is." She hooked her elbows over the back of the bench. "I was gonna bring something to Jim, to cheer him up. What would?"

"What makes you think he needs cheering up?"

She looked surprised. "Boy, you aren't paying attention.

He's a real nice, real sad guy. I never met anyone who needs more cheering up. If I could, I'd take him to an amusement park or something. But if Mohammed can't come to the mountain—"

"James isn't the amusement park kind," I said. I regarded my sandwich; it looked like an ottoman with the stuffing leaking out. "I do pay attention."

Patty Flood nudged my calf with the toe of her shoe. "Maybe *you* need to go to an amusement park. There's one out Nantasket, I hear. Nothing wrong with you a good roller coaster wouldn't fix."

I resisted the urge to kick her back. Library patrons walked up the path, past the bench; some of them smiled, some didn't seem to recognize me without the circulation desk around my waist.

"There's nothing wrong with me at all," I said to Patty Flood. "Roller coaster or no roller coaster."

"Listen." Her voice got soft and personal. "I know you. I know you better than you think I do—"

"What's my name?" I stared at her, sure she did not remember. I wanted to quite literally strike her quite literally dumb.

But Patty Flood laughed. "Oh, ma'am," she said, "that's one detail I don't know. But I know you're someone who thinks she's smart just 'cause she's miserable. And I know you think I'm a fool. I used to be like you: smart and sad. Then I found Jesus Christ, and I'm dumb and happy."

"Ah, well," I said. My sandwich was falling apart in my hands; I tried to put it in some kind of order. "Jesus Christ. That would explain things."

"Yeah." Patty smiled. "He explains everything. Back when I was like you, back when I was so *intelligent*, I thought that was my job, to explain everything. And you know what? That's *God's* job. Without God, there's no explanation, not for the smallest, most meaningless puzzle. No wonder I was desperate: I was looking for nothing! My husband's like you. A lotta people are, billions. Y'all think you feel *deeply* just because you feel *miserable*. But here's the thing: happiness is deep, and so is faith. There's a lot of perfectly good emotions besides despair."

She stood up and visored her eyes with her hand. "Pretty town, that's for sure. Maybe I'll see you later. Remember Jesus loves you." She made it sound like a threat. And then she started down the street without another word.

I wanted to chase her, to say something, to push her over. But I sat on my bench instead. The polka-dot dress, the ludicrous red patent-leather belt that made her look like—well, she looked like a doll I'd owned as a girl: a blond pretty girl on top, and when you turned her over and flipped her full skirt inside out, another doll, her twin, except dark, beneath her. I felt like that upside-down girl, blood cupped in the bottom of my skull, in the dark, no hope for daylight as long as Patty Flood went shining down the main street of Brewsterville. Nobody could see me.

But in that dark I had myself. My old reliable, unlovable self—despite Patty's reminder of Jesus's personal affection for me, I suspected even He favored sunnier dispositions than mine. Jesus might *respect* me, Jesus might think I was a stand-up gal and value me as a friend, but He surely did not love me. Well, who needed Him.

Isn't it funny how the faithful only reaffirm our faithlessness in everything except ourselves?

You were never smart, I thought at Patty Flood, and then I went back inside the library.

Patty Flood was at the cottage when I showed up that afternoon. James was painting at his easel, and she was painting her toenails. She balanced her heel on the edge of my chair and dabbed at her big toe with the tiny red brush. James held his own brush still a second, fascinated.

"I've never seen this before," he said.

Patty leaned as close to her foot as she could and blew at the polish. "It's easy, once you get the hang of it," she said, as if James were watching her debone a fish or tap-dance or turn water into wine. She extended her leg to admire her work. "Not bad," she said to her foot, and then, to me, "Today was a busy day. We had, what, five visitors?"

"Six," said James.

"Six!" said Patty Flood. "Somebody brought taffy. Want a piece?"

"No thank you."

Patty reached over to a box on a high table and grabbed a wax-paper bow tie. "It's good. You sure?"

"Quite sure," I said. "Your husband's at the beach again?"

"Nah. He drove up to Plymouth to see that rock."

"That rock?" I said.

"Yeah. But the guy at the hotel. He said it wasn't any big deal, just a rock with a date carved into it. I mean, *rocks*. Out west, we have plenty of those." She sighed. "That's one thing we aren't short on."

"When are you going back?" I asked.

"Tomorrow," she said mournfully. "I'll miss this place. I'll miss this one." She pointed at James. He looked embarrassed. "Won't you miss me, Jimmy?"

"Yes."

She smirked at him, then slapped at his knee. "Sometimes I forget you're a teenage boy, and then you *act* like one. All mumbly." She looked at her watch. "Well. Don should be getting back. We're going out to some restaurant tonight, some sea captain's house. I need to get going." She blew at her toes again, then tested the polish with her finger. "Close enough." She slipped her foot into her shoe and stood up, gathered her things, walked to James in his chair. Even sitting down he was taller than she was. "Let's see whether you've captured me," she said. But the canvas wasn't her, just a study of her empty shoe careless on the ground. "Not bad. Well," she said to him. "This was the nicest vacation I've had in a long time. Will you write back if I write first?"

"Yes," he said. He didn't look at her, and I realized, astounded, that he was going to miss her, that he didn't want her to go.

"Good-bye," she said, and then quick she leaned in and kissed him on the cheek. She walked as fast to the door as she could without running, and turned. "Well," she said, and her eyes were damp. "Better go hear about that stupid rock. See you." And then she was out the door.

"There goes Patty," I said.

"Oh, she was okay," he said, though I'd said nothing aloud to the contrary. "She's had a hard life. I can forgive a lot of"—he waved his hand—"personality problems if someone's had a hard life. She was a good talker. I get tired of the same questions all day. How are you, how tall are you, how much do you weigh? That kind of company just wears me out. Nice to have someone new around who lasts for a while."

But even Patty Flood had lasted for only two weeks.

"Start the record player, will you?" James asked. I flipped the switch and set the bulky tone arm to the edge of the record that was already there. I hadn't looked at the label. The record popped, and then some fiddles whined. It wasn't the teenagers' music—not Stella music, as I thought of it. I pointed at the record player. "What is this?"

"Molly O'Day," James said. "And the Cumberland Mountain Folks."

"Jesus music."

"Music about Jesus," he said. "Yes. Patty Flood—she gave it to me."

James put down his brush and turned to Molly O'Day's voice, singing now about God gathering His jewels. She meant dead people. He stared at the record player as if it were evidence of God, Molly O'Day a visitation from a particular, southern rank of angels.

"I like it," I said. I was trying to be generous.

"Yeah," said James. "Patty wants me to get religion, I guess. She wants me to get a *lot* of religion. Molly O'Day makes it sound like a good idea."

"Really?" I said. The music made me feel uncomfortable and accused, the way Patty had. If feeling stupid was being faithful, maybe I was on my way.

He laughed. "Don't worry. I'm not convinced yet."

"I met Patty downtown today. She told me my problem was I thought too much and it made me miserable. She promised me if I accepted Jesus, I'd be dumb and happy in no time."

"Don't do it," said James. "But she's right."

"She is?"

"Sure. You'd have to be a moron to think this wasn't a sad old world."

"Sad old world? You're starting to sound like one of these singers."

"Yeah. Well, why not. I don't listen to the radio anymore. This is my new favorite music, gospel. She gave me some Bill Monroe, too. The radio, it's all . . . Dean Martin or Kaye Starr or Elvis Presley, you know?"

"No," I said. "What?"

"They're all singing about *love*," said James. He picked up a brush and started stirring it madly in a glass of water. "I mean, either they're over it, or they're starting it, or they're just talking about having a good time—and it's just this. It's this: I don't want to hear music about things I can't have anymore. I hate to even be reminded."

Molly O'Day's heart was breaking, too; you could hear it in her voice.

"You can have it," I said quietly.

"Please, Peggy," he said. He kept his voice careful, rational. "I understand my life."

"I'm not sure you do," I said.

"I understand some things." He started capping his tubes of paint.

I walked to the record player. "This music doesn't bother you?"

"This?" he said. "This is something I can have, if I want. That's the whole point of it. If I just welcome Jesus into my heart . . . This music?" He closed his eyes and moved his hand as if he wanted to catch one of the fiddle licks. "It doesn't remind me of anyone."

"No," I said.

"It reminds me of *everyone*. Right now, I miss every person I ever knew." He opened his eyes again. "That's okay. That much I can bear. It's just when you get down to particulars." He hit his chest with his fist, a brush sticking up from between his fingers like a cigarette. "That's when."

"When what?" I said, but I thought, *Stella*. Maybe that was wrong. Maybe he'd been a little in love with Patty Flood and couldn't figure out whether her wanting to save his soul was personal or not. If he'd asked me, I would have said, *it's always personal.*

He shook his head, smiling sadly. He was like me. He had no vocabulary to even talk about these things.

He bit his lip and said, "I have to protect my heart, Peggy."

Once upon a time he'd listened to love songs, even if now he'd sworn them off. I'd heard his radio, seen his records, though now I couldn't find any evidence of that teenage music in the cottage. Only those Jesus singers sung there now, loving God and thinking not too much of man- and womankind. He'd gotten rid of Pat Boone and Dean Martin and the Platters and one particularly deplorable but lovely Elvis Presley record, a gift from Stella. I was worried that it would take a turn, that he'd reverse his early decision and start to believe in God, become religious, think that faith could fill his empty hours. Probably it could. But he didn't, and in fact the reason he liked the Jesus singers was because they were broken up over an emotion that wasn't familiar to him and took no energy to receive.

Maybe some nights he craved a brokenhearted singer the way another man might crave whiskey. Maybe those nights he got all the way to the radio, had his hand on the dial before he stopped himself. Slow down, man. One love song and you'll do nothing but listen to love songs. One love song, and you're around the bend. And then he'd drop Molly O'Day on the record player again and listen to her explain, carefully, that God tested us every day and every day most of us failed.

His Heart Shares in His Proportions

I want to tell you about his body.

I want to describe his feet, now (he was eighteen) size thirty-seven, triple A. The store in Hyannis still made his shoes. I'd had to call and ask them to rush and make a new pair to replace the old ones, and they told me how to measure everything, instep, width, length. Now I did it regularly. We set his foot down on paper—not typing paper, which was too small, but some stuff cut from a roll at an artists' supply shop, and traced. I did this. His feet left damp marks on the paper; his second toes were longer than his big toes, and I wondered whether this was a sign of something, either in medicine or folk wisdom.

His calves were unmuscled things. I know because I held on to them while I traced. This was late in the day, eight-thirty or so—we wanted to get his feet at their highest swollen ebb—and I'd slipped my hands up under his pant cuff to hold on.

His thighs—

I want to say that they were like railroad ties, and they were, they were solid and blocky and no wider at the hip than at the knee, but I promised myself I wouldn't turn his body into something it wasn't, I wouldn't compare it to other things. People always did that. They made him into a redwood tree, a building, the Eiffel Tower. I'd never thought about it before, but now suddenly, with so many strangers around, so many new people making guesses, assessing his girth, arm span, I couldn't help doing it myself. I vowed to stop.

I don't want to leave you with a man assembled out of household goods, a scarecrow with hands big as toasters and arms long as brooms and glasses the size of a child's bicycle. I want to detail only facts. For instance, his neck was fifteen and a half inches long, thighs three feet—but that's how you describe the Statue of Liberty, Mount Rushmore, and it means that his body is getting away from itself again.

I want to say, *his body was just a man's body, only bigger. His thighs were the thighs you have met before in your life, but longer. It was any body you've ever known; there was just more of it.*

There's a limit to what I knew then. Oscar gave him sponge baths all his life. I knew his feet best, from measuring and from cutting his toenails. They were my inheritance, my territory. Mine to wash and to diagnose. Every evening I asked him to take off his shoes and socks so I could look for all the danger signs that the doctor had told me about.

One late night, in my apartment, I looked at my own feet. My toenails needed cutting. How did they grow so fast, I wondered. My big toes were calloused, turning in; the nails of my little toes small scabs. All blank, unlike Patty Flood's blood red bouquet. They were the feet of someone who paid no attention; the feet of a woman who knew that no one would ever be there, at the end of the day, to watch shoes get kicked off, stockings pulled free. The feet of someone responsible for her own weariness. Still, I was tired, and I did not even think about going to the bathroom to take care of matters: I took care of *James's* feet, not my own.

* * *

It was a doctor—the one from the Midwest, the one who specialized in giantism—who soured me forever on James's measurements and statistics. Caroline and I did not think James should agree to a visit from him. The article he sent, ripped from the pages of a medical journal, could scare anybody. It was illustrated with photographs of a tall naked man standing next to a short clothed one. The point was that this was a circus giant who claimed to be eight foot two but barely cleared six foot seven; the photographs had been taken by a man who wanted to prove the claim. The doctor exposed him as a fraud; he discussed all the ways a tall man can make himself look taller, the tricks of photography and posture.

The circus giant was skinny, smiling, clearly used to posing for photographs. His hipbones cast shadows over his private parts; all you could see were some vague oval shapes. His nakedness seemed terrible to me, as if it were a demeaning costume he'd agreed to wear in hopes that his personal dignity would compensate.

James wanted the doctor to come. "A specialist," he said. "That means something." James had seen specialists in Boston, but they were gland and bone experts; they were as startled by his height as anyone. This new doctor, whose name was Calloway—surely he'd seen it all. Surely our James would just be another note in his life's work. I didn't like the tone of the letter. "I have read you are eight feet tall," he wrote, and you could tell he didn't believe it.

"Let him come!" said Oscar. "He won't be disappointed, that's for sure."

James read the clipped article over and over again, looking for hope and information. I could have told him, having read the damn thing only once: all the doctor had done was measure the nameless circus giant, that's all. A carpenter could have written it.

So James invited the doctor, who telephoned, and said that James would have to wait five months, he was terribly sorry but he could not get away, would that be all right?

"By then I'll be even taller," James said into the phone. "Yes, still growing."

Meantime we were getting letters from circuses. Small and big, they all wanted him to hire on, but it was Barnum and Bailey who offered the most, of course—private cars on trains, unbelievable fees. They called. They sent free tickets. One day a man in a dungaree suit showed up at the cottage.

"My outfit's playing Providence," he said. "Come down and see. Nice folks. We'll treat you right."

Though James liked the man, who acted nonchalant about James's height and discussed another giant he had known—"Short guy compared to you, only seven-five"—he declined the offer.

James still wanted to visit New York, still did not know that the shoe store wasn't interested. Maybe he would never have to find out—I thought we could talk Barnum and Bailey into a one-visit contract. James could go up in a hired train car, he could see New York, he could earn a little money for college. We were still talking college in those days. I explained my plan.

"I'll go for the shoe people," he said. "More dignity to it. The circus just wants me to sell more tickets."

"The shoe people want you to sell shoes. The circus has more money," I argued. "They'll send you in style."

"No, Peggy," he said. "I'd rather go cheap and quiet than posh and loud."

Dr. Calloway, the giantist, arrived the next March, 1958. He had a thin chinless face, wide at the top and narrow at the bottom. His cheeks were sharp and scratched up with wrinkles; his ears looked permanently folded up by a too-small hat. Altogether, his head looked like one of those miraculous precarious rock formations featured in Ripley's Believe It Or Not—you couldn't imagine how such a thing kept balanced on its spindly neck. You expected one of his cheekbones to break loose and avalanche down to his collar, followed by his nose, then the other cheekbone, and finally by the total dusty collapse of his entire head.

But perhaps this is wishful thinking.

His eyebrows were the fiercest thing about him, awnings that nearly obscured his dark round eyes. He arrived on a rainy day without a hat or umbrella, and water collected on those brows and fell to his tan raincoat without impediment.

"Ernest Calloway, M.D.," he said to Caroline. James wasn't home yet; he was watching an afternoon basketball game at the high school. I'd told him to call me to pick him up when it was over.

"Hello," Caroline said, Alice weighing down her arm. "Come in. I'm Caroline Strickland, James's aunt. He's not here yet—you're a little early."

The doctor nodded, as if this were a compliment. He took off his raincoat and handed it to Caroline. "Who's this?" he asked, pointing at Alice. Though she was two, she still rode around in Caroline's arms almost all the time.

"Alice," said Alice, pointing at herself.

He asked Caroline, "How is she related to our giant? Not a sister?"

"First cousin," said Caroline. "Let me get you a towel."

Dr. Calloway looked at me. "And you are—"

"Peggy Cort."

He regarded me, waiting for more information.

"Family friend," I said.

"Ah yes," he said. "Well. I'd prefer only family be present for this visit."

"Peggy is family," said Caroline, coming back with the towel draped over one arm, Alice draped over the other. "She's closer to James than anyone."

"This will not be a delicate conversation," the doctor said. He rubbed his hair with the towel. "Family medical histories, et cetera." He pronounced *et cetera* as if it were a sentence of great wisdom.

"As far as we're concerned, Peggy can hear everything. If she hasn't heard it all already. May I get you a cup of coffee, Dr. Calloway?"

"I do not take coffee," he said. He sat down on the sofa next to me. "Nor tea."

Caroline was a devoted coffee drinker, and for a guest in her house to decline was like a Catholic saying to a priest in church, no, I don't think so, no communion for me today.

Days I spent with Caroline I drank so much coffee I went home vibrating and nervous and ate straight from the refrigerator until I realized hunger was not the problem, I'd misdiagnosed that hollow feeling.

"Well then," said Caroline. "Water?"

"Nothing, thank you," said Dr. Calloway. Then he turned to me. "So, where is the celebrated young man?"

"He's due any minute. Actually, he's supposed to call, and then I'll go pick him up. You're early."

"Are you hired?" he asked.

"Sorry?"

"A nurse, a companion?"

"Family friend," I said again.

Then James came through the door. His umbrella hadn't done much good. Even beneath the raincoat, his shirt was soaked through. The ceilings at the Stricklands' were eight feet tall, so James slouched, then bent his knees and leaned against the wall.

I stood up to help him off with his coat. "You were supposed to call," I told him.

"I didn't want to bother you."

"Aha!" Dr. Calloway said behind me.

James looked up, then took off his glasses to wipe them. There wasn't a dry spot anywhere on him, so I took them and cleaned them on my shirt and handed them back.

Dr. Calloway walked over to meet James, who had to hunch over a little in this house. The doctor looked up.

"Good God," he said. "You *are* . . ."

We waited for him to finish the sentence but he didn't. I could see him stand up straighter, as if to challenge James with his own height, but of course there was no contest. "I'm Dr. Calloway," he said. "You *must* be James." He laughed.

"I'm sorry," said James. "I didn't realize it was so late."

"Why don't you change," I told him. "Then you and Dr. Calloway can talk."

"I don't have to change," said James to the doctor. "I don't want to keep you waiting."

"He's early," I said. "You can't sit around in wet clothing."

"Actually," the doctor said, "I *am* in a bit of a hurry. I'm driving to Boston tonight, to talk to some of your doctors there. Get history and so forth. But I'll want to examine you at any rate, so you might as well just put on dry clothes after that."

"Well, at least go around back, so you'll be comfortable," I said to James. "No point in squeezing in here."

"Shall we?" the doctor said to James.

James nodded and put his wet raincoat back on.

"You take the umbrella," he said to Dr. Calloway. "I'm beyond help."

The two of them started out the front door to walk around the back. Dr. Calloway said, "I shall interview and examine James in private. Then may I come back and ask a few questions of you ladies?"

Caroline was sitting on the sofa, rubbing Alice's back; Alice was almost asleep. "Of course," Caroline said quietly.

The doctor was gone half an hour before he came back. "Almost finished," he said. "But I seem to have left my tape measure behind. Do you have one, Mrs. Strickland?"

Caroline pulled a floppy measure from her sewing basket, and Dr. Calloway took it and left. I imagined him gauging James with those three feet of cloth, the way you try to figure distance on a road map with your thumb. James would hold the end of the tape at his head while the doctor unfolded it to mid-chest, marking that spot with his thumb so he could determine where the next three feet led to, finally ending at his destination, James's feet.

Fifteen minutes later the doctor returned. He'd carefully folded the tape measure and held it at its center, as if it were a rare butterfly with peculiar markings that he wanted to study but preserve.

"He is, I must say, gargantuan. I heard he was tall, people sent me clippings, but all the reports differed as to his exact height. I'd assumed all the lowest estimates must be closer to the truth, and even then I'd assumed they'd been exaggerated."

"He's tall," Caroline said. "Why would he lie about it?"

"I didn't think *he* would. But journalists always want the best story, and someone who's eight-foot-four is a better story than someone who's seven foot four. Eight foot four," he said. "I wouldn't have believed it."

"That tall," said Caroline. "What do you know."

"Tallest in the world, no doubt," said the doctor. "Maybe the tallest ever. Still growing. Well. Now I have a few questions for you. Where's the child?"

"Asleep," said Caroline. "It's her naptime."

"Ah. Thought I might have a look at her, too." He said this the way a collector will casually offer to buy something off your very walls. We went to the living room to sit down. "No matter. She's about average, correct?"

"Average height," said Caroline.

The doctor smiled. "About now, everybody looks tiny to me. So, no history of this sort of size in the family?"

"Not that I know of," Caroline said. "Not that kind. His grandmother—my mother—was big."

"How big?"

"Fat," said Caroline. "Extremely."

The doctor wrote this down on his pad. "How did she die?"

"In a chair," said Caroline, smiling almost wickedly. "At night."

"But what of?"

"Of fat, I always thought. Or Nephritis, that's a disease, isn't it?"

"A condition." The doctor scribbled.

He was more interested in the fat grandmother than in any of the other human frailties—diabetes, heart murmurs, cigar addiction—that Caroline supplied to him. She wanted to tell him about family accidents: the distant cousin who'd lost a finger to a saw ("the little finger of his left hand," she said, "thank God"); her father's limp, caused by a boyhood fall and complicated by arthritis.

"Well, that runs in the family," the doctor said. "Young Jim's back is somewhat arthritic."

He was disappointed that we knew nothing of Mrs. Sweatt's

background, but said he'd heard that the doctors in Boston had gathered some of it years before. Myself, I was impressed by Caroline's knowledge of her family's bodily quirks. I could not even supply true hair color for any of my relatives.

"Do you think his sense of smell's normal?" the doctor asked.

"I don't know," Caroline said. "I would think so. Peggy?"

"As far as I can tell."

Finally the doctor capped his pen and straightened his papers. "That should do it, I think. If I have more questions, I'll call. No doubt talking to the Boston doctors will turn up more."

"So?" Caroline said.

Dr. Calloway stood up. "Do you have a question, Mrs. Strickland?"

"You examined him. What do you think?"

"I think," he said carefully, "that he is suffering from giantism. My examination was mostly anthropometric."

"Anthropometric," said Caroline.

"I measured him. I'm chiefly interested in his rate of growth, and much of that information I will get in Boston. I'll examine photographs, X rays, records, et cetera. I came here just to confirm things."

"But what's the *prognosis*?" Caroline said. "That's what James invited you here for. He knows he's tall already. Do you think he'll be able to lead a normal life?"

Dr. Calloway laughed. It was a dull, clattering sound, as if he were searching his pockets for his smallest loose change. "Has he so far?"

"Yes," said Caroline. "He has."

"In that case—if you think living in an oversized garage and painting pictures of oversized furniture is normal, then he is leading and will continue to lead a normal life."

"What about travel?" I asked.

"What about *marriage*?" asked Caroline.

Both the doctor and I looked at her. I didn't know whether this was a joke, like her grandmother's death in a chair.

"I wouldn't rule out careful travel," he said slowly. "I *would* rule out marriage."

"Why?" said Caroline. I looked at her: her face was pale but angry. Maybe she wanted to make him say something so rude she could throw him out, insult him. I knew the feeling. I didn't want this man to make a clean getaway either.

"Practically speaking? No sexual function. In pituitary giants, that's to be expected. His genitalia are fully formed, but very small. His testes are descended. Am I being too specific? No? I wouldn't say that he even thinks about sex. I'm sure he doesn't miss it."

"Did you ask him that?" said Caroline.

"I know he likes girls," I said.

"I'm sure he does," the doctor said, in a slightly kinder voice. "I never said he didn't. I just don't believe he's interested in them sexually."

"But you didn't ask him," Caroline said.

The doctor picked up his coat and shook some lingering rain out of it; it splattered on the floor. "Mrs. Strickland, I suspect you are a romantic. But as I'm sure your mother told you, romance and sex are not the same thing, now are they? Some people believe that the secret to a happy life is mind over matter. To my way of thinking, this is backward. It is the body that is stronger than the mind, more determined, and more usually correct. One must trust one's body. One must not second-guess it. Hypochondria kills more people than cancer. Hypochondria is the result of too much romantic thinking."

"Romantic thinking runs in the family," said Caroline. "Bad as arthritis."

"Well then," the doctor said. "Perhaps he'll die of that." He put on his coat; I could tell by his displeased expression that it was still cold and wet. "That is not a diagnosis, mind you. I am not qualified to diagnose romance."

"I'm sure you aren't, Doctor," said Caroline.

I went back to the cottage once we'd rid ourselves of our unpleasant medical guest. James jumped when I walked in.

"Thought you were that doctor, come back for more," he said.

"How was your talk?"

James made a face. "Don't know. He's nosy."

"Doctors are."

"I know doctors, Peggy. I know what kind of questions they normally ask. He'd write something down, and then say, Do you always hold your hands like that? And I'd look at my hands and say, I suppose so, and he'd write something down that was a lot longer than 'patient says, I suppose so,' so I'd ask him what it was, and he'd just smile. It wasn't much of a medical examination, I mean, he did a little. Looked me over, felt my stomach, asked me did I think my sense of smell was normal."

"He asked us that, too. Is it?"

"I *think* so. Now I'm not so sure. I mean, how would I know?"

"Did he say anything useful?"

"Not really. But he said he'd have an article out about it in six months, maybe. *Journal of the American Medical Association*. They printed his last one." He stretched his legs out and regarded them, as if to reassure himself that they were just legs, not hatch-marked and numbered at every unit of measurement. "All he really wanted to do was measure me."

"Well, you're expanding your places of publication at any rate," I said. "Soon I'll expect you to be on the cover of every magazine in the country."

"Not if I can help it," James said.

But the article proved to be one we would not save. "Giantism: Report of a Case" was hateful. I had not known that science could be hateful. It described his impressions of James, though of course his impressions were presented as solid facts. No conclusions, no prognosis; just endless rude sentences about "the schoolboy giant." James was preacromegalic. That was one medical term. He was also colossal, stupendous, Gargantuan, phenomenal.

Also: slow to respond to questions, introverted, morose, short of attention. *His motor co-ordination is not good, or else he is unduly sloppy by nature. He is careless in his dress. His handwriting is untidy and poorly legible.*

"Did he request a writing sample?" I asked James.

"He picked up some notes from my desk. I was tired. I was cold."

He shows a vapid interest in seeing any memoranda made by a questioner. His sense of position, for his arms, hands, legs and feet, is very poor.

Dr. Calloway described James physically piece by piece, forehead to nose to ears to feet, not liking a single detail. *His fingers are "double jointed," and they curl themselves up in bizarre positions and assume ungainly and gruesome postures.*

His beautiful, useful hands!

His chest is barrel-shaped. The scapular borders are straight, and the curves of the clavicles are straightened out a little from normal. His heart shares in his proportions.

I'd already grown to hate metaphorical descriptions of James. Here was a catalog of his every part by a man who would not know a metaphor from a semaphore, and it was so ugly I could barely read it.

He has been bothered much by the curious, who want to see such a freak.

The last three paragraphs were a discussion of circus giants and their humbuggery. *The Life of Barnum, Written by Himself* was one of the footnotes.

I could not imagine how this quack—this man-measurer who couldn't even remember to bring a measuring tape—could have met our James and come away being anything but astounded. James was nowhere in any of it, except in the table charting his growth.

Perhaps young Ernest Calloway, M.D., was tortured by bedtime stories, perhaps he heard "Jack and the Beanstalk" and was thereafter pursued in nightly dreams by a giant. That the giant died at the end of the story was not enough; little Ernie grew up to be a man who intended to prove that there was no such thing. Men who claimed to be eight foot four were really six foot seven. They wore lifts in their shoes and huge feathered hats. They were just trying to scare you, trick you, but they were frauds.

When he met a man as tall as the rumors, as tall as a bedtime story, he had to dispose of him in a different way. The giant is stupid, the giant is slow, the giant is ugly. The giant is no match for Ernest Calloway, M.D., giant-slayer.

An Average Oddity

Dr. Calloway's article proved one thing to James: no matter what, people would think terrible things about him.

He could hold his paintbrush while he talked to them. He could discuss nineteenth-century artists, or thirteenth-century royalty, or twentieth-century comic book characters; he could look at a speaker evenly, listen expertly, ask questions. "Where in Maine?" he'd say, or, "Is accounting rewarding work?" hoping that if he showed enough interest in a visitor, they'd be a little less interested in him. It would just be an ordinary conversation then, the sort that goes on in diners, or across the seats in a taxicab, or during an insurance transaction.

But nothing worked. In the end visitors went away, remembering only that they had talked to the Tallest Man in the World, whose name they had probably not bothered to learn. After a while he started asking money for photographs. "A little money for my trouble," he said, charging more to people he thought could afford it, to those he did not like.

* * *

That summer, New York beckoned.

It had been beckoning all along, of course. Not the way Cape Cod is always beckoning, its curled finger saying to the whole rest of the country, come a little closer, till on the Fourth of July weekend the rest of the country is unaccountably standing on a beach in Provincetown, wondering: How did I get here? And: Is this all there is? New York's call was neither subtle nor polite, and it came in the form of a nineteen-year-old boy who said to me and his aunt and uncle: I have to go. When we expressed doubts, he said: I have to go before I die.

"I'll go with the circus if you think that's the best thing," he said to me. He'd written a letter to Hugh Peters, the president of the shoe store chain, who never responded. Yes, I told him with relief, I thought it was.

"It's time for me to get over my stage fright, I guess," he said. "Not that it's the stage I'm frightened of."

"What, then?"

He looked wistful, the way fear sometimes resembles wistfulness. "It's stupid. Fire."

There had been a famous awful circus fire fifteen years before. Exits had been so badly marked that people died in an avalanche of audience pushing to escape. "But you won't be in a tent. That was the problem. This is indoors. Fire exits marked. And think about how much more careful they have to be now."

"No, that's not the fire I meant." Still, he shivered, thinking of it. "I meant all of those Barnum fires. The one where the giantess had to be lifted out by a crane. That was an indoor fire."

Well, yes, and how did he know that? Years before I'd given him books, practically a blueprint of what he should plan to be terrified by in years to come. "They're prepared now," I said. "And if there's a fire, I promise you'll be rescued first. We'll have it written into your contract."

"You'll come with me?" he said.

I was startled—not by the request but by the realization that

I'd always assumed I would. It seemed only sensible that I chaperone. It was summer and Oscar was busy with his hotel, and Caroline, as always, was busy with Alice. Of course I would go along.

So we wrote a proposal to Barnum and Bailey. An appearance in New York; private hotel rooms for him and for his chaperone, Miss Peggy Cort; the center ring, not the sideshow. If everything went well, he'd consider other appearances.

He read his letter aloud to me. " 'Perhaps I'm asking for a lot, but as you have no doubt read, I'm not an ordinary . . .' I can't figure out what word to put there."

"Man? Performer? Attraction."

"Oddity," he said. He gave the word a French lilt; it was a term he'd probably pulled from a book. "I am not an average oddity."

In two weeks the circus sent a contract with every condition met. Once he'd signed, they sent an advance of a thousand dollars, along with a photographer to take pictures for the program.

"I can do magic tricks," James told the photographer. "Do you think they'll want me to do some?"

"Yeah? What kind?"

"Card tricks."

"Aw, that's no good. You're playing Madison Square Garden! The only person'll be impressed is the ringmaster, 'cause he's the only one who'll see. Learn to disappear an elephant, and maybe you got an act."

The circus wanted to fit him for costumes—a cowboy suit, perhaps. No, said James. How about a tuxedo, they said, with a nice top hat.

"I'm tall enough," James said, remembering Dr. Calloway's descriptions of giant fakery. "I don't need any gimmicks." The circus people couldn't disagree.

With some of the money, he ordered two nice suits.

I myself hadn't been in New York for years. At one time in my life I'd thought I'd want nothing so much as to live there. I had a college friend whose parents had an apartment near Central Park; I visited them once a year. They took me to dark wooden restaurants, to museums and concerts. The colors of everything from the red flannel hash to the faded brownstones were beautiful, and I was filled with the sort of longing a particularly handsome man in a black and white movie can induce, a longing so intense and fruitless that it feels like nostalgia.

What I did not take into account was that it was spring, and my friend's family was rich. Enough fine weather and money and a few memorable meals make any place desirable. As soon as I realized that, New York lost much of its charm for me.

So I resolved to look at the city differently this time. I would be a simple, easily dazzled tourist. I planned to crave hot dogs and roasted chestnuts from the street. I wanted to visit the zoo in Central Park. In short, I was traveling with a nineteen-year-old boy, and I intended to tour the city indulging nineteen-year-old tastes.

I hadn't taken a vacation in the nine years I'd been at the library. Astoria agreed to work that week for me—not that I'd wanted to take that much time off, but James wanted to see the city, and the Cape Cod–New York trains only ran weekends. So the circus booked our seats, and Oscar drove us to Hyannis in my car, and first thing in the morning on a Saturday in late August, James and I rode to New York City, to begin what turned out to be his public life.

Caroline had packed us a lunch, full of odd sweet sandwiches—she had a weakness for chutneys. "I'll miss you," she said to James. "You've never been away from home before."

"I was in the hospital," he said. "That was four months."

"That's different," said Caroline.

"Give me a kiss, Alice," James asked. He was standing up, so a kiss from Alice was an awkward operation. Oscar lifted her up into the air, and she smacked her mouth against James's cheek, using every muscle in her face, the way children do.

"I'll send you postcards," he said, and then we climbed in my Nash, and Oscar drove us to the station.

The circus had offered to hire a private railroad car for James, but he'd turned it down, and the train people had agreed to remove seats in the parlor car to make room. We'd both packed lightly, one case apiece, and Oscar dragged them on board for us.

"We can get a porter to do that," I said.

"Oh, save your money," said Oscar. The porter gave him a dirty look. "Besides, I want to see the inside of the train. I have half a mind to just stay on board, go with you." James followed him, bent over inside the train, which was wide but not tall enough. In the back of the car we found the missing seat; it was on the aisle, so I sat at the window; James sat down so that his legs could keep the businessman a row ahead company.

Oscar threw our bags into the rack overhead.

"I have half a mind . . ." he said again, but then the conductor tapped his shoulder.

"We're ready to go, sir," he said, and Oscar said, "Goodbye!" and almost ran off the train.

The line was advertised as "The Fun Train"; an accordion player walked up and down the aisles, asking for requests and singing. He didn't stop playing even when he leaned over to us, saying, "What can I play that will make you happy?"

As we pulled into Providence, James leaned across me toward the window.

"Rhode Island," he said under his breath, as if Rhode Island were someplace he'd dreamed of seeing all his life. But every station the train pulled into, every little Connecticut town, stunned him equally. Another place he'd never seen, another place that was not Cape Cod.

Hours later, we hit the tunnel that led to Grand Central. A shame, I thought, that trains couldn't just ride straight into the city, proud and unhidden. Trains had to sneak up on Manhattan, underground, in the dark. I felt like an uninvited guest.

We came to a stop, and let everybody else disembark first. A porter came to get our bags. We followed him.

James stepped out of the car onto the platform. Then he unfolded his body, planted his cane, stood his full height. You could hear people suck in their breath, an unmistakable sound that meant, *we knew he was tall, but this?*

Somebody said, "Look up," and then took a flash picture.

Somebody else whispered, "Christ." The circus people had called the newspapers. Maybe we'd expected to be met, maybe we thought that there'd be a band in the station, cheery men like the accordion player, uniforms, music stands. But the silence, the intake of breath, one or two quiet oaths and the splash of a flashbulb were James's "Hail to the Chief," played without variation wherever he went in the city.

A thin gray man in a suit stepped forward.

"Jim," he said, in the warm tone of an official stranger. "Pat Anderson. I work publicity. Glad we got you out here, son."

"Nice to meet you," said James.

"First time in the city?" a reporter asked.

James nodded.

"Like it so far?"

James laughed. "Haven't seen enough to complain yet."

"You guys'll get a chance to talk later," said Pat Anderson to the reporters. "Let's get you to the hotel." He looked at James's cane. "There's an elevator to take us up to street level." A porter came behind us with our bags.

"I don't like elevators," said James. He looked for me, beckoned me over. "This is Miss Cort," he said. "She's come along, too."

"A freight elevator," Pat Anderson explained to me. "More than tall enough. Then we'll catch a cab, get you settled."

James shook his head. "I'm not sure a cab—"

"Checker'll do the trick. Miss Cort"—he turned to me—"will ride in front. We'll follow. We're bound for the Hotel Astor."

"You've thought this through," I said.

He tipped an imaginary hat to me in reply.

He was right—a Checker cab was fine, James sitting diagonal in the back, me next to the driver. Pat Anderson took a second taxi.

Clearly the employees at the Astor had been briefed: a very tall boy is coming; be polite. But the people on the street—the cab driver, customers coming out of the hotel restaurant—had not been warned. We were used to it in our town, where the tourists stared at him the way they stared at everything. James was Plymouth Rock, he was the ocean, he was one more thing we had and the Midwest didn't. Here the stares were serious, weightier. These people had been surprised at home.

It isn't that I ever forgot that James was tall. No way to forget, not when everything in the average-sized world conspired to remind both him and others. But I could forget that it was something that people would not be prepared for, that the sight of a body like his would cause them to think: *but that's not possible. It can't be true.* You cannot imagine what over eight feet tall means until you see it. The tallest people we see on the street—the men who are asked constantly about basketball and weather—are more than a foot shorter.

"Stilts?" the cab driver asked hopefully.

"No," said James, almost enjoying it. Maybe he did. "All me."

I heard a mother say to her child as we stepped into the lobby, "No, dear. It's not real."

They'd thought of everything, these circus people. James's room had an extra-large bed, a large wooden chair, a bowl of fruit; my room adjoined, a nice bottle of wine on the dresser.

"Boy," James said. "I had no idea this was circus life."

"They're trying to convince you to sign a long-term contract," I said, examining the fruit, so lustrous and beautiful I'd first thought it wax. "Sign on, and then it's boxcars and pup tents."

"No, no," said Pat Anderson, walking through the door. "Just want you comfortable. Got the bed specially delivered. Thirteen feet—that's long enough?"

"More than," said James. "Bigger than my bed at home."

"Well," said Pat. "This *is* a luxury hotel. Here, I brought you this." He thrust a rolled-up magazine at James. "Program. You're featured. Page twelve. Also some pub shots." He reached into his briefcase and pulled out a pile of glossy photographs, then handed one to me and one to James.

There were two shots on one sheet. The first was James standing up in the Stricklands' house, his head just missing a light fixture, Oscar posed beside him to show scale. James slouched to fit, and steadied himself with a hand on the ceiling.

The other was a baby picture someone had faked up, neither James nor his parents. They'd taken a dark photo of a couple in a garden, and an overexposed photo of a baby sitting on a patch of grass, and married them in what was once called a composograph. The baby was ludicrously large, as big as the grown-ups, and the artist had not been fastidious in his work. You could see the white edge of what had surrounded the baby in his native snapshot, a strange halo separating him from the dark-haired couple who looked only at the camera.

"Doesn't look like anyone I know," James said.

"No," said Pat. "I'm not so crazy about that kind of fake, but." He sat down in a wing-backed armchair by the door, bounced a little, and rubbed at the upholstery; he leaned back and stuck his legs out, taking that elegant chair for all the comfort it was worth. I guessed he wasn't used to luxury hotels himself. "So, listen. Order anything you want on room service. We got the money, you might as well spend it. The rest of the outfit's due at the end of the week. You folks gonna sightsee tomorrow?"

"Yeah, we'd planned to," said James.

"Mind some company? Might as well get a little publicity out of this, dontcha think?" he asked. "I'd love the papers to see you at the top of the Empire State Building. 'Tallest Man Atop the Tallest Building.' "

"If you think they'd be interested."

"Sure would."

"The Empire State Building," James said thoughtfully. "I'd like to see that. There's a lot I'd like to see." The dresser was an ordinary height, and James reached down to pick an apple from the strange fruited tree of the gift basket.

"Boy," said Pat Anderson. "There are some guys I wish coulda met you. Our other big guys. Hugo of Belgium. Jack Earle. You woulda liked Jack Earle, you remind me of him. He wrote poetry. Nice guy, sad." He let his neck relax, and one of the wings of the chair caught his cheek like a loving hand. "How much you grow last year?" he asked.

"Two inches," said James.

This seemed to depress Pat. "Is there going to be no end to it?" he asked.

"I hope there is," said James, gently.

We'd planned to eat room service upstairs, but the hotel convinced us that we should celebrate our first night in New York in the dining room. "On the house," the manager told me when he called upstairs, and I almost explained that it didn't make any difference, the circus would pick up the bill if the hotel didn't. But the dining room sounded like fun, so two bellhops came to carry the big chair down to the restaurant.

"You should ride down in the chair, like a Persian prince," I said. At this the bellboys looked nervous. You could see them appraising James, wondering how many steamer trunks he was worth.

The maître d' took us to a table in the back; the chair had already arrived and been installed. The room was beautiful: high ceilings, dim lighting. Pillars flanked the tables, plaited with wreaths of painted vines and leaves.

"Some place," said James. He fingered the tablecloth. They gave us menus without prices, and though I know it was meant to be a politeness, it discomforted me; I felt as if I'd been loaned a yacht without a compass.

"What are you ordering?" I asked James.

"A steak?" he said. "Veal? I don't know."

The sommelier appeared at our table with a bottle of champagne. "Compliments of the house," he said, and I worried that they would announce this at the arrival of every course to remind us that the soup was free, the salads gratis, the entrees honoraria. "Thank you," I said.

"None for me," James said as the sommelier lifted the bottle to the lip of his champagne flute.

"Have a sip," I said.

"Well, okay. Just a little," he said to the man.

"I will only dampen your glass," the man answered.

And though there were other people in the room, other customers, the waiters, the boys in white jackets who refilled our water glasses after our daintiest taste, it felt like we were the only ones there. The room was dark; perhaps people could not see us. Or perhaps they were polite, used to seeing famous people.

James took a sip of his champagne and made a face. "It's awful," he said.

"You think so?"

"You don't, obviously." He smiled. "Well, you can have my cut."

"We'll just leave what's left over," I said as a man appeared to pour me another blond glassful. Even the candles on the tabletop burned politely, elegantly, without dripping to the cloth. I drank my champagne. "Why can't life always be like this?" I asked.

"I think even this would get boring," said James.

"So. What do you think of New York so far?"

"I don't know, Peggy." He twirled his glass by its stem. "I'm not so sure this is such a great idea."

"You're in New York," I said.

"But what for? To stand and be looked at? Shouldn't I have some other skills?" He made his glass dance to the edge of the table, then back in front of him.

"You do," I said.

"Yeah? What are they? Name me something else I could do for a living. See? That's what's shameful."

"No shame in it," I said. "Welcome to the world of grown-ups. You might be good at math, and somebody pays for that, but what you really love to do is sing. Do you think Oscar prizes above all else his ability to book guests into a hotel?"

"No."

"The sad fact of the world," I said, "is almost nobody exactly chooses what they get paid to do." I reached over and grabbed his traveling glass. "Stop that. You're fidgeting."

"Sorry," he said. "What about you? Don't you get paid for something you love?"

I tried to locate a spot on the table out of his reach for the glass, but of course, such a place did not exist. "I'm one of the lucky few. I was to the library born."

"How did you know?"

"I don't know."

"Really, I'm curious."

"Well," I said. "It seemed like the sensible thing to do."

"That's Peggy," he said, "always sensible," and I thrilled the way I always do when someone takes care to say something about me and says my name aloud.

"But," he said, "there are other sensible things. You could have been a nurse. You could have been an insurance salesman. There must be something about librarians you liked."

"Sure. A lot of things."

"For instance?"

"I liked . . . I liked the idea of taking care of things. I like order, good manners, and—because I'm basically a stingy person—I like being able to counteract that stinginess by giving people free things all day long. I like knowing things other people don't. You know my favorite part of the library? Our little local history section. Nobody in our town ever goes into it—you never have, have you? It's small. There's the voting records, and the census, and one book a man wrote twenty years ago, called *Brewsterville, My Home*. Boxes of posters for summer fairs, tickets to concerts. And it's all necessary, it's all things you can't find anywhere else, and I'm the one who owns it. The genealogists come in, wanting information, and I give it to them, the desiderata, the ephemera, everything."

"The what?"

"Ephemera," I said. "Stuff that doesn't seem to be useful, that you think will only be around for one use, like a ticket, but ends up being collected."

"And the other word?"

"Desiderata?" I let the word knock at my front teeth. That word was like toffee to me—I never thought of or missed it, but once tasted it became unspeakably delicious. "That word, it's the best thing I learned in library school. It means—well, it's sort of like, what's desired and required."

"Desired and required? Which?"

"Both," I told him. "Some things are both."

James cheered up a little. I realized he never really went to restaurants, certainly not one this fancy. He took the waiter's every suggestion, which resulted in a stultifying amount of food delivered to our table. James enjoyed it, I think: fancy restaurants have the formality of great magic, the whiteness of the tablecloth, the silver plate covers lifted suddenly to reveal not quite what you expected.

Not until the end of the meal did a stranger approach us, a man in a checked jacket, with ashy hair and a complexion to match. He'd had a little too much to drink—I could smell whiskey on his breath—but the fact was, I'd had two and a half glasses of champagne myself and was filled with the milk of human kindness.

"Hi," he said. "I was wondering something." He looked at James. "My friend and I have a bet. How tall are you?"

"How tall do you think?" James asked.

"Well, I say, seven feet at the most. Louise says you're at least seven five."

I laughed. "What do you stand to win if you're right?"

He looked delighted; clearly he thought he was victorious. "We haven't negotiated yet."

"What kind of betting is that?" I asked. "Go back and decide, then we'll tell you whether you win."

"Oh, come on," he said. " 'Fess up. Whatever she has to pay, she deserves it."

I leaned back to locate his friend. Across the room a woman in a green dress and red eyeglasses smiled embarrassedly, then waved.

James smiled at the man, then at me. "Sound fair to you?" he asked.

"Absolutely."

"So?" the man said. "Who's right?"

"Louise," James answered.

"Damn," said the man. He leaned against the nearest ivied pillar. "How tall?"

"Eight six," said James.

The man looked at me.

"It's true," I told him. "Don't feel bad. Don't begrudge Louise. Remember: something she deserves."

He was looking across the dining room then, and he turned

his palms to the ceiling, as if to say, *what can I do? you're right again.* Then he blew her a kiss. "No," he said. "I never begrudge her anything." He looked at us. "Are you two married?"

"No," I said, surprised. "Just friends."

"No, not to each other, or not at all?"

"Neither one of us," I said.

"Son," he said to James. "Quit dilly-dallying. Women only wait around so long." He turned to me. "How long you been waiting on him?"

"No comment," I said.

"Roses," said the man to James. "Love poems. Write your own, don't copy 'em out of a book. What do you do?"

"I'm a performer," said James.

"Ah. And you?"

"Librarian."

"Okay," said the man. "Son, all you have to do is figure out what rhymes with Dewey Decimal."

I burst out laughing.

"I'm serious."

"How long has Louise been waiting on you?" asked James.

The man looked at his watch. "Since the twelve o'clock train from New Haven," he said. "And I think she's getting impatient. Good to meet you both. You make a handsome couple."

"He was drunk," James said when the man was gone. But he didn't look mad.

I poured myself another glass of champagne. "Oh dear," I said as the bottle slipped out of my hand and splashed into the wine bucket. "Maybe we have that in common."

"You're drunk?" James asked. He grinned at me.

I stopped to consider the question. In other company I wouldn't have owned up. "Tipsy," I said.

"We'll have to get the bellhop to carry you up in the chair."

I leaned on the table with my elbows. "I'm sure it won't come to that," I said. "Unless I fall asleep."

"You're right," said James, "I could take this life for a while." His plate was beaded with juice from his lamb chops.

"Tomorrow will be a big day," I said. I looked at my watch. It was already ten o'clock. "We should think about sleep."

"Let's eat dessert first. Let's take the hotel for everything they've got."

"Deal," I said.

After dessert and coffee—after I had, in fact, consumed my cut of the champagne and James's—we got up to leave. I didn't feel drunk except when I tried to speak, and then only because I had thoughts that did not arrive at my mouth intact.

"You *are* drunk," James said fondly.

I shook my head, then shrugged.

We stepped onto the plush carpet of the lobby. I was glad for the cushioning; it felt less precarious than the parquet of the dining room.

We went to our separate rooms. I immediately washed my face and felt a little more clear-headed. Part of me knew it would be a good idea to change into my nightgown, but I felt suddenly too exhausted. After a minute I heard a knock, and I realized it came from the door that led from my room to James's. I went to it.

"Here you go, Peggy," he said. He handed me a folded piece of hotel stationery. "Good night. See you in the morning." He closed his door, and I closed mine.

The stationery said:

Love Poem for a Librarian

Although her love for me is infinitesimal,
Her eyes are as Dewey as any old decimal.

I lay awake for what seemed like hours but was probably minutes, repeating those two lines in my head. Sometimes I could not quite get the meter right; sometimes the syllables all fell into place exactly. James was on the other side of the door. I strained to hear what he was doing—pushing aside the drapes to look out, turning down the sheets of his bed, maybe un-tucking his shirt before taking it off. I thought I could hear the brush of fabric against fabric that might have been any of these things. Life should be like this always, I thought again, and in my drunken state I wondered how I could make it possible. There has to be some way, I thought. Then I fell asleep.

*

"Clear day," Pat Anderson said at ten-thirty the next morning, when he met us in the hotel lobby. There was a crowd around James, reporters and gawkers, asking questions. One man in an awful plaid jacket shook James's hand again and again. "Perfect Empire State Building weather!" Pat said. "Who knows—maybe we'll go out to the Statue of Liberty."

"We can't get to the top of that," I said.

"No, but good pictures there anyhow." He looked at his watch. "I'll go flag the taxi. You flag Jim."

James was reluctant to leave the crowd. The plaid man was still shaking his hand, then pulled out a business card. I saw that he was the drunk man from the dining room.

"Nice people," James said absentmindedly, pocketing the card. "Wow. What's today?"

"Tuesday. Empire State Building Day. Remember to tell me when you get tired. No point in wearing yourself out first thing."

"No," said James. He climbed into the back of the taxi.

"You already sound tired. Are you up for this? Maybe you need to rest."

"No," he said. "I'm in New York. I guess I should be allowed to do a little sightseeing."

"Okay," I said. "Okay. I just—"

"Peggy," he said, "you're not my mother, and I'm over eighteen, and I can tell when I'm tired." He looked at me. "I promise." You would have thought he was the one with the hangover. I didn't feel sick, exactly, just dried out and slow-witted.

The Empire State Building's lobby was big enough that had he stood in it alone, James would have looked quite in scale. A pack of reporters trailed us, from the daily papers, from the newsmagazines. A man in a derby, who said he'd once been mayor of New York, shook James's hand.

"The only thing that rivals you is this building," he said.

We couldn't avoid the elevator, of course, but it went so

fast—so alarmingly fast!—that James didn't have to crick his neck for long. Then we stepped out.

James immediately went to the observation deck. The ex-mayor followed him. "Winds are thirty miles," he said, and as I stepped outside, I could feel it. I hadn't imagined it windy up here; I thought for sure we'd left all the weather on the street. The ex-mayor took off his hat, put it back on, and clamped his hand down on its crown. Photographers took pictures of the three of us.

"Well, Jim," he said, "New York isn't such a big place when you look down on it, is it?"

"It's a pretty good size," James said.

Reporters wrote this down.

"You keep growing the way you do," the ex-mayor said, "and you'll be able to get up here without using the stairs or elevator."

Below us, New York went on as usual. It was so sunny even the dirt looked clean and monumental. The East River sparkled like some big scaled animal turning over and over in bed. "Where's the hotel?" James wondered, and Pat Anderson went over to help him locate the neighborhood.

"Quite a kid you got there," a reporter said to me. He was one of those men who seemed to have walked to the edge of adolescence, looked over, and then stepped back in horror. Thin and high-voiced and baby-faced, as short as I was. I wasn't used to looking at a man at eye level. "How much did he weigh at birth?" he asked.

"I'm not sure. An ordinary weight. Nine pounds, perhaps."

"Eats a lot?"

"Not really. A little more than average. Not much."

"What's his father do?"

"I don't know."

"You're not an overproud mother, that's for sure," the reporter said to me.

"I'm not a mother at all," I said. "I'm James's chaperone."

"Aha!" said the reporter. "What's your name? I'll make you famous."

"Peggy Cort."

"Miss or Missus?"

"Miss."

"Even better," said the reporter. He stopped writing. "Whatcha doing tonight?"

This so flabbergasted me I couldn't think of what to say.

"Don't look so scared," the reporter said. "You want to grab a sandwich or not?"

"No," I said. "Thank you."

He shrugged. "Bigfoot over there your boyfriend or something?"

"Mind your own business," I said.

"Yeah, the tall guys get all the luck. Even the short girls like 'em better. Well," he said, "he's not the tallest this building's ever seen. King Kong's still got the record."

Then several reporters hushed him, and the wind rushed in, too, lifted up the ex-mayor's hat, and deposited it in the wire nets meant to discourage suicides.

James loved public spaces. I did, too, of course; it was one of the reasons I became a librarian. But we liked them for different reasons. I loved buildings where anyone was welcome, where no one could throw you out, wonder whether you belonged. And while I was not an admirer of people in the specific, I liked them in the abstract. It is only the execution of the idea that disappoints. I have always loved strangers a good deal more than my own family, will be politer and friendlier on a bus or in an airport than I am at a dinner table. You have nothing to lose with strangers: they will like you or not and most likely never think of you again, and conversation becomes that much easier. Love and hate are not on the menu.

James loved public spaces for this reason: they were big. Even my small-town public library had ceilings high enough that he'd never have to worry. Town hall was the same, and the high school, and some stores and restaurants.

New York was filled with such places. Hotel lobbies, train stations, museums, department stores—it was as if, having used up so much ground outside, they'd decided they needed wide inside spaces. Outdoors it was all claustrophobia; inside, atriums and staircases that made you look up to see where they ended.

We took them slowly, of course. James was right: he knew when he got tired and said so, and we taxied back to the hotel and rested. We had to tell the desk clerk not to let up visitors. Then we'd go off again, to the Metropolitan Museum, the Frick, to Macy's and Altman's. "Go see a Broadway show," the bellhop told us, though of course James wouldn't have fit. He said he wasn't interested. It's only now I realize that we could have called a theater and asked them to figure something out. James was a celebrity; they would have done it. Of course, I would have pitied whoever sat behind him.

Pat Anderson came to the hotel with clippings every morning. CIRCUS GIANT BUSY ON FIRST DAY HERE, the *Times* headline said, and then, in smaller print, EATS NORMAL-SIZE MEAL. There was a picture of the ex-mayor peering up at James through one of the Empire State Building telescopes.

The reporters fell off after the first couple days, but the crowds continued. It got tiresome, though people were always nice—when we stopped to get a hot dog off the street, a stranger would always rush up to buy Jim's.

"Just one?" they'd say in disbelief. "Have a couple, you must be hungry! No? Just a snack, huh?"

The circus manager had a thick southern accent. "Ease as pie," he said. "For the p'rade, we'll drive you 'round the rings. Then, 'bout midway through, you'll come out by yourself. Wanna walk or ride?"

"Ride."

"Ride's good. Bigger surprise when you step off. Ringmaster'll 'nounce you, ride in, step off. Leila rides with you."

"Leila?"

"Smallest woman in the world," said the manager. "That's our story, anyhow. Jus' stand there, the two you, wave, get back on the truck. Nothin' to it. Ten minutes. Y'manage that?"

"I think I can," James said.

The animals stank up the back of Madison Square Garden. Performers whirled around; their costumes were frayed this close up, and their faces bore little resemblance to the glamour of the program. Their teeth were bad, their skin was bad and paved with makeup. But they were nice, and impressed with James.

"You're the real thing," a clown said, looking up.

In a corner by the stairs, a thin woman painted at an easel. Another clown was sitting for her, in full makeup, a T-shirt, blue jeans.

"You gotta hurry up, Blanche," he said. "I gotta get dressed."

"Oh, you have plenty of time," said the woman. Her voice was girlish and powdery. "Hold still."

"I'm holding still maybe thirty fucking seconds more."

"Well, promise to sit for me later."

"Sure thing," the clown said, standing up.

James walked over to the woman. "What do you do?" he asked her.

She was rubbing a brush clean with a white cloth. "I paint," she said. "What do you do?" She put a huge straw hat on the back of her head, as if she'd just smelled the animals and had taken it as evidence she was in a meadow.

"I'm here, right now," he said. "Appearing for the circus. But I paint, too."

"*Do* you," she said, delighted. The clown she'd just been painting came running past her and pinched her bottom. "Good girl, Blanche," he said. She smiled slightly and lowered her head. "What do you paint?" she asked James.

"Seascapes," he said. "Still lifes."

"Bowls of fruit," she said.

"Not so far," said James. "But I've never had one lying around to paint. Do you work for the circus?"

"No," she said. "For myself. I don't like bowls of fruit either. I paint clowns."

"Nothing else?"

"No," she said. "Clowns. They're so innocent." She turned the painting of the pinching clown around to show us. He looked sweet as a schoolboy. "They bring people so much joy."

Then Leila, the Smallest Woman in the World, came out in a green-sequined dress with matching satin shoes. Whether she was in fact the world's tiniest I didn't know, but she was at least two feet shorter than me, Italian and glamorous, perfectly proportioned though stout and buxom. Even backstage of the circus I could smell her perfume, spicy vanilla set to low simmer.

"Jimmy Sweatt!" she said. "You gonna change for our show?"

"No, I'm fine."

"Don' get paint on your suit," she said. "I'm Leila. This you know already." She turned to me. "Hello. Don' worry about your boy. Blanche is nice only crazy."

"I am not crazy!" said Blanche.

Leila smiled sweetly at me and adjusted her girdle. "Better get ready," she said to James.

He walked over. She barely came up to his knee. I could see where her girdle ended: her stomach rose up over it like a sequined bolster. The circus paired them so they'd exaggerate each other's size, but they in fact looked right together, the way opposites often do, sequin and poplin, frivolous and studious. Leila looked like some fizzy obsolete green drink from a nineteenth-century novel, one that puts you to sleep and gives you dreams that explain your life; James, like the country doctor who'd visit you the next day to break the news that you might never recover. Leila the energetic drug, James the antidote, distilled from the same plant but with different inclinations.

Leila did not even bother to attempt to look him in the eye when they were standing. "Good way to break my neck. So Jimmy, where do you buy your clothing? Same place I do, I bet. Help me on this truck, okay?" He offered his hand; she looked at it and laughed.

"Too big!" she said. "We are a *pair*. Afterward, we will go dancing." She put her hand out to the truck driver instead. James got in next to her, his cane across his lap.

"You wanna go to your seat?" the manager asked me.

I didn't, but I went anyhow. Tomorrow I'd wait backstage,

but for opening night they'd saved me a seat in the front row, just to the right of the center ring. I left Leila and James on their truck, ready far in advance for the starting parade.

The parade was only a minute; James didn't even get off the truck. He and Leila waved as they toured the arena, but they waved the same way the bouncing girls on top of elephants did, and the clowns, and the acrobats in their lamé suits.

Then the circus started. Sitting that close dizzied me. As a child, I sat up high in the back of Boston Garden, where I could keep my eyes on all three rings at once; down here my attention was scrambled by the poodles with their fur shaved in ruffs and the ponies in feathered crowns. Really, I was just biding my time till James came back for his featured performance. I wondered what the audience would think of him. And then I wondered whether everyone in the circus had someone like me in the stands—not in New York, necessarily, but down the road, a mother in a hometown, a pretty girl met on the street in Miami, a barely-known cousin in Des Moines: one particular person looking with particular interest. I wondered how Mrs. Sweatt, in this audience, would look at James. Some pride perhaps, a lot of worries. Mostly, I imagined her sitting still, saying, *my son, my son, my son.*

And then I tried to view everyone with this individual interest. The showgirl with the red hair and blond eyebrows. The lantern-jawed clown dressed like a schoolmarm. The red-faced roustabout whirling the elephants' steel pedestals through the cutaway into the center ring. It got oppressive, as if by paying this attention I created the need in them. Not a profound need: the showgirl was not offering me her soul, just her legs in thick not-quite-skin-colored stockings, her spangled doublet, her face smiling up at the audience in general. But surely she needed to be looked at; why else would she have joined up?

Finally it was time for James and Leila. The ringmaster announced them from the center, and the truck was revealed in a splash of lights. Leila stepped out first, almost bouncing, waving. Then James. I waited for the gasp, but there was none. The light glinted off his glasses, though he barely moved. Maybe he was sniffing for the first rich hints of a fire from a dropped cigarette. First I looked across the arena to the people on the far side: the few faces I could divine seemed, well, unimpressed. The people on either side of me watched James with no wonder at all; the kids squirmed in laps, stood on thighs to face their parents. They'd seen women swinging from their long hair, men pedaling bicycles across wires, tigers complaining like retirees as they lay down, rolled over, sat up. The cheapest seats were so far away that nothing looked big to them, not even James. Just a man, just an ordinary man, leaning on a cane as tall as the ringmaster. They'd have preferred the cowboy outfit, a mile-long leotard.

Leila climbed up to a high platform that put her at James's eye level, and this the crowd liked—funnier to have the height difference beneath her. The lights bubbled off her sequins, green, intoxicating.

"You were terrific," I told James after the show. I'd gone backstage as soon as possible.

"Not much to do. But I was nervous."

"You seemed like an old pro." I reached up to smooth the lapel of his jacket. He'd been sweating, from nerves or exertion I didn't know, and the fabric had darkened in spots. "Maybe we'll get this cleaned tomorrow."

Leila came up to us, riding on the back of the truck. "My chauffeur brings me everywhere." She punched the arm of the man behind the wheel, who didn't even smile. "Where you staying, Jimmy?"

"At the Astor."

"A snob!" she said happily. She stood up on the back of the truck. "Me, I stay with everybody else. So. We'll have lunch. Me and you." It wasn't a question.

"Sure!" James said. "Great. Tomorrow?"

"Tomorrow, yes. Where do you eat? Your favorite place."

"Anywhere. Where do you eat?"

Leila shrugged. "When I get hungry, I stop and eat. Wherever I am. Not so fancy as you, so you choose."

"The Automat," said James.

Leila laughed. "Not fancy, but good. You will reach the top drawers and I the bottoms. Good."

"What time?" I asked.

"Ah," said Leila. Then she turned to James. "She wants to be invited. She's afraid I will do something to her boy."

"No—" I started.

"She thinks I will kidnap you to the circus forever. She thinks I will make you elope." She looked at me again. "I will not. But maybe—" She sat down, not next to the driver but on the platform behind him, her legs dangling off the edge. "Maybe the boy wants to elope himself. So! To make you feel better, have dessert with us. For lunch I get him for my own, then you come. If we elope, we do this with your blessing. Right, Jimmy?"

"Yes," said James. "Of course."

"Twelve o'clock the Automat," said Leila. "One-thirty for dessert." Then she slapped the driver on the back as if he were a horse who'd fallen asleep, and the truck went lurching off.

Before I went to meet them at the Automat, I looked through my suitcase for something to wear. How had I managed to assemble such a dowdy brown wardrobe? I put on one outfit, then tried a belt to dress it up and show off my hips, then decided that my hips were no prize and shouldn't be highlighted. Leila would know what to wear, I thought. Then I was appalled with myself: now I was jealous of a midget with an accent. Which gave me something else to be appalled about, characterizing her in such a way. I finally put on the dress I'd worn the day before and went out to hail a taxi.

The Automat was crowded with a combination of tourists—after life in Brewsterville, I could identify any sort—and regulars. The visitors peered through every single food window; the New Yorkers had the locations of their favorites memorized. I'd pictured Leila in a child's red vinyl booster seat, but instead she perched on top of a stack of metal chairs. She was in the middle of some story that made her spread her arms like a fisherman describing a lost catch.

The lunch china was still there, thick and yellowed and

edged in gray marcelled waves. One solitary, ludicrous iced sweet roll sat on a saucer almost exactly the same size.

"Welcome," she said. "We have saved this bun for you to eat."

"No thank you," I said. "I see you haven't eloped."

"Not yet!" Leila pounded the top of the table. The sugar pourer jumped into the napkin dispenser. "Actually, it is a tragedy. I forgot, I already have one husband."

"*One* husband!" said James.

"One husband at once," said Leila primly. "That is a rule I don't break so far. Five husbands in a row, not all together."

"You've been married five times?" I said.

"See, Jimmy? She is surprised. She thinks I am too small for husbands. She is curious." She pulled a rhinestone cigarette case out of her bag and lit a cigarette with a matching rhinestone lighter. I had a feeling Leila owned matched sets of everything. "They say, to smoke makes you short. I must not lose my job, and so I smoke much. Also it helps me eat less. Yes." She pulled an empty plate over for an ashtray. "Five husbands so far."

"Five husbands, for anyone—"

Leila hoisted her coffee cup and blew some smoke across the top. She said, gravely, "God has been good to me. This is all I will say."

"Have your husbands been"—I couldn't think of a tactful way to say, *In the circus*. "Show people?" I tried.

"You mean short," said Leila.

"No, no. I meant. Well."

"My first husband, Al, was tall to me, short to everyone else, five foot. Next one, Francis, taller. They get taller, boop, boop, boop—" She made her hand climb some invisible steps to show the evolution of her husbands, her cigarette dragging smoke behind it. "Rafe, my newest, is maybe six feet tall."

"Really," I said.

"Such a surprise?"

"Six feet is—well, isn't that a *lot* taller than you?"

"I like tall," said Leila, winking. "I like *big*. My mother told me look for short men because they are used to less, they will be satisfied for me. Now I think, but am I satisfied for them? All my life, I eat less than other people, breathe less air, less material for my clothes, less wood for my furniture. Some things I should be allowed to have more of, isn't that right? So I decided: never again am I stingy about men. The more man, the better. This is why I like your boy. You know this song?"

She paused, as if we would know what song she was talking about, even if we'd never heard it. Then she started to sing. She had a sweet, deep voice; her accent and the cigarette made it seem, briefly, as if we were in a cabaret instead of an Automat.

" '*I got a man that's more than eight foot tall, four foot shoulders and that ain't all. . . .*'

"No?" she said. "You never heard this?"

"I don't listen to the radio," I said.

"Oh, no, this song was never on the radio. Julia Lee. She is colored and a little, mmmmmm, *risqué*. Records and jukeboxes. I heard for the first time in a bar in Kansas City. I own the record, and I will send it to you. '*They built the Boulder Dam, the Empire State, and then they made my man, and is he great!*' "

Then she moved away the sweet roll so she could put her elbow on the table, propped up her chin and gazed at James like a starstruck teenager until he looked away in embarrassment. "Ah," she said. "You must not be shy."

James looked back at her and gave a wry smile that dimpled one cheek. I'd never seen that smile before. "You make me shy. Usually I'm not."

"Oh," said Leila. "I don't want to make anyone this way." She turned to me, and suddenly I felt the shyness fall over me like a tossed blanket. Her eyes were black and damp as olives. She regarded me with what seemed to be great affection.

"You're a pretty girl. Maybe Jimmy will be my next," she said. "But Rafe I just married. In a few years Jimmy and I meet again, run off. Meanwhile, he should marry whoever he likes. You, maybe." She picked up her cigarette, looked at it, and put it back down. "Maybe you and Jimmy, right?"

"No," I said. "Do you mind if I get some coffee?" I looked around for a waitress, then remembered where I was.

"Why not?" she said. "Are you already married? You have no ring."

"No."

"See? Jimmy's not, too. Everyone should get married. We will drive to New Jersey. I will be matron of honor. I like all weddings."

"Well, Leila," said James. "Not everyone likes to get married that fast."

Suddenly I saw us, in an office somewhere—me in a cream wedding suit, James in the top hat and tails the circus tried to talk him into. Leila, I was sure, would wear white—any opportunity to look like a bride—sequined certainly, perhaps trimmed in white fur. She'd look like the sugar pourer, luxuriously full and sparkling. She'd give away the groom, humming the wedding march, holding on to his pant leg. At the altar she'd stand right up on her tiptoes to get a good look at everything. There'd be no way to get the three of us in one snapshot.

"I haven't got a dress," I said.

"Oh, dresses. They think they need dresses to get married. They think they need rings and cake. No. You need these: man, woman, minister, flowers, honeymoon."

"Flowers?" said James.

"Must have," said Leila.

"Well, maybe we'll do it," I said. "You make it sound so sensible."

"And for honeymoon you will go to Niagara. I went there."

"Which husband?" asked James.

"Most. Niagara is best. So we'll go now? To get married? You look fine," she said to me. "Comb your hair. Eat this bun and we will go."

"Oh," I said. "Right now?"

"Don't want to get married? Darling. No. My advice is good. Here—" She pushed the sweet roll closer. "Skinny girl, eat this bun, it will bring you good luck for your wedding. Sweet start, sweet life.

James laughed. "Leila, you're in love with weddings."

"Yes!" she said. "I am in love with many things. Weddings and Niagara Falls and men. I am always in love. See my cheeks? Pink, always, because I am always in love. You too, you be in love and you don't need to sleep so much, think so much. Yes," she said, to herself more than to us. "You must get married. New Jersey is minutes away."

"I'd like a longer engagement," I said.

"You don't need!" she said. "Engagements—they are like a prayer before eating, best quick."

"I'm too young to get married," said James. He was flirting. I'd never seen him do that before either, though of course it was like dancing—easy, if you did it with someone who really knew how to lead. "I think I'll just wait for you, Leila. In ten years, I'll be your husband number eleven."

Leila smiled at him. "Okay. Too bad for your friend, but good for me. In ten years we will meet here again and get married. You—" She kicked me under the table, the toe of her shoe just touching my knee. "You don't want this bun? It's good."

"No."

She picked up the sweet roll, which looked as big as a hat in her hand. "Famous circus lady, Carrie Akers, was the world's fattest short person, or shortest fat person. Three hundred pounds, my height. I try to avoid this. But I will eat the wedding bun, for my own good luck. Ten years we will meet again. You I will marry," she said to James, "and you will be my maid of honor. Okay?"

"Okay," I said. Every day my heart was broken newly, more efficiently. "I'll bring the flowers."

"Roses," said Leila. "Must have."

Late that night, I heard a door open. Not all the way at first, just the tongue of a latch plocking as a doorknob turned. I looked to my right, to the door that opened into the hallway, but it was shut. Then the other door, the one that led to a door that led to James's room, swung open, toward me.

I'd kept it unlatched for this reason, so that if he knocked I could say, "Come in." I'd expected—if I expected anything—

that the knock would come in the morning, when he was ready for the day, or after we'd come home, one last thought before sleep. But except for that first night five days ago, after our meal in the hotel dining room, he'd never used it. Instead he phoned, and we met outside our rooms in the hallway, like any neighbors who went to work together.

Now he stepped in. One small lamp in his suite was on; for a second I could see his outline. Then the first door closed behind him and my room was dark again.

"James?" I said.

He said, "Peggy." His voice was tense, nervous. I sat up a little in bed, my brain still not up to full speed. Slowly my eyes got used to the dark. He was wearing an undershirt and shorts, which were what he'd brought to sleep in—I'd been there when he packed. At home he had pajamas, which Caroline sewed for him, but he'd decided that they'd take up too much room in his suitcase. His shorts just looked like any man's underwear, baggy and a little comic.

"What is it?" I asked.

He sat down on the edge of my bed. "Peggy," he asked. "Do you *want* to get married?"

It was not a proposal. I'd never heard one before, but I knew that much—not the way he stressed *want*, not the way he closed his eyes, confused, when he said *want*, not the way the whole statement leaned on that word instead of *married*. It was just a question: did I, or didn't I, and my answer would be only information, not the start of anything.

"I don't know," I said. My bed was usual-sized, but still he seemed far away from me. He rested a hand on one of the short posts of the footboard. "Who to?" I asked.

He didn't answer. He rubbed the knob of the post. Finally he said, "Me," and that word, in the dark, sounded like it might have been a proposal.

But I wasn't sure. Something in my heart turned, like the latch in the catch of the adjoining door, not open but ready. It might have been a proposal. I didn't know how to answer. *Why do you want to know? What took you so long? Do you think that's a good idea? Yes. Yes, that's what I want.*

I could hear him breathing, could see his sloping shoulders.

"Oh, James," I said.

"I just—" He rearranged himself on the bed. "It just occurred to me you might want to. Get married. I mean, to someone."

"Why do you think that?"

"Because you're a girl," he said matter-of-factly, and O girls, what is said passionately evaporates, it's what's said as a matter of fact that is precious and damaging and lasting as a brand. "Don't all girls want to?"

"I don't know," I said. The neck of his undershirt was frayed, that's how good my eyes were getting in the dark.

"Stella did. Not to me, but even before she was engaged, she had her whole wedding planned. She knew exactly the music, the kind of cake."

"Sounds like planning your funeral," I said. "Not too useful." I thought about sitting up, taking his hand. I didn't know if he wanted me to, and I couldn't think about what I wanted. Not right at that moment. I waited for all those hackneyed, bodily responses to good news—for my stomach to drop, my heart to leap, my lungs to empty, as if every part of me were a spectator readying to catch a pop fly. But every part of me was still, and cruelly rational. Every part of me was waiting.

"Do you want to get married, Peggy," he said. "We could, you know. I mean, I wouldn't be a good *husband*—"

Then I was sitting up, I did take his hand. "Yes—" I said.

"No, I wouldn't," he answered. "I mean, not like a real husband. But we still could. If you wanted."

What I wanted was to drag him into bed with me—not for the sex he was delicately reminding me he was incapable of, not even for kissing. Just so we could be closer. Just so I could explain how little I needed. It's hard, I thought, to have a conversation like this without lying down.

"I wouldn't mind," James said.

I wanted noise, so I didn't have to answer. This was all a dream, I thought, and anything I said would be a bomb thrown in to explode it. I wanted some New York clamor outside the window—a siren, an anonymous scream, someone else's emergency—but this was a fancy hotel and the walls were thick and we were protected from any middle-of-the-night disturbance. All I could hear was the agitated ticking of my travel alarm clock, and I had to stop myself from picking it up to wind it, from the delusion I could calm it down.

I asked, "Do you want to?"

"I don't know. I mean, it seems like I should get married before I die. Which means the sooner the better."

"You don't know—"

"Like planning your own funeral? I mean, Peggy, I have. I have planned it. And I know what my tombstone will say—just my name, nobody else's, just the dates of my life. And people will walk through the cemetery, making up stories the way they do, and mine will be one of the graves they think is saddest. They'll add up the dates, and then they'll say, so sad."

I lay back down, still holding his hand. "Is that a good reason to get married?"

"It's the best one I have. And to make you happy, if it would."

"Oh, James Sweatt," I said. I couldn't think of what to say. Then I tried, "I can't marry you."

"Okay." He started to move his weight to stand up.

"Stop. Hold still. Don't you want to know why?"

"I don't think so. You don't want to, that's all I need to know."

"I do want to," I said. "But James, I can't marry you if you're doing it just to make me happy."

"Why not?"

"Because. No matter what Leila says, getting married is a big deal, not a weekend trip. And because doing things to make someone else happy won't guarantee your own happiness."

"But Peggy, that's what you do. That's just what you've always done. Aren't you happy?"

I began to cry, a little. It surprised me.

"I guess that's my answer," he said.

"My answer is," I said, "yes."

"What are you answering?"

"Yes," I said, crying a little harder, "I am happy."

"Shhh," he said. "It's not like I'm doing you a favor. Peggy, I'm doing everything I never wanted to do. I'm making a spectacle of myself. In the realest way. I'm standing in front of people and telling them to gawk at me and making money off it. That was one thing, truly, I never wanted to do."

"They'd gawk anyhow," I said quietly. "You know that."

"Yeah. And the worst thing is, it's not so bad. I mean, it's bearable. I feel like my life is turning out to be just this: every day I learn I have a little less dignity than I thought. So maybe I should change my life. Get married." He took his hand from mine, then reached back to put it on my blanketed foot. "I want you to think about it," he said. "About getting married, I mean. If you want to, we should do it. I feel like an idiot I didn't think about it before. I should have asked you years ago."

I laughed. "What, when you were twelve?"

"If you needed that much time to make up your mind, from then till now, then yes: I should have asked you when I was twelve. Now you don't have so much time to mull it over. But you promise you'll think about it, and tell me. Take it seriously. We won't talk about it until you're sure, one way or the other." He squeezed my foot. "I'm tired," he said.

"Yes. You should get some sleep."

"I will." He sighed.

And then, though he was sitting on a perfectly fine bed in a perfectly fine room, he stood up and walked away to his own. He was just a boy; he didn't know not to leave a woman crying in bed. "I'll see you in the morning," he said, and then nervously, tentatively, disbelievingly, "Sweetheart."

The rest of the circus performances went better than the first, partly because Leila advised James to wait till she hit the ground, then stand up very slowly. She wanted him to pick her up, too—"I'm so light you wouldn't believe it"—but he was afraid for his balance. Instead she leaned against him off her platform, put her hand on his shoulder, and whispered in his ear. He told me later she said, "Shall I step off? Shall I step off? When we get married, this is how we will go down the aisle."

End-of-Movie Kisses

We were engaged. That's what I told myself, though we didn't discuss marriage again. Not in New York. Not when we got back home. I thought about it nearly all the time, but I could not bring the subject up myself. I was terrified he'd say, *oh that. That was just an idea I had, a bad one*. Or perhaps, *didn't you know I was sleepwalking*? The words themselves, *okay, let's get married*, felt like a bomb in my throat, a bomb I felt like pitching through windows, into living rooms, up through the glass floors of the library, knowing it would explode everything. What would Oscar and Caroline say if I approached them, asking their nephew's hand in marriage? What would the town say if we applied for a license? At best I'd be met with laughter; at worst by plain refusal. Even the basic facts: a thirty-three-year-old woman and the nineteen-year-old she'd known since he was a child. *You cannot have this*, they'd say. *Maybe this is all you've ever wanted, but we're sorry. Think of how it would look.*

So I held on to my bomb, a Molotov cocktail I could taste, sweet like a cocktail in my throat as long as I kept it there.

It wasn't until we got back from New York that I saw how much the trip had taken out of James. I don't think he'd seen it either. In New York he had been busy with people and busy with his camera. He wanted to make sure he'd taken enough pictures; even as we pulled out of the city, he clunked his lens against the glass and snapped a photo. "To show Aunt Caroline and Uncle Oscar and Alice," he said, though of course it was more. I understood, finally: tourists do not take pictures as souvenirs. They want to assemble a new country to tour later, they outfit it with the best parts of the last place: this doorway, that rough-bricked street, a straw-hatted horse, a cheese shop, an empty bedroom. Some want their families there and include them in so many vistas that their new flat world is entirely populated by crowds of the wife and children. The photographer is native and stranger in his glossy dream city, invisible but significant, as natives and strangers often are.

Once home, James started to sleep late. He told me he stayed up until four in the morning and got up at two in the afternoon. He took naps in between.

"Do you feel all right?" I said. "Perhaps you should see a doctor."

"I need to rest, is all," he said. "I'll be fine."

I myself was an early riser. I couldn't help it. Two Sundays a year I would manage to sleep until ten, and then I felt as though I'd wasted most of the day.

Now, though, my day couldn't start until I knew James was awake in his house across town. His being asleep so much of the day felt like a terrible absence to me, although weekdays I never saw him until after five anyhow. Asleep, he was not really in the world. I'd have been up since six, as always, had washed my face and dressed and neatened my apartment and walked to the library; I'd have emptied the book drop and refilled the scrap paper holders and perhaps catalogued some books; I'd have checked items in and out, dispensed advice and collected fines and kept myself busy in all the usual ways, but the day could not really begin, was not really a day, until two-thirty when James was sure to be awake and there was a possibility he was thinking of me.

He might phone; he sometimes did, to ask me a question or request a book. We'd put in a phone line at the cottage at last, to save the Stricklands from answering calls all day. He might pick up a book I'd brought him and think of me—wouldn't he have to? Now he was reading Dickens, one fat volume at a time. I'd planted myself in as many ways as possible in his house, in the record player and records and boxes of the kind of bulky pens he liked; in the loaves of bread I bought him and the articles I clipped from newspapers. Every day he'd have to deal with at least one object whose presence in his life was my doing.

At night I tried to keep myself awake, because he was awake. That we were not in the same room or building made no difference. Perhaps he was in the big armchair; the telephone was on the table next to it. He used a pen to dial, like a lady with an elaborate manicure. Perhaps he was reading, or writing, or painting. Was he thinking of me now? How could I go to bed?

But I couldn't stay awake that late. I listened to the radio, to the talk shows he favored; I thought that way we might be thinking the same thing at the same time. I read. I lay across my bed fully clothed, with all the lights on, in case he called, so that I could tell him, *no, I haven't gone to bed yet*. Sometimes I phoned him those late nights, pleading insomnia.

"I knew you'd be up at this hour," I said.

And we'd talk, and he almost always ended the conversation the same way: "Well, if you're still awake later, feel free to call. I'll be up for a while yet."

Whether he said this out of pity for my imaginary insomnia or really wanted me to call, I don't know. Anyway, I never could stay up later, even though I sometimes set my alarm clock for three-thirty A.M. I slept right through it and finally had to stop trying when Gary, my landlord, said he could hear it through the floor.

"You can call me, too," I told James those nights. "You feel free, too."

But he never did.

Alice, who was three, picked out a kitten for James from a box in front of the supermarket. Caroline had told her she could have one, and Alice insisted on both a white-and-black cat who looked like he was wearing a toupee, and a dark calico. James got the calico. Oscar suggested Peggy as a name, but both James and I were revolted by the idea.

"It's a compliment," Oscar said.

"All I need," I said, "is to hear, 'Peggy ruined the upholstery on that chair. Have you cleaned Peggy's litter box? Peggy kept me awake all night coughing up a hairball.' "

"I get the point," said Oscar.

So we called her Kazoo, because though she was only three months old, she already had a nasal, scratchy voice, a smoker's meow. We did not get along, much to the delight of everyone else, especially James. He liked to imagine that Kazoo spent her catnaps dreaming of ways to torment me.

"She doesn't see herself chasing mice," he said. "She sees herself chasing Peggy."

Oscar had decided to start an art school by mail. He'd gotten this idea from James, who was taking a correspondence course from a school in Vermont. Now that Alice was three, only a little tall for her age and pretty, her father no longer feared sudden giantism; by the time James was her age he was already enormous.

Oscar asked James for advice. "How much is too much for one lesson? How do you think I should grade?"

"People are going to send you paintings in the mail?" I asked. "Won't that get expensive?"

"No, just cartoons. I'll specialize in cartoons—everybody wants to do comic books. So Jim: start with funny characters, move onto serious? Vice versa?"

He tried to recruit students from the tourists who visited James, but it was like the end of a summer romance. Write to me, remember me, won't you? They never did. They remembered only the prairie of mattress, the chair as big as a haystack, sent their friends and came back themselves.

"Charge money," the tourists said. "Charge money," said Astoria, and Oscar, and even Leila, the Smallest Woman in the World, who sent a package from her winter home in Florida. Inside was the promised record: Julia Lee and her Boyfriends singing "King-Sized Papa." I'd almost thought she'd been making it up, but we listened: *I got a man that's more than eight feet tall.* . . .

"You make people pay to look at you in New York," Leila wrote in her tiny messy handwriting. "No problem to make them pay to look at you at home. Better in fact."

But James couldn't make himself do it, and I was inclined to agree. Somehow charging money for posing for photographs was different, a clear transaction. Asking admission to his house was worse. There was a line that you crossed when you decided that you existed for other people. There were a million ways to cross it. You married and changed your name to Mrs. Roger Husband; you went to medical school only because your parents wanted you to. It was a selfishness, to deny yourself like that. I knew. You took care of other people all your days, you gave up your own plans. In these ways you abdicated responsibility: you became an exhibition in someone else's life. Oh, I knew it, I did, and perhaps I didn't like people—haven't I said that enough, that I didn't like people?—but I liked myself a good deal less, I could not bear to be alone, I needed my library patrons, I needed Oscar and Caroline and cranky little Alice and, of course, I needed James above everybody else. If I'd had the choice, if people were offering, I would have charged admission to myself. Maybe it would have made more people interested.

But James was better than me. In every way he was better, and I didn't want him to succumb to needing either strangers or their lousy spare change.

•

"Alice," James said. "Come here." Now that Alice walked, she sometimes came toddling down the path to drag Kazoo to the front house for a visit. That made the cat worth something,

James thought; any creature who brought Alice around was worth something. He asked Caroline and Oscar to bring some of her toys and books over to the cottage.

"Yah?" she said. She came up to the edge of the bed.

"How are you, Alice?"

"Good. You sick?"

"No. Will you read me a story?"

Alice went to get a book. She couldn't read yet, of course, but one didn't dare tell her that. She climbed on the bed from the seat of the step-chair Caroline had brought over for this purpose.

"There were dogs," she said. James closed his eyes. "And they got in a car and they drove away, and then they crashed and they crashed and they crashed and they crashed." She stopped for a minute, fingering the page.

"Then what?" James asked.

"And they crashed and they crashed and then they got up and they turned around and they crashed and they crashed and they crashed."

"A sad story," said James.

"No-oo-o," said Alice, looking at the book. Then she let it slide off her lap onto the floor, where it flopped spine up. I went to retrieve and close it.

"Peggy doesn't like it when you treat books that way," James said. But Alice didn't look at me. She crawled up to James's face and began to pat it, as if it were one of those crashing dogs.

"Good girl," Alice said, patting James.

"Me or you?" James asked. "I'm not a girl, and I'm not sure how good I am. Maybe you mean Kazoo." The cat was asleep on the far corner of the bed.

"She's a girl," I said. "But she's definitely not good."

"Good girl," said Alice. She had her palm open, dabbing at James's face. "Good, good girl."

Now I can look back on those days six months after New York and see he was dying. Although strictly speaking he wasn't—there was nothing for him to be dying of yet. Height wouldn't kill him, after all; it was just that his height made him susceptible to other things. But he was weakening, worn out. I sat by his bed some evenings while he napped. The circus invited him to go to Boston for the 1959 spring tour, and he wanted to—now he was interested in all cities and their mysteries. I stuck signs on the cottage door that told the tourists to go away, but they still pressed their faces to the window, still knocked on the glass. If James was asleep, I didn't even turn my head to look at them. They thought I was stubborn or deaf. That was fine.

When he was awake, he'd call out in his thick husky voice, "Come in." They would, but he wasn't so interesting when he was in bed. Impressive still, but even tourists turned uncomfortable in the company of a man under a blanket, a sick man. The room smelled like an old quilt, a mixture of history and mildew and a huge, on-the-blink body. They didn't know what was wrong with him. They thought he was dying of too much of himself. "Some place," they'd say, looking around, and then they'd hustle their children out. Only when he sat in the armchair—shabby now, after several years of teenage use, even looking a little small for him—would they stay and talk.

One night I sat there reading. At least, I had a book open on my lap. Kazoo, growing out of kittenhood, jumped on top of the book, and then up to the bed. She dug her claws into my arm to push off.

"Bad cat," I said to her.

James opened his eyes. "Good cat," he said absentmindedly. "Are you torturing Peggy? Good cat."

"Rotten animal, through and through." I put my hand out, hoping just once she'd walk under it to be scratched—she did it for everyone else—but she rubbed up against James's shoulder instead.

He made a clicking noise with his tongue, and the cat sniffed his nose, then curled up beneath his chin. "Aunt Caroline says I should be careful, I'll roll over in my sleep and kill her."

"Doubtful," I said.

"I don't roll over. I'm too heavy. The cat's safe anyhow. She likes to sleep on my pillow."

"She knows that's where you live."

"What do you mean?"

"In your head," I told him. "You live in your head. Everybody lives somewhere in their body. Hands, heart, private parts. Some people live anyplace but their head. Remember Patty Flood? She, I believe, lived in Jesus."

"Where do you live?"

"Oh," I said. I didn't answer.

"You have a habit," he told me, "of asking questions of others that make yourself blush."

"That much is true."

"Where do you live, Peggy?"

"Me?" I closed my book and looked at him. "I live in a whole other room from my body. I live down the block."

"Not really," he said.

I put down the book and climbed up to sit on the edge of the bed. The cat jumped off. She didn't even pretend to like me. "My body is a dull place. Who'd choose to live here?"

"I might," he said. "If I could move. But here I am." He pulled one arm free from the covers; his pajama top was striped a cool blue. "At least the view was good. And you. I think I know where you live."

"Where?"

He slapped his right leg, three times. "Here. Me. Vicariously, I mean. Bad choice. You should have picked someone who has more fun."

"You have fun," I said. A stupid comment.

But he said, "Yes, sometimes." He put his hand on mine. I held it a second.

I didn't know what would happen next.

"You should go back to sleep," I said.

"I wasn't asleep. I was just sort of pretending to give you some time off. When I'm awake, you feel obligated to talk to me." He threw the blankets off the top half of his body. "But I don't know what people sound like sleeping. You know—I try to get the breathing right, but I don't know how it goes. Then I thought maybe I'd talk in my sleep to entertain you. My mother did that. I don't remember what she said, but sometimes I'd hear her voice from the other room. Is that common? Do people talk in their sleep as often as they snore?"

"I think everyone eventually does," I said. "I guess. I've watched you sleep enough, but you haven't talked yet."

"Another thing I don't know. When you stop and think, there's a lot I'm stupid about."

"Me, too."

"You?" he said. "You've lived more a life than me. You know a lot of things."

"I don't think so," I said. I held on to his thumb. "I think everything worthwhile I know I probably learned from you."

"There's a lot of things you know that I don't. I don't know what people say in their sleep. I don't know how to ice skate. I've never been in a plane. I don't know—I don't know what somebody looks like when they're about to kiss you."

"Like this," I said, and just like that, I leaned in and kissed him. One short kiss on the cheek. He hadn't shaved lately; he did that in his bed, a towel across his chest and a mirror leaning on his knee, though he never had much of a beard. Then a kiss on the mouth. And then I looked at him, and I was about to kiss him again, for real. For real, whatever that means. But he caught me as I was leaning in, he put his hand on my shoulder.

"It's too late," he said.

I nodded. But then I had to ask, "Too late for what?"

"It's too late, Peggy."

I put my own hand on his shoulder. I tried to çurl my fingers around, but there was too much of it. "You should go to sleep." I'd wanted—at that moment—to kiss him because I thought he should be kissed, but maybe it was better he didn't know. No, it wasn't better. I wanted to give him something that could make him forget he was a young man, dying; I wanted to give him a kiss so good he'd forget it was his first. But I wasn't the woman for that kind of work. I imagined getting Stella to help me out again, though she was long gone, married and a student at a college in Maryland; even so I imagined calling her up and explaining my problem.

Then James reached up and smoothed my hair—it was late, I'd taken it down—smoothed it on either side of my face, with just the tips of his fingers. It was the sweetest way he'd ever touched me, so planned and a little clumsy.

"I guess you didn't want to marry me after all," he said.

"I did. I wanted to, but you didn't."

He closed his eyes, smiling. His hand was still by the side of my face. "But I think I did. I mean, obviously I love you."

Then I leaned forward and kissed him, and this time he didn't push me away. *Obviously he loved me*. His lips were hot and his mouth was dry and I had my hand on his shoulder; he let his teeth part a little. He didn't know quite how to do it. When I sat up, his eyes were still closed.

"We could still get married," he said.

"You're not dressed for it. I think even Leila would frown on pajamas at a wedding."

"When I'm feeling better. In Boston, maybe. Leila could be there."

I wanted to kiss him again, but he had his hand on my cheek, bracing me up. His eyes were open a little. I could see how chapped his lips were, though I hadn't felt it.

"When I'm feeling better," he repeated.

"You look tired," I said.

"You must be tired yourself, saying that so much. Lie down." With some effort, he scooted himself over; first his hip, then the rest of him. "We're going to Boston soon. You need to get some rest. Lie down with me and take a nap."

So I did, my back to him. He'd stretched out one arm for me to lie down on.

"So that's what people look like," he said.

I was quiet.

"Who was the last man you kissed?"

"You," I said.

He laughed. "Before that."

"I only remember the last boy I've kissed."

"Come on, Peggy."

"It's been a while. Since college."

"Did you love him?"

"No," I said.

"Did he love you?"

"No. That's why I didn't love him."

"Tell me."

"Just a boy," I said. "A philosophy major. A nice boy, nice enough."

"Does he have a name?"

"I don't remember. George Baker. You aren't interested."

"I am," James said, and I could tell by his voice that he was.

"He was older by a couple of years. Too handsome for the likes of me."

"And you kissed him."

"Yes," I said. "I kissed him."

I remembered the way this boy had kissed; it didn't seem like a good story. He didn't like deep kisses at all, just gentle slow ones, our lips and tongues just touching. Lovely one-note kisses. He'd recently broken up with his longtime sweetheart. I liked those kisses, but I wanted other sorts, too: bruising, end-of-movie kisses, someone saved from a villain or shipwreck in the arms of another who suddenly realizes *everything*. Impolite kisses. A catalog that I could now describe to James, to let him know there are as many kinds of kisses as there are kinds of conversation. But no matter how I tried to convince that boy otherwise with my mouth, he went back to his gentle kissing. Finally I concluded that I was at fault, I simply didn't know how to kiss. That, of course, was not the problem. The problem was that his mouth had just come from a five-year stint with somebody else's, somebody who'd taught him to kiss that way in the first place. The problem was he was giving me some other girl's kisses.

"I kissed him," I said again. "It was a long time ago. I didn't love him, but I kissed him."

I could feel James shifting behind me. "I'm trying to see your face," he said. "I think maybe you did love him."

What could I do for him?

All he wanted was something of a fair return. For years he'd lived, and I'd had something of a life because of that; I'd had a job and a purpose. Maybe all he wanted was a small piece of me. Oh, I should have greedily taken his proposal the night it was offered. We should have called Leila to the Hotel Astor, told her to bring a minister and a bouquet. In the time it would have taken her to taxi over we could have dressed. I could have combed my hair. He was so warm in that bed we wouldn't have had to light the furnace all our married life.

I turned my head and looked at James. "You're right. I loved him. He had green eyes. He played the trumpet."

"Good," said James. He let himself fall back to the pillows. I thought I felt him kiss the back of my head. "I'm glad. Where is he now?"

"I don't know. Last I heard, somewhere in the South." I closed my eyes.

"A southern boy?"

"Yes, damn him."

And then I felt James's hand on my hip. I had forgotten that I owned a hip that could be touched instead of merely clothed. That sounds odd, I know, but when I said I didn't live in my own body, I wasn't lying. James's magnetic hand pulled my steely self out of that formerly abandoned hip, and then rolled it down the slope of my hip to my waist, to my rib cage. And to the back of my neck, where I could feel his humid breath. He had a touch of pneumonia, though I didn't know it then.

"He probably loved you back," said James. "He was just too shy to say it."

I tried to concentrate on that lost southern boy—to concentrate, as I always had, on what was being said instead of what was actually happening. "This boy wasn't too shy to say anything," I said.

James's other hand—the one attached to the arm under me—reached up. Tentatively, it touched both my breasts. Well then. Something was happening, even I was not too dumb to notice. He kept that hand there and with the other drew my skirt up and touched my hip again.

I tried to turn over.

"Hold still, Peggy."

I didn't want to. I bumped my head into his chin.

"Ow!" I felt him laugh into my shoulder. "I'm not very good at this—"

"Who is?" I asked. He was holding me still with the weight of the arm reaching around me, intrigued by my stockings, the waistband of my underwear—the dullest underwear in the world, I was a woman who patched everything for longer use. "I just want—"

"Peggy," he said. "Peggy, be quiet. There isn't anything more you can do for me."

"I'm going to fall asleep here," I said later. By then, I'd rolled over to look at him. We were still dressed—me partly, him completely. Without his glasses he had an untroubled, hopeful look. Only twenty, and he already had the hint of wrinkles, a line on one side of his mouth. But that didn't bother me; in fact, I liked it. It was evidence that he was growing older, that he wouldn't die in childhood.

"You should," said James.

But I couldn't fall asleep like that; years of falling asleep, of living alone, made me claustrophobic at the worst times. I turned my back to him again and settled; I thought there was plenty of time to get used to things. I would regret turning later, but what wouldn't I regret?

James asked, "What do people say in their sleep?"

It had been so long. There was only that one boy I'd ever spent the whole night with, and as far as I knew he never said anything. But maybe I hadn't been paying attention. Maybe, so pleased with everything, I'd slept soundly, paying attention only to myself. If I'd been told, all those years ago, that this would be it, I would have learned it, the way if somebody said of a song I loved, *you will never hear this again*, I would try to memorize every little false note and trill and would play it in my head until it became my favorite song, until I was the one singing it.

"They talk nonsense," I said. "And when you repeat it back in the morning, they don't remember dreaming anything close."

"Go to sleep." I felt his arm move beneath me, then relax. "Say something."

"What do you want me to say?"

"I mean later. When you're sleeping. Try to talk in your sleep. Make something up."

The Altitude of Man

He died.

He died, of course.

He died, not that night, the one I fell asleep on his arm and slept soundly. I don't know whether he did, too—it was only nine at night when he made room for me, half a day before his usual bedtime—but when I woke at five the next morning, his arm was still beneath me, and his faint snores weren't much different from his speaking voice. I got up and went home alone to change for work.

He died a week after this, two weeks before the circus hit Boston. Feeling better, he'd gone into town by himself. He did that every now and then, to admire a store's high ceilings, get a touch of admiration from the tourists. Ever since New York, he'd liked that: seeing people watch him, people who hadn't been forewarned.

He went to the little grocery store in town to buy a Coke. There were two tourists there, men from Boston, getting things for a picnic in a more picturesque town than ours. They filled their baskets with packages of cheese, a loaf of Italian bread wrapped in white wax paper, and then they caught sight of what looked impossible: a man whose body had refused to stop, an ambitious body, beyond what they'd imagined architecturally feasible. First they thought it was some kind of costume, two men dressed up in a dark suit, a papier-mâché head on top of the top man. Was it advertising something? Wasn't it hot in there, hard to balance?

Then the thing said something. "Mary," it said, "could you open that for me, please?" The clerk pried off the crown cap of the Coke; it plunked off the glass and fell into a basket beneath the counter. The tourists realized in steps. The face was real, the head was real, that whole enormous span of body was a true thing, no fake, no hoax. He smiled at them, then turned to the door. Still precarious looking, as he bent down his head to leave, started across the parking lot. You could understand why people thought at first he was two men: he moved like that. Like each part of him was a piece of furniture a little heavy for the rest, his Laurel and Hardy legs moving his piano-torso down a flight of stairs. Clearly his body regretted agreeing to this unwise proposition, getting James across the street.

It was halfway across the street that he fell, about two blocks from the library. Nobody came running to get me. He would have told them to, I think he would have, but he had a sudden fever and was not making much sense. The tourists got to him first; they dropped their bread and cheese in the middle of the street, as if they were the ones who'd fallen. Then Mary from the market arrived. She called the ambulance and then Oscar and Caroline. The paramedics couldn't get him on a stretcher; he was too heavy, he wouldn't fit. The tourists—they were good people, real estate brokers on vacation—said they'd help to lift him. The doors wouldn't close. By this time James was back in the world, and Oscar was there.

"I want to go home," James said. "I'm fine, I just want to sleep."

"Think you better go to the hospital, Jim," Oscar said. "You look terrible."

"I feel *fine*," said James. "I just want to sleep."

So he sat up on the floor of the ambulance and they closed the doors and drove him home.

I found out an hour later, when two boys came into the library. "You hear about the giant?" one said to another. "Got hit by a car."

"Naw, he tripped over some kid," said his friend. "Killed 'im."

"What?" I said. "What are you talking about?"

"That giant fell on some kid and killed him. Squashed him flat," said the second boy.

"Did *not*," said the first.

I immediately called the Stricklands.

"Oh, good, Peggy," said Caroline.

"What's happened?"

"Jim had a little accident. Nothing serious. He fell in town, didn't hurt himself, but I think he must be sick—he's sweating, he feels terrible. We can't get him to go to the hospital. Oscar's over there now. We were just about to call you. Maybe—could you get away from work? Is this a good time?"

"Of course it is, of course I can." I wondered where Astoria was, I wondered exactly how fast I could get out. "In a couple of minutes." And then, as I hung up the phone, I did something I'd never done before: I yelled in my library. I didn't care who heard me.

"Astoria!" I hollered. "Come here! I need your help!"

She came running up on her pointy little movie-star shoes. "What is it?"

"Take the desk. I need to go. I don't know when I'll be back."

I left her there, calling after me. "Peggy? Just wait a minute, Peggy—"

He wasn't asleep when I got there. I thought he would be; I'd imagined I'd have a few moments to think, to discuss things with Oscar.

"Peggy!" Oscar said. "How nice!"

"I'm not going," said James. "I don't have to."

"I'll just leave the two of you alone," said Oscar. "I'll be over at the house."

"Had a fall?" I said.

"I had a fall," said James. "Then I got up, and I came home, and I want to recover *here*."

I put my hand on his head. "You have a fever," I said.

"Well Jesus, Peggy, maybe I have the flu like a normal person. Maybe I feel a little lousy, and I fell because of that—my balance isn't great in the *first* place—and now, like a normal person, I want to sleep in my bed and drink orange juice and feel better in a few days. If there's anything that'll make me feel worse, it's being in a hospital."

I nodded. Maybe he was right—how could I tell?

"Okay," I said. "Do you mind if I stay?"

He sighed. "I don't plan on being real entertaining."

"I've watched you sleep before," I said, "and you're right, you're not exactly enthralling."

"Okay." He gave me a grudging smile. "I'm going to sleep now."

"I've been warned."

He took off his glasses and set them on the windowsill beside his bed. When he was asleep, I called Astoria and asked if she could handle the library by herself. I was sorry, I said, I knew I had taken a lot of time off lately—

"Peggy," she said softly. "You've barely taken off any. How much vacation time do you think you've got stored up?"

"No idea."

"Call town hall," she said. "I bet it's a record."

And then I sat there and watched him. Maybe this was the night he'd talk in his sleep. I even thought I'd claim he did; I thought he'd like that. Caroline came over at dinnertime with some soup and crackers for both of us.

"How's the patient doing?" she asked.

"Okay, I think. Maybe tomorrow morning we can take him to the hospital, when he's not so scared. I think the fall shook him up."

"Naturally," she said.

"Naturally."

An hour later James said something. I thought he *was* talking in his sleep, and I leaned closer to hear what he said. It was my name. Then he opened his eyes.

"Peggy," he said. He put out his hand. I moved closer, put my hand in his. "Don't," he began, and I took my hand away, but that wasn't what he meant, he closed his hand around mine, made it disappear, and held on.

What he said was, "Don't let them boil me."

"What are you talking about?"

His eyes were glossy, strange paperweights in his face. "Like Charles Byrne."

"Who?"

"You gave me a book," he said. "A long time ago. Charles Byrne. He was a giant and he always thought this doctor, I forgot his name, was going to steal his body and boil it for the skeleton."

"What a thing to be thinking of," I said.

"And then he died and he'd paid his friends to take care of him but the doctor got his friends drunk and stole Byrne's body anyhow and now it's in some museum hospital. You think they'll try that? With me?"

I felt his forehead. It was slick and warm. "How do you feel?"

"Don't let them. They want my bones."

"Nobody wants your bones. They just want you to get well."

"Peggy," he said, "don't let them boil me!"

"I won't," I said. "I promise."

Then he started to shiver. Not the way I'd ever seen anyone shiver in my life, a brief electrical jolt that can be explained by anything, medicine or superstition: a goose stepping on your grave, your body working up heat. This was ongoing shuddering.

"I'm cold," he said, and God help me, that explained everything. He was cold. He needed to be warmer. Later I would know it was the sign of a fever spiking; maybe I knew that before, too. But at that moment, standing next to his bed, all I knew was that he was shivering like someone who was cold, and that he said he was cold. This was something I could solve, despite the fact that all my suspicions were confirmed: me, my careless supplying of books, was the source of all his habitual nightmares.

I pulled the covers up, right to his ears. I unfolded an afghan and draped it over him. He still shivered. "I'm so cold," he said, and I went to the closet and got his overcoat out and threw that over the blankets. I arranged the tweed arms like a muffler around his neck.

"How's that?"

He nodded. Soon he fell back asleep. He didn't shiver in his sleep. Tomorrow morning I'd call the doctor over. Maybe he could talk some sense into James. I wondered why I hadn't thought of that before.

I'd lied, of course. Somebody did want his bones: me. Not just bones, or the quilted muscles that wrapped them, or the resistant but assailable cartilage in his ears. I wanted to ladle together my hands and dip them in him and cast from my netted fingers a net of blood onto the floor to read, untangle what was wrong and fish it out, *see, no wonder you felt poorly,* this *was in your blood*. Hard work will solve all problems. I imagined fingering white and red cells as if they were beads, sorting them.

Not just blood, or flesh—everybody wants that. I was worse than vampire, worse than cannibal. I wanted everything. *Every* cell of him, an airy room with an atrium and walls you could hear the neighbors through. I would have stuck my face into his to get the curiously cold mist off a sneeze. I wanted the ephemeral oxygen that visited his lungs and exited, deflowered. His urine, which (this is a scientific fact) was sterile. I would have taken his shit—there should be a lovely word for it; the ones I know are clinical or vulgar—I would have taken what his body had deliberated over and rejected as useless. And I would have been amazed: it had been somewhere I could not venture, another part of him I could not know.

By now you think I sound desperate and sick. I'm just cataloguing all the things I could not have, *desiderata, desiderata*. By now you are tired of me insisting, *but it wasn't sex*. Well, it was, in this way: all I wanted was to become a part of him, to affect him physically. Maybe that's all anybody ever wants, and sex is the most specific and efficient way to achieve it.

But that night I did not want sex. I wanted to drape myself over his body and be absorbed, so when I left (and I knew I would have to), we would average out: two moderately cold people, two moderately sickly people, two—well, two extraordinarily tall people. Still the two tallest people you'd ever seen. But we'd have each other, we'd share that burden.

I was tired. A week before I'd slept in that room, in bed with James, and for a minute I considered climbing in with him again. But there really wasn't room, not unless he made it for me, and I didn't want to disturb his sleep. I reached under the blanket and felt his ankle, which, because of his bad circulation, was cold. I gave it a rub to warm it up, but it was too big a job and I was exhausted. Finally I crawled into the big armchair and curled up. And in the morning, when Caroline came in with Alice and breakfast, I was the only one who woke up.

Whatever Was Essential

Taking care of James was difficult work when he was alive, but at least he was there to help us. Caroline took Alice back to the house and got Oscar. I could hear the two of them, Alice and Caroline, crying from the front house. Probably Alice was crying only because her mother was. Finally we had to call a neighbor to go sit with them. Then we phoned a funeral home two towns over.

I went back to the cottage. Most of the covers, including the overcoat, were in a hill on the ground. Oscar had pulled the sheet over James's head, the way they do in movies, and I thought this was wrong. Doctors do that, or clergymen. Standing there, I thought it was as if Oscar had tried to improvise the last rites because a priest wasn't available.

So I walked to the bed. Beneath that sheet, he was still in his street clothes, the shirt and pants he'd fallen in. He's dead, I thought, that's a simple fact. It wasn't him anymore. Anything I decided to believe, science or religion, told me that whatever was essential to his existence was gone now, soul or cold mechanical bloodworks. The sheet lay flat along the length of him, not moving at his mouth, nor at the rib cage over his lungs, nor at his hands or knees. It was still. *Whatever was essential.* That was the problem, what scientists and ministers forgot. It was all essential. *His soul has departed the earth,* the minister would say later, and I wanted to answer, but his soul forgot something, his soul didn't pack for that long trip. I thought I was thinking of his body; really, I was thinking of myself. The two things, my self, his body, were not distinct entities. This is how I'd always allowed myself to love him: I hired on as caretaker of his body, because his self, his soul if that's what you wanted to call it, had no reason to need me. I needed to be essential, too, but I was still here, I hadn't gone, I was standing by the bed, my hand still out to the sheet. He had done an awful lot in the past twenty-four hours without my permission.

No profit to this thinking, I told myself, *so stop it.* I could not lift the sheet. What was I doing? That's right, waiting for the men from the funeral home, better get ready. This place needs dusting, I thought, and I opened the top right desk drawer, where I kept a cloth. I dusted the sashes of the windows, the roses Oscar had painted; I spat on the cloth and rubbed at a stubborn spot.

I had my back to him. Can I tell you something? It wasn't so bad. Not so bad at all right then, me scowling at the dirt, James in his bed, the way it always always was. Look, if that's all that happened, if his dying just meant that I would be waiting for him to say something instead of listening to him say something, it would have been fine.

But then Oscar arrived. He walked to me, took the cloth from my hand. And still, if he hadn't said anything I could have gone on and got the cottage ready for whoever would come by to visit.

"Peggy," he said, his voice not up to even these dumb syllables. It was Oscar's breathy bad voice that made dusting seem like the wrong thing to be doing. "Let's wait somewhere else," he said. "Let's not stay here." And he put his arm around me, dropped the cloth to the floor, and led me to the front house.

Caroline had Alice on her lap, Alice had a book on hers. They weren't looking at the book. The neighbor we'd called came in carrying coffee.

"Oh!" she said, when she saw me. She hoisted the pot. "Would you like some?"

I shook my head.

"I'm making cookies," she said. She was alternately smiling and looking grief-stricken, not sure what her role in all this was. "I mean, I'm about to." She was a nice woman, wearing one of Caroline's gingham aprons. She stuck her hand in its heart-shaped pocket. "Maybe Alice would like to help me."

"Maybe," said Caroline. But she didn't look like she wanted to let go of her daughter anytime soon.

"Cookies," said Oscar. He sat down on the sofa and patted the cushion next to him. I sat down.

"This isn't right," I said to him.

"No. Of course not."

"No," I said. "We should be doing something."

"There's nothing to do, Peggy."

"There's something." I rubbed my hands on my knees. And then he took my hands in his and held them in such a way I could believe he needed them, that I was being useful, lending Oscar my hands.

Is it possible that I knew all along that he'd die, that he'd be taken away from me, and that's why I'd loved him? I don't mean in any selfless way, but in the most selfish, the way that so many of us—we unhappy, I mean—want only to assure ourselves and the world that our unhappiness is justified and real. This is why the dying are so easy to love: it's a magician's trick, a paper vase with an invisible sleeve. Did I love him because I knew this moment would come, when James, who I'd poured my love into, would be gone, because I knew my love, my pourable love, was limited, and if I'd decanted it into someone whose prognosis was better I would have run out by our fifteenth anniversary (is that tin? paper? steel?) and would have then become the bitter empty person everyone knew I was destined to be, only with the company of my unfortunate husband?

Maybe I'd loved him because I knew he'd leave me. Maybe, once. It wasn't worth it.

We hadn't explained things to the funeral home, and they'd sent over a regular-sized hearse. "My God," the driver said. "*This* is who it is?" He folded his arms across his chest. "No way. No way to do this."

"Yes, there is," I said. And they seemed to believe me. With Oscar's help they lifted him to the back of the hearse, tied the doors shut.

"We'll take him to the hospital—" one man started.

"What?" said Oscar. "Why? Is he—"

"No," the guy said, and then, more gently, "No. But we need to get him declared dead by a doctor." And they drove down the street, neighbors watching from their porches, and took James away from us.

I stood there, waiting for him to sit up, part the pleated curtains of the back window. Those curtains looked like coffin lining—why did the dead need so many folds of fabric, so much luxurious privacy, everywhere they traveled? I waited for him to wave at me. He didn't, of course. I went back to the cottage and made his bed. I crawled into it for a second, wanting warmth. But it had been hours since anything warm had been in that bed, the sheets were cold, and I did not want to be the one to warm them.

What killed him was an infection caused by a brace rubbing his leg, the sore spot so far away from his brain he never felt it at all. This is not poetic fancy, but fact: the news from his leg was never delivered. He hadn't noticed that he'd lost feeling that far up. Neither had we.

He was just three months past twenty, eight foot seven inches, four hundred and fifteen pounds.

There were other things to do. Funeral arrangements, for instance. Caroline took charge of that. He needed two burial plots. There was money—James's circus money—to buy them, but the ones for sale were by themselves, away from family. Caroline and Oscar donated theirs, by James's fat nephritic grandmother and limping arthritic grandfather. With the money they bought themselves a spot in the new part of the cemetery, knowing they would eventually have each other for company.

The funeral was attended by neighbors, reporters, friends, even the real estate brokers who saw him fall. Stella came up from Maryland with her husband and, incredibly, a baby, plump and pink-cheeked and pretty like her mother. I did not talk to her, nor to the reporters, not even to Caroline and Oscar. They had asked me to sit in the front with them—wasn't I family? Didn't I know by now I was?—but I said my heart couldn't take that. "The front of a church is not the front of a roller coaster, Peggy," Caroline said gently, "it's going to be bad no matter where you sit." I thought differently. A stranger might have concluded that I worked for the church or the funeral home, standing as I did at the door welcoming people, handing out programs; sitting as I did at the back, by myself, so I could see what was going on; comforting, as I did, some old lady who didn't even know him but had shown up after seeing the obit in the paper. "He was so young," she said, sobbing into my shoulder, "so young, and such an unhappy life. God is strange. God is good, but God is strange."

For the second time, James made *Time*'s "Milestones" column.

He left a will, of sorts. Any money in the bank was to stay there for Alice's education. The cottage belonged to Oscar and Caroline; only sensible, since it stood on their property. Anything else—letters, paintings, books—was left to me. I could do what I wanted with them, though he hoped I would consider requests from friends who wanted souvenirs. He'd underlined the word *friends*. Dr. Calloway called from Illinois, wanting to buy some things. "I have quite a collection of memorabilia, and I'd be interested in adding some of James's effects," he said.

"Dr. Calloway?" I said. "Doctor? Go to hell." He hung up on me immediately; I knew he was that sort of man.

You seem to be taking all of this very well, somebody said to me. I don't remember who it was. That person was wrong, although I didn't know it then. I was taking it the worst possible way.

I believed then that the thought *James is dead* would be the key that swung open my heart and then broke off in the lock. It would ruin me. I believed I was making a choice. I could carry on, I could do my work and think of him and iron my clothes in the morning; or I could become so wrecked by grief that I wandered the streets, my fingers stuck in my hair and my hair stuck in my mouth, strangers running from me as I said, *wait a minute, I only want to tell you about somebody.* I thought these were the only two paths before me, that they diverged so wildly that, as I stepped onto the sensible ordered path, my lifelong choice, I would not see or think of the other path again; it would lead to another neighborhood entirely. I did not know that walking on one, I would be always in sight of the other; that they crossed one another sooner rather than later; and then crossed each other again, and again.

I offered my help to Caroline in closing up the cottage. "We'll leave it for a while," she said. That put me out of a job. I boxed up my inheritances without looking at them, emptied his desk drawers, rolled up paintings, and put them in my car.

And then I went home to my apartment.

Part Three

The Reverse Orphan

Caroline opened the cottage as a museum three weeks after James died. Oscar painted a sign that said, JAMES CARLSON SWEATT HOME, and then, in smaller letters, (THE GIANT'S HOUSE). They hung this in front of their house, visible from the street, so that visitors knew to come there first, pay their admission, and wait for the tour.

Some people thought that was heartless. At first I was one of them. But in fact Caroline was just being sensible. The tourists still came by, as they had when James was alive, and now they were insistent. They didn't understand that, were James living, they'd be invited in only through his good graces. They acted like the cottage was some sort of national landmark, and that Oscar and Caroline's reluctance to let them in was actionable.

Caroline explained it to me this way: "If I just sent them back, they'd think anything. Nobody there to stop them. But if I go, if I make it a tour, I can say things. I can explain who he was, and they have to listen to me."

Caroline didn't do a thing to the cottage, didn't bother to dust or put away the huge shoes, one in the kitchen, another nosing the threshold of the back door. It was like they were on their way out, she told the tourists, looking for the one pair of feet in the world they'd ever fit. That was like her: turn every casual thing into something to be remarked upon.

"Custom made," she said. "Well, everything he owned was. James Carlson Sweatt wasn't made for anything store bought."

She charged fifty cents for adults, a quarter for children, and sat in her own house waiting for someone to knock on her door. She was pregnant again, and this was perfect work for her. All day long she knit, put her knitting down, picked it back up. Sometimes the tourists were so desperate for souvenirs they admired her work and offered to buy it before she even took them out back to see the house itself. She stuck their money in the pocket of her shirt and led them through her own house, living room to kitchen to back door, and across a little patch of grass to the Giant's House.

His glasses on the windowsill above his bed—had he taken them off to die?—were as big as horses' blinders. That's what the tourists wanted to hear, *as big as*. They didn't care about *Big enough to fit him* or *Couldn't ride in a plane*. You would think seeing the things themselves would drive out all thoughts of comparison, but the tourists craved those easy metaphors, wanted more, didn't even care if they were true. Those glasses got bigger and bigger. As big as a child's first bicycle; one lens the size of a toboggan.

He hadn't taken them off to die. He took them off to sleep, I watched him do it.

The tourists skulked into the corners of the cottage, giggling, wanting to find the bathroom. Sometimes they asked.

Generally, of course, James used the front house—no endorsements for oversized commodes, so he went without—but toward the end he sometimes had to rely on bedpans. He was an invalid, after all.

It was a reasonable question. But she could never think of a way to make it sound natural, not so bad.

"Closed to the public," she always said. "Tour's over."

* * *

So there was something else for me to think about: how to turn the cottage into a proper museum. I'd have the paintings framed, maybe some newspaper clippings, too. We'd make up a plaque describing his life. I imagined scripting a tour, instead of the jumble of facts ("he liked birds; he read a lot of books; I never heard him sing") that Caroline presented. There were clippings I could frame, photographs—dozens of the celebrated man's late mother, who hadn't even lived to see the cottage, never mind set foot in it. But I couldn't look through the papers until we decided to really make it a tourist attraction. I couldn't start until I had to, not until it was a job and there was some purpose to it.

Caroline didn't want anything formal. "He's not history yet, Peggy, even if the tourists think he is. It's just his house, still."

"But if we made it professional," I said.

"No. Someday in the future, maybe. Not yet."

The difference was that Caroline hadn't spent that much time there, and now she was there several times a day. If she left it James's house, she could believe he might be coming up the front walk for dinner at any moment. When she took tourists over, she could pretend he had just stepped out, he was at the library, out watching birds. Don't move anything, he'll be back, he wants everything just so.

But I had once been there several times a day, and now not at all, and I wanted the cottage changed. If we turned it into a museum, moved those heartbreaking shoes and made the bed again and put solid framed things on the wall, maybe then I wouldn't wake up in the morning, wanting to walk over. Maybe I wouldn't sit at my kitchen table at night, still waiting for the phone to ring.

Unlike Caroline, I could not bear to keep thinking he might walk in at any moment, because every moment of the rest of my life he wouldn't be, he wouldn't walk through that door, he wouldn't telephone me, and I had to stop expecting he would.

* * *

So some days after work I stopped by to make my case. I never went to the cottage; I relied on Caroline's descriptions of its success. They banked all the money in Alice's account. One Friday, two months after James's death, I heard Caroline talking to someone in the dining room as I walked through the front door.

The man Caroline was speaking with turned and looked at me. He had round blue eyes and a slightly ashen face, fluffy hair that stood out in peaks. He smiled at me.

"Peggy," Caroline said. "This is my brother, Calvin."

"We've met," he said. Then he said to himself, almost immediately afterward, "No, we haven't."

"You haven't met," said Caroline. "You were long gone by the time Peggy moved to town."

Caroline's brother. She didn't look happy to see him. Then I realized: James's father. Mrs. Sweatt's husband. *Your father, C. Sweatt.*

"Yes," I said. "You've been gone a long time."

"Hometowns," he said. "Sometimes they get pretty scary when you think about them. But I figured it was time to come see where Jimmy lived."

"Well. I guess it's bad news for you. He's dead."

"I know that," said the man.

"He knows," said Caroline softly. "He's here for his fucking inheritance. He's here for the money."

"Not like that, Carrie," he said. "I just asked if there was any."

I leaned on the doorjamb and rubbed my forehead. Caroline sat down at the table across from her brother.

She said, "Well then, you have your answer. No, none."

"None?" The man smiled at me. "Circus, shoe stores? All those journalists, wanting to know the story?"

"Clothes," Caroline said. "Furniture. Medical expenses. *Coffin.*" She looked at the man. "Specially made coffin. Cemetery said he needed a double plot."

"End to end?"

She shook her head. "Diagonal. Concrete for the coffin."

"Concrete?"

"To keep the curious—kids, doctors, entrepreneurs—from digging up the body."

"Nobody would do that," said Mr. Sweatt.

"It's happened before. He wasn't taking any chances, and rightly so. It was his money."

"Maybe. He was my son."

"What could he owe you?"

"Respect." He gave the kitchen table a cheerful thump. "A little respect, and a little remembrance."

"Calvin *Sweatt*," said Caroline. "What for? What did you ever do for him?"

"Genes," said the man. "That's my investment. I supplied half of 'em. I was his father. Look at your daughter. Pretty tall. Must run in the family."

"James favored his mother in every way," I said quietly.

"I have photographs I could show you," Caroline told him. "The two of them had the same face. Wasn't a bit of you anywhere in James."

"Maybe not in the face," he said. "That leaves the body. Law of averages says I'm responsible for a good part of him. Without those genes, would he have been tall? No. Famous? No. Hired by the circus or the shoes people? Got his picture in the paper? Earned a living? No."

"Been happy?" asked Caroline. "Yes."

I looked at this man, who looked back at me, still smiling. "You tell me," he said. "Was he happy?"

I said, "I don't have to tell you anything."

The next day Mr. Sweatt walked into my library. "Ah," he said. "The illustrious librarian."

"Mr. Sweatt. Good morning."

"So far, not so good. Off season in vacationland. I find it depressing. Though not as depressing as the summers. I forget how *small* New England is: it's like the whole place was built by dwarfs," he said. "No offense."

"No," I said. "Well, this isn't the West, that's for sure."

"New York's my town, actually. Full of good-looking people."

"Nice." I turned my back to him.

"So maybe you could show me around town," he said.

"You know this town," I told him. "Didn't you grow up here?"

He took off his hat and twirled it on his hand. "A lot's different. Just here. Now, as I recall, fiction used to be here in the front room. Whydja change that? I figure, fiction is most popular, and you put your biggest mover out front."

"This is a library," I said. "Not a business. We arrange things for space."

"See? Just that's interesting. Tell me more."

"Mr. Sweatt—" I said.

"Cal."

"Mr. Sweatt. Please. I cannot help you."

"Coffee?" he said.

"Across the street. No food or drink allowed in the library."

He sighed deeply, put upon. "I mean, have coffee with me. My son died. I know I don't seem like the kind of man that would bother, but it does. My son died, and my sister won't talk to me, and I come back to my old hometown—suddenly I'm a villain, with nothing to console me, not even my son. I'm a—there must be a word for it; you're a librarian, you tell me—I'm the opposite of an orphan."

"You didn't seem to care about James when he was alive," I said. "So I don't know why you should miss him now that he's gone."

"I did care for him. I did. After I saw him in New York—"

"When did you see him in New York?"

"Oh, what, a year ago? He was in town for the circus thing, and the paper covered it, so I showed up at the hotel. We did meet, you know. In the hotel. The restaurant." His face softened. "You were there, and you were wearing a brown dress. See? I'm not making it up."

I looked at him a little more closely. The drunk man. Louise's friend.

"I didn't introduce myself so well that night. I got scared. But I talked to him in the lobby the next morning, and a couple of times on the phone in his room."

And James had never told me. Would he have? If we'd married, would we on our honeymoon have spilled all those secrets we had kept?

"Talking to him in a hotel a year ago," I said, "is not proof that you cared."

"But not just then. I called him at home, too. His number was BL7-8928. He knew mine, too. Find his address book, I'll betcha I'm in it. He wrote me, too. I have the letters, I can show them to you. Me, I was never too good at that. But a couple, I sent. Was Jimmy a saver?"

"A what?"

"A saver. Did he save things? Letters, I mean. Well, postcards."

"A saver," I said. "Yes, he was. Well, I'll look."

"If Caroline didn't throw 'em out. She's not feeling kindly toward her old brother, I know that much."

"No, she isn't. But I have those things. If he kept them—if you sent them—they're at my apartment."

"You'll find them," he said. "So have coffee with me. I have a couple of questions I need to ask you."

"What about?" I said.

He looked surprised. "Jimmy," he said. "I want to know about my boy."

Why did I agree? I was lonely. And I kept telling myself, James would have wanted me to. My job, I thought, my new job, was not to let this man off the hook.

"Come back at lunch," I said. "I'll answer your questions."

We went to the coffee shop across the street. Mr. Sweatt flirted with the waitress, who was not charmed. Somebody had told this man he was charming, and he believed it, and maybe it would work on some. But not me and not the waitress. He had a strange habit of starting a story and then laughing, as if he thought his own laughter was a sterling endorsement of the quality of what followed.

"Nice hair," he said to me. "Permanent?"

"I hope so," I said.

He laughed. "No, I meant your curls—they a permanent wave?"

"What curls?"

"Curls, wave, whatever you call it. Your hair's got a nice shape to it. Just wondered whether it was natural."

"Entirely," I said.

"So tell me about Jimmy."

"You want me to give you his life story? You have a lot of catching up to do."

"Give me a chance," he said. "Am I a good man? Probably not. A good father? Definitely no. However—" The waitress brought him a bowl of clam chowder. "Thanks, sweetie," he said. "However, as I was saying, I am good at some things. I am a good poker player and a good listener. A world-class listener, in fact. So whatever you want to tell me, you go ahead. The way I figure it—" He reached across the table. For a minute I thought he was going to try to hold my hand, and as appalled as I was I didn't take it out of his way. Instead he picked up the salt. "The way I figure, I need to do some listening and you need to do some talking. We're going to get along fine."

"James," I said. "Well, James." Then I stopped. "I don't know what to say."

"He was a smart kid?"

"Yes, very."

"So tell me about that," he said. "What was he smart about?"

So I started with the books James read, the subjects he followed. Mr. Sweatt gave a low whistle of approval. "And he had friends?" he asked.

"Plenty."

"Plenty of friends," said Mr. Sweatt. "So. Elaborate."

He told the truth: he was a good listener. Mr. Sweatt was, in fact, a ruthless truth-teller. As bad a man as he might have been—and it wasn't that I was revising my opinion of him, exactly—I don't think he ever told a lie. Later I would find four postcards from him in a box marked *Correspondence*; they were badly spelled, clearly written in haste. Instead of using punctuation he merely left large spaces between sentences. I had seen one of them arrive; I hadn't thought of the card since James had died. Truthfully, I hadn't looked through any of those papers; I couldn't believe I now had permission.

Mr. Sweatt listened, and I talked, and when I thought I'd talked myself out, he'd ask me a question that would get me going again. He was a tourist in his son's life, an interested tourist, armed with just enough information to ask the right questions. He smoked cigarettes he rolled himself, smashed them out, and soon the ashtray was filled with the ends of them, tiny scorched bouquets.

A bald man walked by the table. Mr. Sweatt gestured with his coffee cup. "See that? Gimme another ten years, and that's me." He shivered theatrically. "That's my fear, and afraid it's my curse, going bald. My granddad on my mother's side, he was bald, and they say that's what counts. So far, I've been lucky." He caught me looking at his hairline and said, "I've always had this high forehead. Same as it ever was, pretty sure. I keep checking."

It was at that moment I began to like him a little better. In fact, he was going bald. I could see the shape of his skull, the shell-pink scalp, quite clearly when he crossed his arms on the table and set his face down on top, which he did every now and then, brooding or thinking. I never knew anyone else who would do that while you were talking to them. It made me want to brush his head.

"A high forehead is distinguished," I said.

Cal was embarking on the sort of baldness that is most treacherous: the hair to the left and right of the center of his forehead was sneaking back, as if to secretly tryst behind the lock in the middle. Eventually he'd be left with a bare horseshoe path of scalp. He would notice it all of a sudden one day, and it would horrify him.

"So, more," he said. "Tell me more."

"What else?"

"What else is there?"

"Why don't you answer this question for me: why are you here?"

"Well," he said. He shrugged. "I don't know, exactly."

"Money?" I said.

"Oh, *money*," he said. "No. I'll be straight with you. I'd thought maybe there *was* some money. But that was a later thought. I dunno. Maybe a smoke screen."

"You must be desperate for it," I said. "To ask that way."

"No, what makes you think that? What do I have of Jimmy? Not a thing. A couple of letters maybe. I'm a businessman. People think that money is the hardest thing to ask for, but take my word for it: it's the easiest. Now, you tell me, why is that?"

"I don't know."

" 'Cause people can tell you no and there's no hard feelings, or they give it to you and it's yours to spend. You ask for anything else in this world, and what happens? The answer might be no, or the answer might be a lie, or the answer might be a can of worms you don't want to open. Ask for a compliment, ask for love, ask for an explanation or an apology—either you don't get it, or what you get's counterfeit. But money: if it exists, you might get it, and it'll be as good as the money you get anywhere else. Look," he said. "Jimmy was my family, and I never forgot that. If I'd died before he did, who do you think would've gotten *my* money?"

"No idea."

"Jimmy! Of course. We were each other's closest relatives." He dribbled some coffee down his tie. "Damn," he said, dipping his napkin in his water glass. "I can't eat a thing without getting it all over myself. Well, I'll never starve. I can just boil my clothing for soup."

"So money's not why you came," I said.

"No, no. I came back because I missed my family. I mean I guess now I've *missed* my family, my wife and my son, I've missed that chance. But there's still my sister and my niece, and I should probably say hello to them before it's too late."

"Why did you leave in the first place?" I asked.

"Ah," he said. "The tables have turned. Okay, I'll answer your questions. But I want you to promise me something. I want to see Jimmy's paintings, his photographs. I asked Caroline; she said you have them all. I thought maybe I could get one. She says there's lots."

That stopped me. I'd had an idea Caroline wasn't speaking to him, and I couldn't imagine what she'd think of me, lunching with the enemy. "Yes. You and Caroline talk often?"

"Not all that often. Every year, maybe. Every year she calls me up, we chat, and then I manage to say something wrong and she decides not to talk to me. This year. . . . Well, this year I guess I came in person to say it. She'll come around, but about now I'm persona non."

I relaxed, feeling safer. This transaction had felt illegal, but maybe the Stricklands wouldn't have to know. Did he count as a friend, as James had specified in his will? Perhaps, I thought. I could give him a picture, a small one.

"I'll bring some to the library Monday," I said.

"No good. I'm leaving Sunday. Can't I come over?"

Why not, I thought. "Okay. So. Why did you leave?"

He grabbed his coat. "Let's go," he said.

"What? Not now." I looked at my watch. "I have to go back to work."

"After work?" he said. "I'll pick you up." He took out his wallet to get money for the check. A snapshot fell out, a pretty girl in a dress.

"Who's this?" I picked it up. "A girlfriend?"

"Girlfriend emeritus," he said. "Gina. Retired as girlfriend some time ago, but still retains some of the rights and privileges of the position."

"Like her picture in your wallet."

He shrugged and reached further into the slot in his wallet. He extracted a small stack of pictures, then dealt them onto the table like a hand of solitaire. The last two were of Mrs. Sweatt, one alone, one holding a baby James.

"I keep 'em all," said Mr. Sweatt. He stacked up his pile of pictures, his neat exosomatic memory, and put it away.

"You haven't answered my question," I said. "Why did you leave?"

He smiled. "Boy, you *are* feisty. Okay. I left because my wife asked me impossible questions, and she never let me get away without answering. And if you want a better answer than that, you're going to have to wait until—what, five o'clock?"

I sighed. "Five o'clock," I said. "Sure."

"I see Mr. Sweatt is charming you," Astoria said to me. "He always charmed the girls."

"Not me," I said. "Not bloody likely."

She smiled. "You know, he isn't a bad guy. I know you might think he is, but Mrs. Sweatt wasn't the easiest person to live with, plus a sick kid—a man gets scared of that sort of thing."

"He wasn't a sick kid," I said.

"Peggy. He died at twenty. He was sick all his life. I'm not saying leaving was the right thing to do, I'm just saying these things aren't black and white."

Cal Sweatt showed up at five o'clock on the dot. "Astoria!" he said. "Glamorous as always. What's your secret?"

"Library work," she said. "It's the fountain of youth."

"This library is," he said, smiling at me. "This library is fuller of pretty girls than Hollywood."

"I'll get my coat," I said, trying to sound icy, because I didn't want to encourage this sort of talk, especially with Astoria around. "Let's get this over with."

But Cal Sweatt didn't want to get it over with. He wanted to look at every single photograph and painting.

"When did he do this one?" he asked, fingering a photograph of a thin couple in matching outfits.

I looked at it. "That one's older, I think. He probably took that when he was fifteen or so."

"Five years isn't so old."

"A fourth of his life," I said, and Cal got quiet.

"You're right," he said. "What about this?"

I hadn't been through any of this since James died. It was a snapshot of the library, nothing in the frame that would hint at the year. "I don't know," I said. He flipped to another picture. This one was a self-portrait, James in the bathroom mirror in the Stricklands' house. He held the camera in one hand, squinting into it; the other disappeared out the bottom of the frame. I knew he was steadying himself on the basin, that his knees were bent so he could look in the mirror.

"This is hard," Cal said. "I didn't know how hard this would be. Look, you think I'm a terrible guy—"

"No—"

"Yes, you do, or you started out thinking it and that's hard to shake. And you know, I get flip 'cause it's easy." He sighed. "No one will ever say that Calvin Sweatt didn't take the easy way out, every single time. But—" He held on to the shot of James.

"But?" I said.

"But the easy way out isn't always so easy. I'm getting old, starting to realize that. Why did I leave, you asked me. I left because it was the easy way out. Mrs. Sweatt was an unhappy person, you knew her, and I am pretty much a happy person, and this caused some spectacular fights."

"Did you love your wife?" I asked.

"I loved her," said Cal, "because I got used to her. I didn't *fall* in love with her."

"No?"

"It pains me to say this," he told me, "but I'm not susceptible to love. Probably I'm immune." He sighed. "That sounds so pessimistic."

"Why are you immune?" I asked.

He took me by the hand and stroked my knuckles. It was a slow touch; I felt it in my stomach. "Well, people become immune to love like they become immune to any disease. Either they had it bad early in life, like chicken pox, and that's that; or they keep getting exposed to it in little doses and build up an immunity; or somehow they just don't catch it, something in 'em is born resistant. I'm the last type. I'm immune to love and poison ivy."

"Oh, dear," I said. "You're invulnerable." He opened my hand and stroked the palm. This was not a good idea, to sit here and take his touch. I decided to concentrate on what he was saying.

"Not at all," he said. "Not invulnerable at all."

"What's your Achilles' heel?"

"Everything," he said mournfully. "I am highly susceptible to almost everything."

"To what precisely?" I asked.

"You'll only use it against me," he said. "Let's see. Strep throat, sex, flea bites, companionship, pillow talk, whiskey, flattery, presents. Most of me thinks that's pretty smart. I'm not convinced that love can offer me anything that the dynamite combination of sex, companionship, pillow talk, flattery, and of course whiskey doesn't already supply."

"There are some things," I said. "So I hear."

"Like what? Nausea, nerves, and stupidity? If I ever get a craving, I'll just increase the whiskey dosage."

I turned my hand over in his hand. He started to trace my thumb—the creases at the joints, the lump of bone where it met my hand. My thumb had never before seemed like such a complicated mechanism.

"Could you get used to me?" I asked.

"Peggy Cort," he said, in a small, sad voice.

"Calvin Sweatt." I closed my eyes. "May I ask you a favor?"

"Shoot," he said.

"May I kiss you?"

I opened my eyes. His were closed. He didn't say anything. I leaned forward and kissed his jaw, then his neck, then the edge of his mouth. Then his mouth itself. We still held hands, and I thought about slipping my hands from his to put to his face, and I cursed myself for thinking this much. Was he kissing me back? Yes, now he was. Now he was kissing me back. My eyes were still open. His still closed.

I leaned back. There was lipstick on his lips. What was it I liked about him? I examined everything. Not his coloring, sandy hair and almost-blue eyes—James had gotten his pink-and-gold from his mother. Not his arched nose or straight eyebrows, not his heavy-lobed ears or curiously unlined skin. This is what I liked: one thin scar on his chin (a shaving accident, perhaps), and my lipstick on his mouth.

"You look like you were hit by a bus," I said.

"Yes."

"Yes, you were hit by a bus?"

"Yes," he said. "Yes, Peggy Cort, I could get used to you."

And I decided to take this to mean he could love me.

Some men—well, one man I knew, anyhow—get braver in bed, the way they get braver fixing a car, or showing you how to shoot billiards: sex is man's work, even a woman's body is man's work, and you won't ever be as good at it as he is but he'll pass along some tips anyhow. Cal Sweatt, however, got shyer, looked more like his son, more like my James, every moment. He snuck his hand between my legs, over my skirt, to rub me there, but I wasn't wearing the clothing for it; mine was a stiff, unyielding straight brown skirt; something gossamer and flowered and loose would have been better for that almost furtive maneuver. Still I whispered in his ear, "That's nice."

"It is?" he said, his voice full of surprise.

I pulled him closer to me, and he moved his hand around my back; I felt his fingers find the waistband of my skirt, pull my shirt from it, snake down past the bridge of elastic between the back belt loops.

I was not in my body, I was somewhere just behind it, as if I were pushing an empty shopping cart through a bright supermarket, taking anything I wanted from the shelves and throwing them into the basket, knowing someone else would pay the bill, knowing the things would never fill the cart.

He said into my ear, "Should we be doing this?" and since he put it that way, a question, I said Yes.

You might think, living alone so long, so seldom touched, I wouldn't know what to do. But I did. Alone in my bed, I'd sometimes tested on myself. I ran a tentative hand along my collarbone; then a confident hand; then somewhere between. There wasn't an inch of skin I hadn't skimmed my fingers along, wondering *would someone else like this?* I thumbed my ears, traced the outer trough with just a fingernail; I strummed my belly; outlined my own nose, mouth, as if they were places on a map I longed to visit, a homeland I had not seen since childhood.

Some lonely untouched people might get used to it, decide they could do without. Not me. I learned to touch myself tenderly to give myself what I could not ask others for. I stroked my own cheek; late at night, I brushed the hair off my own tired, worried forehead.

I knew in what order to caress a face, a back. I knew what would be expected, and what surprising. I remembered: there is bone, and there is skin, and muscle, and other things. You must always remember this, encountering a body, the same way you must remember when you walk around Cape Cod that there are trees, and also dunes so vast that while walking in them you cannot see the ocean or road; there are roads, and the ocean, and the bay, scrubby forests full of things that scratch, and bogs. It may seem impossible to dress in readiness for all these things, but you can, as long as you are mindful.

When I woke up the next morning, Cal was still asleep, turned toward me. If he thought that was just a high forehead, he was even more of an optimist than he claimed.

Late last night he'd asked, "But what do you really think of me?" and I'd answered, "I think I've never met a nicer man with fewer morals."

Then he was awake. His eyes were a little crusty. He put his hand to my cheek, and for that moment things were lovely, and then he said, "Heya, kid. What time is it? I gotta get to Albany tonight."

And I walked to the bathroom, shut and locked the door, turned on the shower, realized what I'd done—in this order, this order precisely—pulled off the sheet I was wrapped in, folded it carefully, and got in the shower and began to cry in a way I am quite sure I have never cried before.

I pounded the walls of the bathtub, sat down in the tub, hit my knees. I couldn't get enough air; I tried to eat it, bite down into it. My mouth filled up with water. Finally I curled up in a ball beneath the shower, as if the water had driven me there, as if I had no choice but to stay.

I'd like to say that, at that moment, I was crying for James, that I'd fully realized his absence by sleeping with the man who, all things considered, might be expected to be most like him, but who was nothing like him at all. I'd like to say that, as I cried, I completely forgot about that balding man outside the door, who knocked once or twice, politely, as if he were overhearing a domestic dispute that he wasn't sure he should interrupt.

In fact I was crying for myself. I was an idiot, and while that wasn't the worst thing—most people are idiots—for some reason I was an idiot who would be lonely the rest of her life. An idiot who had believed, briefly, foolishly, based on nothing, that this might not be so.

Through my tears and the shower I heard my front door open and close; I was listening for it. I waited ten minutes—not crying now, just listening to make sure he was gone—then put on my robe and went into my living room.

I'd expected my apartment to be wrecked. By what I'm not sure, by whatever had happened last night, by Cal this morning. I'd half hoped he'd turn out to be a common thief, a man who'd take advantage of a hysterical but private woman by silently removing her valuables. But my apartment was as orderly as ever, and the only thing Calvin Sweatt had helped himself to was tomato juice; the glass, still glazed red, was upside down in the sink. I imagined he'd probably dribbled some down his shirt.

There was a note on the kitchen table.

PEGGY I hope you are ok I thought I should go I didnt take any pictures you could send me ones you wanted to me Caroline has my adress in NYC thanks I like the one in the bathroom mirrer And maybe a picture of you too if theres any thanks I'm sorry you feel this way Cal

Residence

You can't hide a fire behind paper. This sounds like something a mother would say, some piece of wisdom, although I don't know that it is. Before James died, if someone had said that to me, I would have said, Yes you can, if you work hard enough. If you lay a book down on a fire, wait until the flame has almost bit its way through the top cover, then quick throw down another one, maybe you can hide it. It might take diligence, but I was always a diligent woman.

For years I tried to hide a fire with books, endless books. I think I was born with a little grief in me, a sadness, not unlike Mrs. Sweatt's. I tried my best to hide it. All I did was succeed in making the fire hungrier to finally burst out big. I can't say that I think it did the books too much good either.

Peggy, you might say to me, didn't you think the fire would burst around, creep up the binding? All those words just wicks? Fire is a speed reader, which is why the ignorant burn books: fire races through pages, takes care of all the knowledge, and never bores you with a summary.

I would have said: maybe your fire. But I know my life, and it is a small, hesitant thing. I thought then that the smallest thing in the world would put out the flame, and I had one of the biggest. And then suddenly, he was gone, and I had nothing left to throw down.

That Saturday afternoon, the one after Cal Sweatt drank his tomato juice and moved on, I wept, wretched. I sat in all the chairs in my apartment, stopped weeping long enough to stand up, walk to a new chair, and sit. Then I started crying again. Sometimes I quit just long enough to laugh at myself, the mess I was.

Around four o'clock I got up, took a shower, got dressed in my old gummy clothes. I washed the upturned glass that Mr. Sweatt had left in my sink and filled it with cold milk, then took it back to the table. What I really wanted was whiskey. I don't think I'd had one since Mrs. Sweatt and I, seven years before, had ducked into that Provincetown bar. Sitting in my kitchen, I imagined the way whiskey would ease down my throat, the immediate warmth that followed it, first head, then body, slow enough that by the end of the drink I wouldn't remember the start of it, wouldn't even feel grateful. I'd just be warm and happy and unbelieving I'd ever been anything else.

That was what real love must be like, I thought. Most people get it, most people are used to it. Me, here I was, hung over with something that hadn't even been love. Probably I should swear it off, like an alcoholic. I should just vow never to try it again in my life. I didn't see it ever being offered, anyhow.

I felt left. I felt abandoned. And until that moment in my kitchen, looking at my spinster's glass of milk, I honestly believed that it was James's father who had left me, that it was a man who couldn't bring himself to use a comma saying, I have to go to Albany, that did this to me. I was amazed the way a child is amazed to discover, holding his thumb to his eye, that he can blot out a mountain.

I thought work would take my mind off its awful machinations, all the things I should have done that would have prevented everything: James's death, Mr. Sweatt's return, all that followed. That was what I called it, to myself, *all that followed.*

But the library made me sick. Every day was a little worse, until a month later I could hardly stand it.

It was a Friday, and April, and the building seemed toxic: the brown dust the books gave off, the tropical dampness of the ladies' room, the cracked glass panes in the floors in the stacks that, at the merest suggestion of a footfall, might drop their burden—a patron, me—down to the basement. The patrons sickened me, too. More books! They dropped off their books and demanded more, they spied a best seller and wanted it *then*, never mind the waiting list. Even the books disgusted me that day. Their jackets were plastic-wrapped, to keep clean, and that struck me as sleazy, that they were doing things they needed to be protected from. Library books were, I suddenly realized, promiscuous, ready to lie in the arms of anyone who asked. Not like bookstore books, which married their purchasers, or were brokered for marriages to others. Now my books seemed so filthy, physically filthy, that I didn't want to touch them; usually, when a book seemed unclean, I washed the covers with a soft waterless soap made for the purpose. Now I picked them up gingerly, threw them on the distribution shelves for Darla.

I forgave no fines that day. I searched for no titles for the curious. When one woman came back for a book she'd returned half an hour before, thinking she'd left a letter between the pages, I thought about telling her she'd just have to wait until the book had been reshelved, because I sure as hell wasn't going to look for it. But I hadn't turned that wicked yet. It was a philosophy book, which meant that I'd tossed it up on the highest of the shelves behind the desk. I got a footstool and stepped up, and it was then, reaching, a foot off the ground, that I did a little arithmetic.

I grabbed the book, found the letter, and brought it to the woman. She thanked me, sounding a little afraid.

I went to the doctor for a long lunch hour to set facts straight. The fact was this: I was pregnant.

Maybe I wanted to be; maybe in the back of my mind I'd

planned it, thought this was one thing Calvin Sweatt could give me: those genes. A baby with those remarkable genes. Not as a replacement for James, but a reminder. My life was over and I wanted a new one. No better way, as I thought about it.

I felt my body suddenly. Was that so bad? I'd been absent, for years it seems. I'd set up residence in James's body, and there was room there for me. He didn't use all of it. Plenty of space. And when I went to kiss him that night—James, I mean, not his father—when I leaned forward, punched my arm into the pillow, I still wasn't in my body, I was trying to pay back rent, I was begging not to be evicted, I was knocking on a door I knew was about to be locked, saying, *Just another minute, wait, I've packed, I know, put off the demolition, I just want one more look around*. And he let me, and then he died.

I walked back to the library, to the staff room. I sat down. I didn't have to wait for the test results: I knew. Astoria followed me. Normally we weren't ever in that room together; when one of us was on the desk, the other was off. I was sitting on the awful sofa we'd inherited when the town manager's office had been redecorated. I must have looked like I'd been hit by a truck and thrown onto that sofa, my legs off in different directions, my head flopping back.

"I think you should consider taking some time off," Astoria said.

I didn't speak; like an accident victim, I concentrated on not moving anything.

"You've been through all of this," she said, sitting down next to me, "and you haven't taken any off. You're exhausted. Get away. We'll figure it out here. I know you don't think so, but we can keep this place running without you awhile—and that's not an insult, it's a compliment. You've got this library running so tightly it can go by itself."

My eyes started to tear, because she was lying. I was doing a terrible job, and had been. "It's okay," I said. I sat up. "I'll be taking time off soon enough."

"You will?" she said.

"I will. I'm pregnant."

I can't say that her mouth fell open, but her entire face rearranged itself. Then she bit her lip.

"Wonderful?" she asked.

I nodded. I think I even blushed.

"Good," she said. "But, Peggy—"

"James," I said. "It's James's baby."

I knew, by telling her, that it would get around town. One of the reasons Astoria liked working at the library was to receive and relay gossip. She would tell everybody—strangers, and the regular patrons, and Oscar and Caroline—and she would tell each in a hushed voice, as if they were the only ones she was taking into her confidence.

That night Caroline called me at home.

"Peggy," she said.

"Yes?"

She waited for me to say something, but I didn't.

"Is it true?" she began. I heard Alice nattering on in the background. "Is it true you're expecting—"

"—yes—"

"James's baby?"

"Yes," I said.

"But that's impossible, isn't it?"

"No," I said. "It's more than possible. It's true."

"But that doctor. The one who wrote the article. He said James couldn't . . ." She let her voice trail off, and I felt sorry for her. She was not good at this sort of thing.

"Did that doctor get anything else right?" I asked.

"No," she said emphatically. "That's what I told Oscar." Suddenly her voice flooded with something, and it took me a second to realize it was her usual warmth, which she'd been holding back. "You should come home," she said. "You could live in the cottage. We'll close it down as a museum and set you up. You should live with us, Peggy. Look! I'm pregnant, too—"

"Caroline—"

"We'll have children together," she said, like a lovestruck man proposing marriage.

"Oh, Caroline," I said. "Yes. Okay. Yes."

And that night I packed a few things and put them in the car and drove back to Winthrop Street.

Oscar and Caroline and Alice greeted me, Oscar so full of attention and caution that I thought, if he wasn't already married, he would have offered to make an honest woman of me. They carried my things back to the cottage.

"We'll pick up your furniture tomorrow," Caroline said. "You can't climb up into this bed—"

"I've climbed into it before," I said, not thinking how that sounded.

"Well, yes," said Caroline. "I just meant—later, it will get harder. Believe me—after a while that bed will look like Mount Kilimanjaro. We'll spruce up the place—"

"No," I said. "Leave it. Leave everything."

The town manager called me later that week, to tell me I'd been fired; not bad enough that the library (so he'd heard) was falling to pieces, but surely I understood the *moral* problem here. A *public* librarian, after all . . .

Fine, I told him, fine, and I said good-bye to my library. Oh, I was a scandal. A grown woman, they said, well into her thirties and him barely out of his teens. Not to mention everything else. Maybe they did mention it, some of them, but that talk didn't make it back to me. Some of the more sympathetic and liberal people in town—those who considered themselves artistic—thought I was a romantic figure. Caroline told me a few people even claimed that James and I had gotten married secretly in New York. She'd done nothing to discourage that rumor.

I had a new job, anyhow, in charge of the James Carlson Sweatt Home. Still a librarian—always a librarian—I organized his letters, to and from, I wrote a guide to the newspaper clippings.

You would have thought that first week would have been the worst, but it wasn't. I ate cookies from the bakery, canned soup heated up on the hot plate. I listened to the radio and read the last library books I'd brought to James, which since his death had sat on the night table, collecting fines; I'd known they were there, of course, just never could bear to pick them up. *City of God, From Here to Eternity, Thurber Carnival.* I'd felt like returning them meant I was closing out his account.

Finally one morning Caroline came to the cottage and said, "You can't go on like this."

I looked around the room. I thought she was kicking me out.

"There's someone else you have to think about, Peggy," she said, and she touched my stomach to remind me. "Come to the front house."

"I like it here," I told her.

"For meals. That's all. For meals and a little company. I'm home all day, too; I could use the conversation myself."

So I did that. I took my dinner and breakfast there, chatted with them. I wanted to stay at the cottage mornings and afternoons, waiting for visitors; I wanted to be always ready and present. That is, I wanted them to know that I lived there.

But evenings, I sat on the sofa with Caroline, whose stomach was just beginning to push at her own clothes; soon she'd move on to wearing Oscar's pants, kept up with a knotted scarf. And though I'd thought during the week I'd spent alone in the cottage that it was the way I wanted it—me, the radio, the silly cat leaping from surface to surface—I discovered that it was simply because I could not have imagined the pleasant life in the front house. Oscar offering me something, sweet potatoes or gravy, a homey rich dish, his hands on one side of a warm platter or bowl and mine on the other; Caroline back and forth from the kitchen, her hair tied back; Alice, a good eater always, picking one thing off the plate and sticking it in her mouth till the plate came clean. Caroline cooked and I washed, each according to her abilities.

I'd always thought of happiness as some dramatic talent, or unreal luck; I'd never imagined it could come in this workaday variety. This was something James had done, too, after all: he sat in this dining room, ate Caroline's careful soft food. She was frightened of people choking, and if anyone so much as coughed at her table, she looked alarmed; if it went on, she stood up asking, *Are you okay, do you need some water?* The cougher, red-faced and damp-eyed, had to smile and nod, and Caroline took her place again. Such sweet strange concern was everywhere in that house. It was not my life—I knew that—but it was the life of people I felt comfortable with, and that was enough. When dinner was over, I went back to the cottage and turned on the radio and knit. Caroline had taught me.

After a while I just stayed at the front house till it was time to go to sleep. Caroline and I got bigger and bigger. She was a little disappointed with me—she wanted someone to discuss stretch marks with, to compare swollen feet, and I demurred. But I learned from her, sometimes too literally, as if she were a girl I admired one class ahead. I did everything she did, two months behind: a crying jag at the end of the third month; a passion for salt in the fourth; a two-day superstitious prohibition on mentioning the baby at all in the fifth. When Caroline gave birth to another daughter, they named her Margaret Ann, after me and then Oscar's mother. They didn't realize that Peggy is my given name. Now they call her Ann, because I do.

That gave me two months to meet a baby before being introduced to my own, which seemed like good planning. I was strangely patient. The townspeople were the ones who waited nervously, who called each other up to say, Has it happened yet? Will it be another one, do you think?

Dorothy was born two months to the day after Ann, perfectly healthy, fat, but nothing else. I decided not to name her after anybody.

And so I had James back. I don't mean Dotty, who grew up so much her own person, I sometimes thought she wasn't related to anyone—plump and impetuous, a dear, longed-for foundling. Our girls played together in the yard between our houses. They knew they were somehow related. *Cousin Dotty*, Alice called, and sometimes, mistakenly, *Cousin Ann*, as if all babies born that one year were her cousins.

I told Dotty about her father. I told her about James, because he is her father, in every way. For instance: it is a scientific fact that she shares his genes. We live in his house, among his possessions. And in every way, he is the one who brought her to me, which is one of the reasons I love her—though much to my misanthropic amazement, not the only reason. He was my one, true husband and love, and he would have loved her best, like he loved Alice, only better, because Dotty is his and has his name. And everybody else told Dotty about James; everybody else told her stories about that wonderful man, her father.

•

The girls are gone now. The Strickland girls went to college in Boston and stayed there. I see them when they come for visits. Alice looks like photographs of the old Alice; it's only when she speaks that Mrs. Sweatt disappears. She is certain of herself, and it gives her a weird beauty. Ann is tall enough that we once worried, though the doctors told us not to; she stopped growing in eighth grade when she was five foot nine, as if it were a childhood hobby.

And Dotty is in Chicago, twenty-five years old, older than James lived to be. Still plump, still looking like no one I've ever known. She comes to visit me every summer for a month; in between I rarely hear from her. My address book is crowded with her different houses. I don't think I have the most recent. Sometimes my letters bounce back to me; other times she writes, thanking me for my news. She sends postcards, no place for a return address, saying *I'm fine, I'm okay, more later*. She always signs, *love*. She had parents who were in love with each other, and that is a blow no child can recover from. Everyone I ever knew has turned into a stack of papers.

I have James back because I live in his house. I show the tourists around. Every day I talk about him and sleep in his big bed, dream of him. That mattress is a mess. I can't bear to replace it. It feels warm, as if he's just gotten up, the whole bed warm wherever my skin touches it. Even in the summer, not enough people come. I wait. I read.

Sometimes I try to pull myself into my body. Sometimes I can, I can even feel my self unscrolling from my head down, to my shoulders, my chest, down to my hips, and I try to hold it. It's a physical, definite sensation. But it's as if my self is a stubborn window shade. The minute I loosen my grip, it goes snapping back up, leaving only the faintest wind.

I live in my head and my hands, the mouth that kissed James and the hands that held him. Plenty of space.

I take walks in town with Dotty on her summer visits. We are bold, a scandalous woman with definite proof of scandal, my definite Dotty. The tourists look at us and I see them forming certain questions. But there are some things even a tourist won't put into words.

"I want to tell you about somebody," I say, and they listen. They send me postcards addressed to Mrs. James Carlson Sweatt. When I write back, I sign my letters the same way. It's the first posthumous marriage in history, a true, real marriage. Don't doubt that.

They talk about me in this town. I have passed into legend, even though I'm still around in the flesh. Who would have thought? people say to each other. Now, when I walk past the windows of the library, into stores, along the beach, I am discussed. I know the sound; I heard it enough with James. See that woman? they say.

I am a figure they imagine knocking on their doors, to test them. They don't know what they should do to pass the test: let me in to sit by the radiator, or send me down the sidewalk to bewitch another house. They anticipate me at any moment, thrilled with the possibilities.

My thanks to the following good readers: Karen Bender, Kermit Cole, Bruce Holbert, Max Phillips, Robert Siegel. Ann Patchett's ability to read and reread this manuscript probably qualifies her for sainthood or psychiatric evaluation. Thanks also to Henry Dunow, Kathleen Jayes, and Susan Kamil. Thanks for various types of support and inspiration to: the MacDowell Colony; The Fine Arts Work Center in Provincetown; the staff of the Somerville Public Library; the reference staff of Van Pelt Library, University of Pennsylvania; Sam, Natalie, and Harry McCracken; and Elizabeth Perowsky.